Becoming Lily Kaltyk

Also by Dorothy Brown Henderson

Novels:

The Season for Strawberries

Happy Are Those

Dr. Bloom's Event

Dreaming in Grey

Cookbook:

Loving it Local: Preparing Delicious Fresh Local Food

Becoming Lily Kaltyk

A Novel

Dorothy Brown Henderson

Becoming Lily Kaltyk

This book is a work of fiction. Some people named, such as Canadian Prime Minister Justin Trudeau and a few renowned architects, are ever so real, but the rest of the characters in this story are figments of the imagination of the author. Any resemblance to actual persons, living or dead, in the rest of the story is coincidental. However, the Canadian places in the novel—Emerson, Manitoba, Vancouver, Flin Flon, Toronto, Kingston, Montreal, Quebec City and the towns mentioned in Nova Scotia—are real places in Canada and all are rewarding to visit and explore.

The author has taken some liberty with other facts. There is no Presbyterian church in Emerson, Manitoba, but wouldn't it be splendid to have one? New Hopewell is a fictitious town on the north shore of Lake Ontario, but the reader is invited to go exploring along Ontario Highway 2 in search of the "Old Manse." Likewise, the architectural pilot project is a figment of the author's imagination, but there really *is* a wonderful architecture school at the University of Toronto commonly referred to as the "Daniels Building" at One Spadina Avenue.

Editor and Designer: Tim Faller of Tim Faller Design Inc.

Cover image: Adobe Stock

Issued in print and electronic formats

ISBN 978-0-9938962-7-9

This book is written in love for
Kaya, Noah, Quinn, Adelaide, Malone and Karl

Beautiful beings on the journey of becoming

CHAPTER 1

"Happy? Would you be happy if this was your life? I'm thirty-nine years old. I have a pitiful career, if you can call it that. I've never lived outside of Emerson, bloody Manitoba. I live close to the poverty line and still share a house with my mother who is consumed with bitterness. I have no partner or kids. I can't see how my future can be different or better. Would you be content with this?"

"Lily...Lily...I didn't mean to upset you."

"Oh, Cath," Lily sighed, "Don't feel sorry. It's not your fault. It's just the reality of my situation."

The two women lapsed into silence until Cathy made a suggestion. "You know, Scott has a couple of single buddies. We could arrange for you to meet them, see if you are at all compatible."

"You sound like my mother," Lily groaned. "She is always saying to me, 'You're reasonably good looking and your hair is quite nice but why don't you fix it up? Go out to a dance and meet a nice fellow.' You have any idea how hard that is in Emerson, Cathy? The good men are all taken and the ones who are available are either divorced—for a reason—or drunks or social imbeciles."

It was Cathy's turn to sigh. She could think of no other advice or comfort to offer. Although they had been close friends since kindergarten, they were careful to avoid an unvoiced reality that neither had ever been able to talk about. Both knew that Lily had often been too unsure of herself, afraid to risk new beginnings, hindered by a pattern of shyness, anxiety and uncertainty that had persisted from childhood.

Cathy had invited Lily to spend a weekend on the farm. "Scott's away with the boys at a hockey tournament. Why don't we treat ourselves to a good gossipy girl's weekend? Some old movies, potato chips. I'll get some wine and cheese, pick up some frozen dinners so nobody needs to cook."

On Saturday night, they had curled up on the well-worn living room furniture, the voice of Michael Bublé crooning in the background. The farm collie climbed onto the couch and rested his head in Cathy's lap. "He thinks he's a lap dog," she laughed. "More wine?"

"This has been a great weekend, Cathy. I didn't realize I needed one so badly. I seldom get away."

"You have to go back into town to play the organ at church tomorrow?"

"I begged off. Haven't had a Sunday away in years. I'm not sure what they'll do, but that's not my problem. Maybe they'll have a little more respect for me."

"You think they don't appreciate you?"

"Oh, I'm sure they do. I don't know. I started playing the organ in that church when I was seventeen. The pay back then was seventy-five dollars a Sunday, and twenty-two years later the pay is still seventy-five," Lily sighed. "Every year at the Annual Meeting when they make decisions about the budget, the Chair of the Board says the same thing. 'Of course, we would love to shower our minister, organist and custodian with raises, but our finances just don't allow it. Fuel, electricity, water, repairs and internet keep going up and those are fixed costs.'"

"What! That's so insensitive!" They lapsed into a comfortable silence. "You like the new minister?"

Lily paused for so long that Cathy wondered if she heard the question. Lily was thinking that ever since the Reverend Rupert Cameron had come to be their minister six months ago, she had been more anxious, stumbling through the hymns, starting in the wrong key, having to stop and start again, choosing the wrong tune. She had always had a strong sense of rhythm, but even that had faltered since he arrived. She noticed him glance toward her when these mishaps occurred. She was sure that he counted her mistakes, perhaps even went home and reported them to his wife.

"His wife is gravely ill, I hear. I haven't met her," Lily said, trying to empathize with the man who made her so uneasy. "It must be hard for him." But she wondered, as she had so often in the past months, why he had left a large, established and, as rumour had it, wealthy congregation in Vancouver to minister in the small and relatively unknown town of Emerson, Manitoba.

"Cathy, if I let you in on a secret, do you promise to tell no one? Not even Scott? I just don't want this getting back to my mother until things are settled."

"Sure. What's up?"

"You remember when we were graduating from high school and Mr. Stone interviewed us to discuss our plans for the future?" That conversation with her guidance counsellor had taken place more than twenty years ago, but resentment and bitterness still festered as she recalled a five-minute exchange, a fatherly redirection, that had thwarted her dream for the future. "He looked over my marks and observed that I had done exceptionally well in math and physics and that my English mark was excellent, too. He asked if I had given any thought as to what I wanted to do after high school."

"And?"

"I told him that I had always dreamed of going to university to become an architect. Do you know what he said next? He declared that architecture is not a good profession for a young woman. It's too hard, he said. He looked in my folder and said, 'I notice that you're also good at music.' I told him that I had private piano lessons for eight years and this made it easy to understand the band music."

She didn't admit to Mr. Stone, or even now to Cathy, that when she was eight her mother had scraped together enough money to pay for piano lessons but after a year had discontinued them because of the cost. The stigma of poverty, the sting of never being able to afford things, was never far away in her childhood. Her piano teacher could see that the shy girl who practiced so faithfully had a gift for music, more talent than her other students. She had called on Lily's mom, Krystyna, and proposed a trade: a weekly piano lesson in exchange for a large pan of cabbage rolls and two loaves of homemade bread.

"Yes, yes, I see that, now," Mr. Stone had mused, stroking his chin. "Your music mark is even higher than your physics. And your drama mark is exceptional. Of course, drama's just an empty fun course," he declared, but Lily knew differently. That had been the only drama course she had ever taken, and it was the first time she had ever been on stage. It had amazed her to discover, when she was acting in her role, that she felt like a different person. Her new persona was like a mask at Halloween. Her shyness and timidity fell away, freeing her to forget herself, to become something different. She remembered with crystal clarity the power and freedom of this transformation, the courage that surged through her body.

"Yes," Mr. Stone had advised, "since you're strong in several areas, you would make a fine teacher. Now then…" He had turned around to a bookcase crammed untidily with catalogues of all sizes and shapes and retrieved a booklet. "It will be much easier to find funding for teacher's college."

When Lily had finished retelling her story, Cathy asked, "So what's the big secret?"

"You know that I never wanted to be a teacher, so I just stayed on here in Emerson after I graduated. But, on Monday, I'm off to Winnipeg for a tour of the architecture school at the University of Manitoba. I'm planning to enroll for the fall term. I'm not sure how I can make this happen, but I'm determined to try."

CHAPTER 2

Lily pulled herself up the steep steps of the bus to Winnipeg. Going alone to the city flooded her with anxiety. She rarely left Emerson because she had never learned to drive and, as her mother often said, they couldn't afford a car anyway.

After the driver handed back the return portion of the ticket, she draped her bag over one shoulder and side-stepped down the narrow aisle, nodding politely to people she recognized, then paused mid-way, searching for an empty seat. She disliked sitting close to the odiferous washroom in the rear of the bus. From former times, she knew that the bus, with its top-heavy swaying, made her feel queasy. The bacterial ammonia malodor of the toilet added to her discomfort. How shameful it would be, she worried, to vomit on the bus.

"Is this seat taken?" Lily asked a woman sitting on her own.

"You are welcome. I am alone," the woman replied.

When she had folded her jacket neatly on her lap, she settled back into her seat, took a deep breath and said, "I'm Lily."

"I am Maryeah. It is nice to meet you." The woman, Lily noted, spoke with the slow, careful enunciation of a new Canadian. Perhaps her ESL teacher had urged her to engage in as many conversations as possible, aiming to perfect her fluency, striving to add colloquial touches to her command of the English language.

"Do you live in Emerson?" the woman inquired.

"Yes. I've lived there all my life," Lily told her. "I teach a bit of music at Emerson Elementary school."

"Oh!" Maryeah exclaimed. "My children go to that school. Maybe you are their teacher?"

"Perhaps," Lily smiled, suddenly self-conscious and uncertain, for she was not a qualified teacher and it was only for lack of one in Emerson that the school principal had called and invited her to direct the choir and give some rudimentary voice lessons.

She decided not to mention that she was also the long-time organist of Knox Presbyterian Church. She assumed from the woman's dress that she was Muslim and might not understand that some religious groups in Canada believed that they could not sing unless they had a pipe organ to lead them.

They lapsed into silence and Lily thought back to the day when she had been invited to be the church organist. The former organist, who had a form of dementia it was rumoured, had retired. Her playing had become erratic, which stressed out the choir and embarrassed the minister. When he approached Lily, she protested. "I play the piano," she declared. "I don't know anything about playing an organ."

"Piano, organ, keyboard. They're all the same. If you can play one, you can play the other," he insisted. "Besides, it's easy to play hymns."

In the years that followed, she found all these things to be untrue. She struggled to coordinate the foot pedals and play with hands on different manuals, and because she and her mother had rarely attended a church, she found the hymn tunes stilted and awkward. But she was impressed and excited by the fact that the church paid seventy-five dollars a week, a huge sum to a teenage girl whose father had died and whose mother got by on a small pension.

The bus bounced and growled along Highway 75 as it crawled north following the curve of the Red River. The voice of the woman, Maryeah, broke into her reverie. "Are you going to Winnipeg to shop? Or see a doctor?"

"More or less," Lily replied. She felt reluctant to disclose anything personal to this woman who was a complete stranger to her. She couldn't admit that she was about to take one of the most daring steps of her life, with her plan to enroll in the architecture program at the University of Manitoba. Not wishing to seem rude or unfriendly to the woman, Lily confided softly—she didn't want the couple sitting ahead of them to hear—"I want to buy a new dress. Something bright and modern." She glanced down at her unadorned, navy blue sheath.

"What colour will you buy?" Maryeah inquired. "Red?" she added, smiling.

"Yes, perhaps. Red would be a change, for sure." Lily glanced again at the woman beside her who wore a dark cotton garment with triangular sleeves and a headscarf tightly covering her hair. Lily looked away, then glanced again. She now saw that the coat—or was it a dress?—had beautiful embroidery around the neck and along the side seams of the gown.

Maryeah noticed Lily's glance and smiled. "In Syria, we must be modest. Our husbands do not like us to show our beauty when we are out. When we are at home, we wear what we like. Many Syrian women are very interested in fashion."

"Oh!" Lily exclaimed, realizing that she had never considered what life would be like in the homes of Syrians displaced from their Middle Eastern homeland to the southern border of Manitoba, Canada.

"I tell you a secret," Maryeah said, leaning toward Lily, lowering her voice. "I dress with modesty when I am out, but I always wear red underwear."

Lily inhaled sharply. She didn't know what to think of the woman's intimate and shocking disclosure.

"You see?" Maryeah said, pulling aside two layers of clothing to reveal a red bra strap.

"I see," Lily said, blushing. Both women laughed softly.

"Back in Syria, I am student at university. Here I look after my children and wear my red underwear because it makes me brave. It is important for a woman to be brave. Then she will know that she is strong. She will know that she is herself."

When the bus shuddered into the terminal, the driver called out "downtown Winnipeg," and everyone scrambled to their feet, grabbing bags and jackets. Both women struggled down the steep bus steps. Then Lily turned and said, "It was lovely to meet you. Good luck with your shopping."

Maryeah wished Lily good luck, too, and called out, "Remember! Red."

Lily stood for a moment, smiling a little, watching the other woman stride away. Maryeah seemed to know exactly what she wanted and she seemed to know precisely where she was going. Such robust self-assurance, Lily thought, such a sturdy sense of self.

After she had returned to Emerson, her mother asked, "Was it a waste of time, then?"

Lily shook her head. "Not entirely. I bought a few things that I couldn't find here in Emerson." She didn't tell her mother about the conversation with the Muslim woman. Nor did she admit that she had been disheartened and frightened by the tour of the architecture department.

The young graduate student guide had spewed out a list of options available in the Faculty of Architecture. "You begin with a Bachelor of Environmental Design. After two years, you take another two years in a more specialized stream: interior design or landscape or city planning. There are courses on visual literacy, environmental technology, the history of culture, ideas and the environment. A student can specialize in either interior environments or landscape and urbanism or just stick with the architecture stream where premodern history and theory and modern architecture are the focus. Eventually, you could also choose a PhD in Design and Planning."

Was she interested in interior light and colour? Indoor systems? Digital media? Emergent futures? Principles of urban design? Lily's head ached with confusion and from an overload of information.

How could she possibly explain to this eager, verbose young man that she simply loved looking at historic buildings, that she loved walking around Emerson, fascinated to gaze at the deteriorating first Customs Office built in 1868? Even more interesting to her were the features of the Emerson Court House and Townhall with its neo-classical style, stately columns, grand entrance and richly detailed façade. How could she confess to this impatient young student that her favourite reading was two volumes of *A History of Canadian Architecture*, which she had discovered by happy chance while browsing at a wobbly wooden table at a Saturday yard sale?

Nor did Lily admit to her mother that she had taken the city bus to Valencia Boutique, then to Voilà by Adréanna, but the dresses were expensive and the only ones she saw in red seemed too flashy, too showy, even a bit lurid.

CHAPTER 3

Several generations had come and gone, but the immigration stories of central Canada were still foremost in the hearts and habits of Lily's Ukrainian-Canadian parents. Life was moulded and shaped by an expectation of hard work, troubles and dashed dreams. Their ancestors had been among the first wave of Ukrainians to settle in Gretna, Manitoba, in 1891, leaving behind their peasant existence in the declining Austro-Hungarian Empire, lured to Canada by promises of cheap land and prosperity. In the farmlands around Gretna, they were told, Mennonites who spoke their language had settled, and this would ease the transition of the Ukrainians.

Like most Ukrainian-Canadians, Lily was raised on stories of the diaspora, but her family also stressed the importance of maintaining their language and preparing Ukrainian food, and they relished the relentless energy and clatter of hopak, Ukrainian dancing. It was an insular life, a life within a larger context, and so it came as a surprise, like a stepping stone into a whole new world, when her school friend, Cathy, who was of English-Scottish heritage, invited Lily to her family farm.

Cathy gave Lily a tour of the sheds and barn, then pointed to the hundreds of acres of ripening wheat, the golden expanse of rippling canola fields, and somewhere beyond, Cathy told her, there were fifty head of cattle grazing. When she joined Cathy, her parents and three older, sun-tanned, robust brothers for supper, the table was loaded with steaks, mashed potatoes, gravy, carrots, beans, dinner rolls, great slabs of butter and seemingly bottomless pitchers of milk. Lily was overwhelmed and confused by the bouncing discussion, the myriad of talking points. Everyone, even Cathy and her mother, was actively engaged in running the farm, and everyone had an opinion. Their life on the farm provided plenty of fodder for supper conversation.

"Don't hog the potatoes down there, Robert..."

"Folks up in Ontario don't get that with this much rain, ground turns to gumbo..."

"Be thankful that it's nutrient-rich..."

"I'd be more thankful if the growing season were longer..."

"Yeah, when you're not growing, you're not living..."

"Dad, ya ever think of buying up that acreage to the north?..."

"I'd rather think about doing a better job on the acres we have. Who needs more?..."

"I could use a little more cash than this old farm provides..."

"Ha! Would you be your own boss, then? Here, at least, we can march to our own drummer..."

"If only there wasn't so much risk involved. You can't control the weather..."

"True, but it kinda evens out. We had two bad years in a row. Now a bumper crop this year..."

"It's a lot to juggle when you think of it..."

"There are a lot of moving parts..."

"I can't wait for the harvest to be over so hockey can start..."

Lily was dizzy following the fragments of conversation, which flowed as effortlessly as the bowls of food.

Later, after she and Cathy had graduated from high school and Cathy had married Scott, Lily visited their farm as well. They were always busy, it seemed, juggling farm chores and raising three sturdy, rambunctious boys. It felt like déjà vu to Lily.

"Ma, Bobbie won't pass the potatoes..."

"Sure looks like rain. Wish it would hold off for a couple more days..."

"Dad, why does Newman get to drive the combine? When will I be old enough?..."

"Pass the steaks around again. Lily, help yourself before these little vultures get them all..."

"Heard there's a meeting in town tonight about worldwide marketing..."

"Do we have to be told by another bigwig that farming offers us endless opportunities..."

"The older I get the more I think it offers endless pitfalls..."

"Any more milk in that pitcher?..."

"Ma, who's taking us to hockey? You or Dad?..."

In the winter, Lily knew, farm families settled into a less hectic pace. She had seen families emerge from Border 9 Bar and Grill, men with toothpicks bobbing in the corner of their mouths. There was time now for a meal in town, time to oil and grease machinery, time to have neighbours over for a few rounds of euchre or gin rummy, followed by a lunch of thick ham and Bothwell cheese sandwiches. There was time to make schmoo cake, oozing with whipped cream and melted caramel sauce. There was time to pick up a hot chocolate at the coffee shop before heading to the curling rink. And in the good years, there was always the prospect of catching a flight to Florida to take in some Disney World and winter sunshine.

Life within the more insular Ukrainian community was different, though. Some communities in Manitoba had numerous families of Ukrainian descent, but it was not so in the town of Emerson. All the more reason for Lily's mother, Krystyna, to stay closely connected to their neighbour, Sofiya. She was her mother's best friend, closer than a sister. Most mornings, when their housework was done, the two women met for coffee and snacks, but mostly they met for camaraderie. Lily could count on hearing Aunt Sofiya's cheerful voice at the back door.

"Ah, Krystyna! I smell fresh pampushky. I came at the right time."

"Good day. Come in. Let me put on the kettle," Lily's mother said, removing her flowered apron.

The women had long ago given up speaking Ukrainian when they were together, unless there was something that the children shouldn't hear, but maintaining their Ukrainian connections and customs was important to both. How else will our children know who they are? they often repeated. Each year, on the nineteenth of December, they helped the children prepare for a visit from Saint Nicholas and made spider decorations for their homes, explaining that spiders were considered to be good luck. On Christmas Eve, both women cooked the traditional twelve dishes—one for each disciple—and took care to include no meat or animal products. This was a way to respect the animals who had paid homage to the baby Jesus in the stable, they told the children. Their families gathered with others to celebrate Christmas on January 7, and later in the month, Malanka, Ukrainian New Year. No one wanted to miss that party. In the cold and snowy month of January, with the prairie temperature dipping between twenty and forty below, everyone looked forward to a gathering with food, music and dancing. Later, when the snow had begun to thaw, the two women joined with Ukrainian families from other communities to plan a Maslenitsa feast on the last week before the Great Lent. It was a time to say goodbye to winter and to greet the spring. When visitors arrived at their door, they took care to welcome them with a round loaf of bread, the holiest of foods, and salt. From their long tradition, bread and salt represented hospitality. Then, in the summer, the women grew sunflowers—a Ukrainian favourite—in their vegetable gardens. Maintaining Ukrainian customs and rituals was very important in both households. Above all, they valued family and dedicated themselves to their children.

"So, your little Lily starts to school next month. I will ask one of mine to walk with her."

"Thank you for that. I've been so worried about her. You know how shy she is."

"Yes, but perhaps school will help her."

"You think so? Do you honestly think so? She is so easily frightened. I'm afraid that the older children will..."

"Krystyna, she's your only one. I understand that, but try not to worry. If you fret too much, you'll pass on your worry to her."

"I'm afraid it's her nature—to be timid and shy. She never wants to try anything until she is absolutely certain she can do it. I just wish she would take a few risks, to at least try things out. I want her to learn to skate and learn how to swim. Maybe take some dance lessons." Krystyna paused, then standing to fetch the coffee pot, she added, "She's her father's daughter, that's for sure."

"That's not so bad," Sofiya replied, reaching for another pampushky, sweet fried dough which Krystyna had filled with jam and rolled in sugar. "These are delicious, Krystyna. What's so bad about being like her father? He's a good man. Handsome, too."

Krystyna sighed. "But he never gets ahead. Whenever there's a promotion at work, someone else always gets it. He just doesn't seem to try. He doesn't put himself forward."

Lily had been lying on the living room carpet around the corner, playing with her stuffed knit animals, but she heard it all. She absorbed her mother's words, she heard the worry in her voice, and even though she was a small child, she understood for the first time that she was not good enough. She was a disappointment to her mother. She also realized, as she felt a sharp pain in her chest, that, to her mother, her beloved father was an even greater disappointment.

CHAPTER 4

Every evening after supper, if the weather was fair, Lily's father took her for a walk through the streets of Emerson. "Time for our adventure, sonechko." She loved that her father called her "my sunshine." As they walked, there was no need to say much. It was enough to amble along together, holding hands. They played a quiet hunting game which they called "Could this be our next house?" They sauntered through the streets, counting them off as they strolled. 1st street. 2nd street. Sometimes they made it to 6th street.

"This is a nice one," her Papa said, stopping to survey a bungalow with its long paved driveway. "It looks as if the garage might be heated. A great place for a man to get away in the long winter evenings and weekends," he said with a sigh.

Lily spotted the large vegetable garden at the back of the property. "Mama would like this one," she agreed.

Once, on 5th street, they found a house with a closed front porch, perfect for rainy days when she could play there with her stuffed animals, Lily considered. On the front lawn, there were six mature trees—black spruce, lodgepole pine, Manitoba maple, wild plum, trembling aspen, peachleaf willow. "It's almost like a park," her father explained after he had named each tree for her.

"Do you think this house would make Mama happy?" she asked, anxiety pinching her face as she looked up at her father.

It was on these early walks that Lily first awakened to the enchantment of old buildings. Their evening stroll invariably started or stopped at the corner of Church and Winnipeg streets. "It's a beauty," her father declared as they stood gazing at the Emerson Court House and Town Hall. "Built in 1917, 1918. They say it is a great example of pre-1920 architectural design." In time, as she borrowed more and more books on architecture from the town library, Lily came to understand the features of this majestic building. She was able to describe the massive front portico composed of tall Ionic columns. She could identify the pediment adorned with dentils and modillions. She could describe the neo-classical features of this form, its symmetrical and imposing beauty. But as a child, it simply filled her with awe. She felt as if she were standing in front of a temple, before a monument that described elegance itself.

Lily dreaded the time when she was to start to school in September. In the hot, dry nights at the end of August, when she woke in the night, crying out, Krystyna rushed into the bedroom, scooped her into her arms and rocked her until she calmed and could fall back to sleep. "It will be fine, it will be fine," she crooned to the child, but Lily knew, from deep within her small, slender body, that it would not be fine. And it wasn't.

From the first day, she was afraid to raise her hand to ask if she might go to the bathroom. She could think of only one thing: would she wet her pants and be sent home in disgrace? The playground, too, was a nightmare. The boys raced past her, kicking soccer balls, almost knocking her over as they ran to the monkey bars. The girls huddled in self-appointed groups to play hopscotch or tag. The kindergarten children were given a separate recess, so Sofiya's children were not there to provide a buffer for her. Most days, she stood alone, clinging to the chain link fence, longing for her mother to come pick her up.

When Cathy entered her life, everything improved. Used to high-spirited older brothers, nothing seemed to bother Cathy. On the farm, she had nurtured stray kittens and her parents had given her a puppy to raise.

She tended her own small flock of baby chicks until something—a skunk, opossum or raccoon, her father said—had broken into their pen and killed them. Looking out for Lily was easy for Cathy.

For the first time since she had walked up the long sidewalk leading to the sombre black doors of Emerson School, Lily began to feel less anxious. She no longer shrank back when she had to walk past the school mascot, a frightening, ferocious eagle. Some of Cathy's self-confidence rubbed off on her when the girls became friends. Unexpectedly, in the classroom Lily began to pay attention to the voice of the teacher. Numbers began to make sense, words began to flow into sentences which described scenes. Once, when Aunt Sofiya was visiting and Lily was not supposed to be listening, she heard her mother say, "She may not be quite what I hoped for, but at least she brings home a good report card."

CHAPTER 5

Rupert Cameron slipped out of the house while his wife, Elodie, was sleeping and walked toward the church, hoping to find a few moments to talk things over with his organist. Something had to be done about the dreadful church choir.

It had been a difficult transition, moving from his large and comfortable congregation in Vancouver to the small border-crossing town of Emerson. He'd been looking for a church with less responsibility, so that he might have more time to be with Elodie, who was gravely ill with untreatable cancer.

It had all begun to go downhill in the previous year. Elodie, who had always been healthy, began to notice distressing symptoms. There were foods that she could no longer tolerate, and she often felt too full to eat. When she stepped onto the bathroom scale and realized that she had lost twenty pounds, she knew she could no longer ignore the bloating in her abdomen. They had never had children, so when the doctor informed them that she needed a hysterectomy, it did not seem to be a problem. It was only after the surgery, in the long, sluggish days of recovery, that the doctor gave them the sobering news that Elodie had ovarian cancer, epithelial carcinoma. At first there was talk of the possibility of full recovery, then discussion of a five-year survival rate, and finally, the sobering news that the rapidly growing cancer cells had moved into her liver. Their life, which had previously been a shared companionship of refinement, became a blur of ultrasounds, CT scans, MRIs, chemotherapy and radiation.

Rupert might have taken a leave of absence from his church in Vancouver, but a disagreement with his church treasurer had caused him to change his mind. He had only one criterion for a move. How soon could it be arranged?

When he arrived in Emerson, he knew he had made a mistake. It was such a small town, and the residents cheerfully informed him—it seemed almost a point of pride to them—that the town was prone to flooding in the spring. The church, too, was a disappointment. It was sparsely attended by older, sleepy retirees who looked up at him on Sunday morning with what he interpreted to be dour and impassive expressions.

"At least they are there," Elodie consoled him.

"Yes," Rupert sighed. "I have to keep reminding myself that these are God's children and I am their shepherd." But to himself, he complained, "Why me, Lord? Surely a wealthier, happier congregation needs a shepherd, too."

There was also the matter of the church choir. In his worry over Elodie and his unhappiness with their move, the matter of the church choir mushroomed out of proportion in his mind. It was not a good choir, but no one seemed to notice or even care. There was one bass with very unsteady intonation; there were two tenors who found it hard to catch their line over the wavering foundation of the bass singer; there were no altos and three sopranos, one of whom loved to sing heartily but sang in a monotone. On the rare occasions when Rupert sat in a back pew listening in on choir practice, he cringed in embarrassment.

How did Lily Kaltyk tolerate it? She seemed musical herself and there was evidence that she had been classically trained. How could she guide this motley crew through the hymns and a featured anthem, week after week after week? At the time, he did not know that when Lily described her choir to Cathy, she referred to them as "my dear little canaries," which made both women laugh.

For the choir members, it was a night out, a long tradition to get together to sing, and they belted out with enthusiasm all their old favourites, especially *Will your anchor hold in the storms of life.*

Rupert arrived at the church a half-hour early, hoping to find Lily alone. When he entered the sanctuary, he spotted her sitting quietly in the front pew in a wash of sunshine that shimmered through the western stained-glass window. Her eyes were closed, the palms of her hands open and crossed as she cradled her cell phone, listening to Mozart. Careful not to disturb her, he slipped into the back pew and closed his eyes, too.

The sparkling, dancing harmony transported him to another place. He was in a sunny courtyard, his face turned to the sun. The wind was strong and gusted with the sweeping violin lines while dry leaves skipped and fluttered around him. The sunshine was tender, butter-warm, and for the first time, he felt himself liking Emerson, even seeing some humour in the little dysfunctional choir.

He heard a door swing open and one of the choir members bounced into the choir loft, then abruptly stopped. "Lily, are you okay?" she shouted out. Rupert's eyes popped open in annoyance, but Lily, he noticed, simply turned off her phone and smiled. There is such an enormous peacefulness in her manner, such gentle tolerance and tenderness, he thought in amazement, noticing for the first time her long slender neck, the gentle curve of her breasts under a pale blue angora sweater, her long chestnut hair swept back loosely. He had never really paid attention to how very attractive she was. When the choir member spotted him at the back and called out to him, "Hello there, Reverend Cameron," he saw a flush creep up Lily's neck and turn her cheeks a soft pink, as delicate as a rose petal.

"I was wondering if I might have a word with you, Lily," he said. "But perhaps I could come back when choir practice is over." She looked so uncomfortable that Rupert made a mental note to arrive back in plenty of time, fearing that she might end the choir practice early and bolt for home.

• • •

"How did your practice go?" he asked, when he had returned and the others had gone.

She smiled a little, her shoulders lifting in a small shrug. "The usual. They mean well," she added, "and they are faithful."

"Yes," he said, turning his head sideways as if reflecting. "Faithful, but not musical."

To his surprise, Lily laughed. "You can't have everything."

"But it *is* a choir, and you would think that one of the prerequisites is that they should be able to sing. After all, would you hire a plumber who couldn't install a toilet?" Oh, why did he use a bathroom analogy, he berated himself, but he was surprised when she laughed again.

"What's on your mind?" she asked. He pulled a stuffed maroon chair close to the recessed organ pit, where it seemed to her that he had an unfair advantage since she had to look up several feet to talk with him.

"I'm thinking of switching hymn 343 and substituting 341 instead. The tune is a problem, though. The one printed in our hymnal is Engelberg but we could possibly substitute Sine Nomine or perhaps Camucua. The words of the hymn seem a suitable pre-Advent choice, however. Which tune do you prefer? Maybe Camucua is a bit sombre for this time of year?"

"I'm not sure, really," Lily replied, for she knew neither tune by their names. "In the past, we stuck with the old familiar hymns," she said. "People seem to sing out better." She was remembering how her choir had eagerly belted out *To God be the glory*.

"I see…"

Lily wondered if she should suggest another alternative, perhaps *Praise him, praise him, Jesus our blessed Redeemer*, which the congregation had sung lustily in November for the past twenty-five years. She glanced at Rupert, thinking that tonight, despite his dapper appearance—tan pants, white button-down shirt open at the collar, royal blue pullover—he seemed sad. Perhaps she should inquire about his wife. But then she remembered that when any of the parishioners inquired about her health, he had a standard answer: "She's as well as can be expected. We take one day at a time."

"I was wondering—"

"Have you considered—"

They both spoke at once. Lily felt herself blush, and to her relief, Rupert smiled. "I was wondering," he began again, "what you would think of inviting a paid soloist once a month for the worship service?"

"Paid soloist?" She turned her head and gazed off across the empty sanctuary, already imagining what long-time members, never prone to accepting change, would say to such a suggestion. Not only was this uncharted territory, it also involved spending more money. She sensed tension brewing even as she thought about it. Churches had split apart over lesser things.

"I heard that there is a teacher at the high school who was a semi-professional musician before returning to the classroom. He might be a possibility. And remember, Lily, Winnipeg is only an hour away. My goodness, the possibilities are endless. We could invite one of the performers from the Candlelight Concerts, or even an instrumentalist from the Winnipeg Symphony Orchestra. Maybe I could get in touch with the Virtuosi Director at the University of Winnipeg. A little fine chamber music would elevate the quality of music here in Emerson."

If Lily had found Rupert intimidating before this conversation, she now felt herself flushed with anger and irritation. Several things rushed into her mind, all of them unspeakable in church. Before she could think of how to respond, he leaned over to glance at the sheet music on the organ stand.

"Mmm... *Soliloquy* by Healey Willan. That slow, solemn, brooding bass line might be suitable for Lent but I wonder if it is really appropriate for the pre-Advent season. I remember the one you played last week—*Minuet in Classical Style*. By Armstrong Gibbs, I believe. Such tender grace notes and that lovely modulation between major and minor mode and then that forceful Tierce de Picardy at the end. That might be appropriate for the weeks after Easter. Ah," he sighed, "that long stretch of ordinary time after Pentecost. It's a challenge."

He leaned back in his chair and Lily hoped that he would rise to leave. "One last thing," he said. "You're a very adequate organist, but I was wondering if you might branch out and try some pieces that are a little more upbeat and lively."

"Like *Onward Christian Soldiers*, you mean?"

To her surprise, Rupert laughed. "Oh, Lily, you have a delightfully roguish sense of humour. No, I was thinking more of Bach's *Toccata and Fugue in D minor* or maybe part of Widor's *Symphony No. 5.*"

"Bach's *Toccata and Fugue in D minor*?" Cathy exploded after Lily had related this encounter, mimicking Rupert's comments. "Who does he think he is? Reverend Lord Mucky Muck?"

Lily smiled. "His heart is in the right place, I think, but all of a sudden I feel as if I just don't measure up, that I'm not good enough."

"Hey, you listen to me, Lily Kaltyk, and you listen up good. Don't you let that man—yes! I know, he's a man of the cloth—" she said, gesturing wildly, "just don't let him, or anyone else define you or what you are."

The following Thursday, to her relief, Rupert didn't come to choir practice, and it was only on Friday that she learned that his wife had died.

"Everyone in town is talking about it. Cancer," her mother said with finality. "Not that anyone knew her, but still...with her husband being such a prominent minister..."

Lily watched her mother prepare the red borscht and dumplings that she made every Friday. When Lily was a child, she had loved to watch her mother prepare varenyky, the boiled dumplings so similar to perogies, and she had discovered that by the time she was a teenager, she was as adept at making them as her mother. Sometimes they filled them with mashed potatoes and fried onion, other times braised ground beef and chopped cabbage.

Suddenly, she became anxious. What was she doing, thinking about making dumplings when she had just learned of the death of her minister's wife? She would probably be asked to play the organ at the funeral, she thought in horror. The funeral would undoubtably be at Knox Church, presided over by a visiting dignitary, perhaps even the Moderator of The Presbyterian Church in Canada. Rupert was that kind of man. He would want the best for his beloved wife.

"I hear the funeral is to be from Wiebe Funeral Home in Altona," her mother said as she wiped her hands free of flour and turned to stir cabbage into the beet soup. Her mother had always insisted that the borscht must look and taste like the rich dark soil in which the vegetables grew.

Lily exhaled, limp with relief. She knew that Wiebe Funeral Home used taped music—music that comes out of a pipe, her mother called it. "Who's conducting the service?" she inquired.

"I hear that it's the Lutheran minister from here in town."

Lily pursed her lips, nodded a little and murmured, "Mmm…" It would be a subdued and short service in a town thirty-five kilometres up the road. There would be light refreshments to follow, some egg salad sandwiches, pickles, squares and urns of tea. Perhaps, she mused, I have misjudged Rupert a little.

CHAPTER 6

Christmas drifted toward the new year. On a cold, snowy evening before Ukrainian New Year, Lily curled up in their small, cramped living room, watching the movie *Fiddler on the Roof* with her mother. She hadn't wanted to see the movie again. Instead, she was eager to dive into her new library book about the old houses of the prairies, but her mother had insisted, saying that she liked the music. At least, Lily thought, sighing, it is a very long film. It helps to fill the empty hours that stretch between the drying of the supper dishes and going to bed. *Sunrise, sunset, sunrise, sunset, swiftly fly the years, one season following another, laden with happiness and tears,* sang Tevye and Golde in their plaintive, bewildered voices.

Lily looked across the room to where her mother sat in her worn brown corduroy armchair, watching the movie and knitting. Krystyna quietly wiped away tears. Puzzled, Lily wondered what moved her stoic mother to tears when she heard this song. Was she remembering the sudden loss of her husband in the dreadful car accident so many years ago? Was she wondering how it was that Lily, her only child, was unmarried and middle-aged when Krystyna's friends were surrounded by broods of grandchildren? Was she thinking back to her younger years when she and her sisters played so innocently on their parents' farm? Or did the movie just express the quiet, resigned suffering of the Slavic and Jewish peoples? Lily simply did not know, and she realized that she did not have the kind of relationship with her mother that would allow her to ask such an intimate thing.

Lily and Krystyna had been invited, as usual, to celebrate Ukrainian New Year with some farm families out of town. They crowded into a car with Aunt Sofiya's family, and when they arrived, the farmhouse was sparkling with lights, music and dancing. The kitchen table groaned with food: breads, cheeses, smoked meat, cabbage rolls, perogies, cakes and tortes made with ground almonds. The adults were enjoying glasses of home-distilled horilka flavoured with fruit, spices and red peppers.

Lily squeezed into the group, pausing to admire a new baby, greeting the other women. Despite the noise, confusion and fun, she felt depressed. She wondered if she looked sad. Around her, couples scolded or hugged children, women discussed the price of millet and oats needed to make kasha and bemoaned the exorbitant rise in the price of fabrics, men complained about their bosses or unions and wondered whether they should trade in their truck this year. In the midst of the music and laughter, Lily had never felt more isolated, her aloneness an ache in her belly.

After she had eaten—no one seemed to notice that she was very quiet—she eased toward the back door and untangled her winter clothes from the jumble of jackets and scarves piled on the chest freezer in the hallway. She tugged on her coat, wrapped a woolen scarf tightly around her head and throat, thrust her hands into a pair of thick mittens that her mother had made, and stepped outside.

The air was crisp, full of crystals, making her nostrils feel stiff. The icy blue moon cast thin shadows as she crunched toward the end of the farm laneway. It had been a clear, sunny day, warming the bark on the south side of the double row of deciduous trees that lined the lane. Now that the sun had disappeared, the temperature had dropped quickly to twenty below, causing the trees to crack and groan.

In the distance, Lily heard the howls of coyotes, short yelps that rose and fell in pitch, punctuated with staccato yips. Lily had grown up hearing coyotes, so this did not frighten her. She knew that coyotes are generally shy, but their breeding season continued through February. Their calling told her that they were looking for mates. How strong that instinct is for creatures of all kinds, she thought, that desire to find a partner. When she reached the end of the laneway, she stood looking up at the moon, wondering if she would ever find a mate.

Slowly, she turned back toward the farmhouse, hoping that someone might have missed her. It wasn't time to leave for home yet, but she couldn't imagine that anyone even noticed she was gone. They were all too busy dancing, talking, eating and drinking, the children darting in and out, tagging and teasing each other.

When the party was over and they had arrived back home, Lily and Krystyna crawled out from around Sofiya's sleeping grandchildren in the back seat of the car, unlocked the door of their house and carried their now empty dishes into the kitchen.

"What's this?" Lily asked, pointing to something covered with a tea towel on the kitchen counter.

"I was making one. I thought I might as well make two."

Lily lifted the towel. It was a Kyiv cake, one of her mother's specialties, light spongy layers with a crunchy slice of meringue and hazelnuts between the sponge, slathered with jam and topped with a rich buttercream frosting. No one made a Kyiv cake like her mother.

"It's for the minister. Reverend Cameron. I thought he might enjoy a treat once in a while. It must be lonely for him now that his wife is gone. Some Sundays he just looks so sad. Tomorrow, Lily, you can walk over to the manse and take it to him."

"No!" Lily snapped. Her mother looked at her in surprise, confused by her reaction. "You can deliver it yourself," Lily said, hurrying upstairs to prepare for bed.

"Well! Whatever!" Krystyna called out.

The following day, to Lily's relief, the cake had disappeared, but conversation with her mother was stilted and strained. Neither of them knew how to breach the gap that had been created by Lily's sharp response.

She brooded about the week ahead, dreading the fact that in two more days she had to prepare, once again, for choir practice. A headache pounded at the sides of her eyes. She ran some cold water over a cloth, wrung it out and was about to lie back on the sofa with the cloth on her forehead when her mother walked into the room carrying something in her hand. "I forgot to mention. This came for you."

Lily frowned at her mother and reached for the letter. "When? When did it come?" she demanded.

"I'm not sure. A few days ago."

Lily stared down at the envelope. In the left-hand corner, it read University of Manitoba Architecture Department.

Upstairs, in the privacy of her bedroom, Lily's hands trembled as she tore open the envelope. It contained several pamphlets outlining various aspects of the Architecture Department. She opened the cover letter, which had been neatly folded in three. She needed to read only part of the first sentence: *We regret to inform you…*

Lily crushed the letter into a ball and hurled it across the room. She picked up the pamphlets and with a fierce energy, she ripped them into jagged halves, one after another, and threw them into her waste basket. She kicked off her shoes and lay down on the bed, straight and stiff, then draped the cold wet cloth over her forehead, waiting for her pounding head to ease, waiting for her heart to calm.

CHAPTER 7

The weeks of February and March crawled forward without a hopeful hint that just around the corner there would be green swelling buds and soft melting breezes. Lily taught her music classes to bored and listless children. Had they picked up on her ennui or were they truly not all that interested in music?

She trudged week by week to choir practice. She was relieved that Rupert had stopped talking about paid soloists and alternate hymn tunes and appropriate music for the season of Lent. But one night in March, he popped into the church as the choir was gathering, waved and turned toward the vestry. One of the choir members called out, "Will you be coming to the pancake supper on Shrove Tuesday, Reverend Cameron?"

He paused, looking bewildered. "Oh, yes, yes. Of course. I nearly forgot. Since my wife died, I just seem to be in a fog. I'll see you on Tuesday night."

On the following Thursday, Rupert entered the church a half hour before the choir members. When Lily arrived, he said, "Please," indicating that he wished her to sit beside him in the front pew.

They sat in silence for a few minutes, until Lily said in a gentle voice, "There's something I've been wondering."

"Yes?"

"In your years in ministry, I'm sure you've had to guide a lot of people through a time of grieving." Rupert glanced at her, nodding. "Does it make it any easier when you have to go through it yourself?"

To her horror, Rupert started to cry, long shuddering sobs. She sat paralyzed, sweat pooling in her armpits, breathing quickly. She had no idea what to do. Should she say that she was sorry? Should she pat his arm? In the end, she opened her purse, pulled out a packet of tissues and handed them to him.

When he had composed himself, he turned slightly toward her, stood up and said, "Thank you," and then he left. When the choir members began to arrive, Lily found herself still shaking.

"Are you okay, Lily?" someone asked. "You look a little off tonight."

When she admitted that she was feeling poorly, one of the sopranos said, "Now, you run along home and have a good hot rum with butter. An early night is what you need. Don't worry about us. We know how to practice the hymns."

Rupert sauntered home, feeling drained but emotionally rested. He had been slightly embarrassed, breaking down in front of Lily. But, he mused, she always seems so calm, so reassuring. She doesn't fret over me with words of comfort like some women might. She just accepts me for who I am.

When he was upset or struggling with an issue, it seemed to Rupert that his thoughts invariably turned inward to his unhappy childhood in Flin Flon, northern Manitoba. These were memories that he preferred to suppress: the humble houses perched on ragged rocks of an old volcanic belt from two billion years ago, the insolated boxed pipes carrying water from house to house over the rocks—it was impossible to put water pipes underground—the endless lakes and menacing shadow of trees, the huge mining shaft that dominated the town, the rhythm and well-being of the community precariously dependent on how the mines were doing. He recalled that most schoolyard disputes were solved with fists as hard as stone. He remembered his father, stooped and dirty, home from his shift underground, sucking on a beer bottle and shovelling food into his mouth before collapsing into bed. He recalled how his mother would demand that Rupert take a Saturday night bath before making him go to church with her on Sunday. He resented this. "Dad doesn't go," he shouted, but his anger arose from fear; his friends didn't go, either. If they found out, there would be no end of torment for him.

When he was twelve, something happened to change him forever. A new minister came to their church—straight from Ireland, everyone said. Until that time, their Presbyterian ministers had always been Scottish or of Scottish descent. The Reverend Boyle was flamboyant, a marvellous storyteller, and had the ability to put a fanciful spin on the most ordinary of things. Rupert was fascinated with his fine car, his quality coats, his beautiful young wife and their two small, perfect, blond-haired children. Later, when Rupert had taken all the steps needed for approval to enter ministry, he never admitted to anyone that he had never felt a genuine sense of call from God as so many other ministers claimed to have. What he felt, instead, seemed even more powerful to him. He was called to leave Flin Flon and he was called to have some of the fine things that a life in ministry might give him. He would be admired, honoured, showered with gifts, and have a place of respect in the community, he believed.

In his more honest moments, he acknowledged that it was impossible to truly slough off his childhood, but when he sat in his fine living room in Vancouver and when he drove his powerful car through the splendid suburb of Shaughnessy, he preferred to believe that the confused and angry boy in Flin Flon was not him. He had transformed himself into something tasteful and refined. He had married a handsome wife with impeccable taste, and together their life was dignified and copacetic.

After Elodie died, he was lonely. Once or twice, James, the Lutheran minister who had conducted Elodie's funeral, had invited him to the coffee shop, but it was not the type of companionship for which he longed. An even greater angst was troubling him. He felt a powerful tug to leave Emerson. He didn't sense a call to a particular place, but he had an almost claustrophobic need to leave. The town filled him with unhappy darkness.

When the phone call came inviting him to meet the parishioners of New Hopewell church in Ontario, he had been remarkedly unsurprised. It was what he expected. The process had started. He felt its tug. Perhaps, though, he considered, he should talk it over with James.

CHAPTER 8

The vestry at Knox Presbyterian Church was a small, non-descript room, but it served multiple functions. There was a cupboard in which Rupert could hang his vestments—preaching stoles, a black Geneva gown, a white alb. In the corner of the room, there was a small desk where he could review his sermon notes before Sunday worship. In another corner, a triangular cupboard with a glass door held the vessels for communion—the silver plates, the chalice for the minister and the round silver trays with individual cups for parishioners' communion wine. There was space, too, for several padded wooden chairs, so the room could sometimes double as a small meeting room for the Sunday school teachers or for counselling. Beside the desk on the back wall, there was a second door that opened into a space that was more like a closet than a room. This was called the "choir cupboard," and it was here that Lily stored her collection of easy-to-sing anthems.

On the Wednesday before Palm Sunday, she walked into the church, hoping to find the music for *Hosanna Processional*. The choir and a few Sunday school children had sung it several years before and she remembered that it featured a joyful retelling of the ride into Jerusalem. She stepped into the choir cupboard and began her search. Where was it? Not on the west or north walls. Perhaps it had been stored on the east wall, but the only way to access that shelving involved shutting the door between the choir cupboard and the vestry. She had barely time to do that before she heard footsteps. Someone was entering the vestry.

She gasped, her hand over her mouth. She heard two voices—Rupert and another man. Should she burst out of the cupboard while there was still time or would that startle them? It seemed an awkward and bad idea. The entire scene unfolded in a few seconds, but it felt to Lily like an eternity. She had hesitated too long. She had no choice but to sink to the floor and wait until Rupert and his guest had gone.

She could hear their voices quite plainly.

"It was so good of you to come, James. You have no idea what a comfort you have been to me since my wife died."

"Rupert, my friend, it was nothing. Nothing at all. I know you would have done the same for me if the circumstances were different." Lily recognized the voice of the other man as that of the Lutheran minister who had conducted the funeral. Now he asked, with concern in his voice, "How have you been? Are things getting any easier?"

"I've been coping, but as for living happily…no. It's been more tough than I thought. When we moved here a year ago, the doctors told us that she might have a year at most. I wanted to make that year as good as possible, and that's why I left my church in Vancouver. A smaller community like this, less pressure, fewer expectations…but it has been hard."

"I can only imagine."

"James, I invited you in to ask for your counsel. I have some serious things to consider, and I could use your guidance."

"I shall do my best, God willing. What's on your mind?"

"I've been here only one year. It's a short time, I know that, but I'm considering moving along. It just seems wise to make a fresh start. A church in New Hopewell, Ontario, has issued a call to me. It seems to be a strong congregation, larger than this one, and a new beginning would let me leave this painful year behind."

Lily, listening in the choir cupboard, held her breath, waiting through a long quiet pause.

"Do you feel God's hand in this?"

"To tell you the honest truth, I don't know. I only know that staying here brings me back over and over to painful memories, but starting afresh means new possibilities. Is that a call from God or is it my own desperation?"

"Ultimately, Rupert, what do you think God asks of you?"

Lily waited through another time of silence.

"I've always taken my life calling to be the words of Micah 6:8—Do justice, love mercy and walk humbly with God."

"Ah...you feel called to justice, mercy and to walk humbly with God," James mused. "In other words, God calls you to do good work."

"Well, of course, sure."

"So where can you do good work, my friend?"

"Anywhere, I guess."

"Precisely. You can live out justice, mercy and a humble walk with God wherever you are. So, my next question is this: in which situation would you be happier and more able to do this? Here in Emerson or in the new place?"

Crouched in the small space behind the door, Lily wished desperately that she had never come into the church today, that she could escape this dreadful situation.

"I need to leave," Rupert said. "I need to make a fresh start. It isn't fair to this congregation. I know it has only been one year and it will be hard for them, but I need to look after myself, too."

There was another long time of silence.

"You seem a bit troubled by this decision."

"Yes...and no. I know that I need to leave. That part is easy. The problem is...in the past year I've become interested in someone in the community."

Lily heard the conversation stall again. The Lutheran pastor seemed as taken aback with this revelation as she was.

"A woman?"

"It makes me feel guilty and untrustworthy. While I was busy caring for my dying wife, I became enchanted with another woman. I've been so drawn to her...attracted to her simple goodness, the innocence of her spirit, her kind and gentle ways."

"Was she one of your wife's nurses?"

"No," Rupert replied. "She's my church organist. Sometimes I come to choir practice so I can watch her kindhearted dealings with an unlikely bunch of non-singers. Sometimes I come to just watch the way her lovely neck flushes until the blush reaches up to her cheeks."

CHAPTER 9

In the weeks after hearing Rupert's preposterous—in her opinion—secret confession, Lily was determined to avoid him. In uncharacteristic fashion, she arrived late for choir practice. She made sure to leave with one of the choir members, sometimes asking for a lift home. Sunday was easier. Rupert was busy, preoccupied with last minute details of the worship service and busy greeting parishioners as they arrived and left.

One day, though, when Lily was simultaneously boiling cabbage leaves, frying ground beef with onions and garlic, and simmering tomato sauce, she heard a knock at the front door. Her mother, who had been cleaning at the front of the house, welcomed the visitor, and when Lily turned around, Rupert was in the kitchen. She blushed and quickly wiped her hands with a tea towel.

"It smells delicious, whatever you're making."

Lily knew that this was a half-truth, for the umami redolence of frying beef, onion and garlic could not mask the skunky odor of boiled cabbage. "I'm making holubtsi, cabbage rolls," she stammered.

"Oh. I've never tried those. I'm sure they're very tasty."

Lily stared at him, then glanced away. Two questions rushed into her mind. How could a man as old as Rupert never have eaten cabbage rolls? There was a bigger question, though: Why had he come?

"I was wondering," he said, "if I might take you out for a cup of coffee?"

"Now?" Lily waved her hand toward the stove. Clearly, he could see that she was in the middle of preparing a long and complicated dish. From behind Rupert, her mother gestured in a way that seemed to indicate go, go.

When she had slid into the front seat of Rupert's car, she felt even more uncomfortable. The vehicle—an Audi A4—reflected the style and quality that Rupert exhibited in his clothing. The car was sleek and silver with creamy leather seats.

"May I help you with your seat belt?"

"No, no. I can manage."

"First," Rupert said, "I would like to show you something. Something that has been on my mind." He swung the car away from the front of her house, heading not to the coffee shop but somewhere else. They rode in silence for a while, until he pulled into a wooded area beside Crow Wing Trail. "There's a nice bench over there," Rupert pointed out, "and it's a lovely day."

Walking to the bench, Lily worried that her legs might give out and she would collapse onto the wood-chip path. When they had settled, the only sound was the loud ringing chippy-chipper song of a bird. "That's a Connecticut warbler," Rupert said. "I fancy myself a bit of a bird expert."

"Oh."

Again, they lapsed into silence until Rupert cleared his throat. "There's something I need to tell you," he began. Lily glanced at him, waiting. "I know it may come as a shock to you, but after my wife's death, I've given a lot of thought to the future and I have decided that I need to leave Emerson. A larger church in New Hopewell, Ontario, invited me to preach for a call last month. You remember that Sunday I was away?" Lily shrugged slightly and nodded. "They've invited me to be their minister, and I intend to tell the elders and church Board members this evening that I am leaving."

"I see," she said, flooded with relief. She understood now; he had simply wanted her to know before telling the church leadership.

"I know this will be hard on the church members here, but I felt—and still feel—that this is the right decision."

"Yes, I see your point."

"Do you? Do you really see my point, Lily?"

"I imagine that you want to make a fresh start. You must have painful memories associated with Emerson after your wife's illness and death." She was about to add that perhaps, though, he might do well to focus on his grieving, for his loss would surely follow him to Ontario.

"That's what I appreciate about you, Lily. I've never known a woman who is so tender, gentle and thoughtful." Lily held her breath. "I've come to the conclusion that I can't bear to part with you."

Startled, Lily released her breath. "You want me to move to New Hopewell and be your church organist?" she blurted.

Rupert roared with laughter. "I love your sense of humour, Lily. No, of course not. I want you to come to New Hopewell with me as my wife." She watched in horror as he reached into his pocket and pulled out a small, blue velvet box.

Cathy was aghast. "How in heaven's name did you answer?"

"To be honest, I was so astonished that I said the first thing that came into my mind. I told him that I had never considered us to be a match made in heaven."

"And?" Cathy laughed.

"Like you, he laughed." Lily smiled. From the vantage point of a few days later, she was finally able to see a little humour in the situation. "I told him that I need time to think about it. Then he asked me how much time. I said I didn't know. Enough time to think things through."

"Well! Yes!"

"I mentioned the fact that his wife had been dead only a few months, and he responded that when you live with a spouse with a long-time terminal illness, you do most of your grieving beforehand. He said for him there was even a sense of relief when his wife died, glad that she did not have to suffer anymore. There are so many indignities at the end, he told me."

"Do you believe that? That he has done a lot of his grieving already?"

"Honestly, Cathy, I don't know. I don't know what to make of the whole thing, and I have no idea how to answer him."

The two women sat quietly, both lost in their own thoughts, until Cathy broke the silence. "Lily, my dear friend, it was only a few months ago that you sat here in this very room and told me that your life is miserable—no partner, no children, a stalled career if you can call it that; you're a middle-aged woman living on the poverty line with her mother. Honestly, Lily, think about it. What have you got to lose?"

"Cathy! I can't believe that you would think that way! I have a great deal to lose. You, mother, Aunt Sofiya, my sense of belonging." Even though she had often railed against Emerson, the only town in which she had ever lived, she realized that her experience living there had been safe, sheltered and, in its own way, nurturing. In that moment, she appreciated the comfort and stability created by the repetitive rhythms of her life. How could she leave all this behind?

There was something that Lily hadn't shared with her friend. Sitting on the wooden bench with Rupert, she had turned toward him and said, "There's one major problem here, Rupert," using his Christian name for the first time. "I don't love you and you certainly don't know me well enough to love me."

"Love," he sighed. "Sometimes I think that love is highly overrated in marriage. There are so many things that bind a man and woman together in marriage: mutual interests, respect for each other, sharing good food and wine, humour, companionship, a bit of travel thrown in. Those are some of the things that glue people together. I think we could be very happy together, Lily." He had reached out to take her hand, but she tucked it quickly into her sleeve.

Lily could no longer put off having a conversation with her mother about Rupert's proposal. Once it was public knowledge that Rupert was leaving, she raised the subject with her mother, telling her just what she had told Cathy. Krystyna did not seem very surprised. She had simply murmured in Ukrainian, "What is meant to be, will be." Does every language have a phrase that espouses such patient fatalism? Lily wondered.

"How will you answer him?" Krystyna demanded.

Lily sighed. "Mother, I simply don't know. I don't know what to do."

"Let me ask you this—is this how you want to spend the rest of your life, living in a small town on the edge of Manitoba, directing an out-of-tune choir, unmarried and living with your mother? Or do you want to take a risk? Step out into the great unknown?"

"Mother! I hardly expected to hear that from you! The man is almost twenty years older than me and I barely know him at all."

"Still...I think you can count on the fact that he is a good man."

For several days, Lily was in an agony of indecision. Could she leave her familiar life behind and step into an undetermined future with a man she knew only superficially? It seemed not only unwise but reckless and irrational. She had made up her mind; she would not move to New Hopewell, Ontario; nor would she marry Rupert.

But something nagged at her mind. As her mother had said, he did seem to be a good and kind man; he was confident and sure of himself. She admired the meticulous way he dressed, which somehow communicated to her that she, too, would be looked after in a careful manner. But really, Lily, she scolded herself, is that a basis for marriage?

CHAPTER 10

It was the last choir practice before summer. There was no year-end choir social or barbeque. Her choristers just drifted away, relieved to be starting their vacation from church. The congregation did not seem to mind at all that there was no choir to lead them in their plaintive, sparse summer worship. It was a time in Manitoba, perhaps in all of Canada, where even the most devout Christian believer would rather be at a lake, in a cottage, a cabin, a camp site. This summer, Lily thought, it would be even more disheartening than usual. Their minister was leaving them and no one would feel an ounce of allegiance to a preacher who takes over when the regular minister is not there. There would be a faithful core of dull-spirited worshippers who would never notice that Lily played the same prelude week after week.

She walked around the choir loft, picking up and sorting out the leftover anthem booklets. When she had finished stashing away the music and had pulled shut the door to the choir cupboard, she heard someone walking toward the vestry. She stood paralyzed, knowing that it would be Rupert and he would be expecting her answer. She took a deep breath. If ever there was a need for courage, it was now.

"I have something wonderful to show you, Lily. Quite wonderful!" She could hear the excitement in his voice. "Look," he said, suddenly boyish, tugging at the inner pocket of his sports jacket, "here are photos of the Old Manse where we will be living. I had a walk through it when I preached for the call, of course, but I was waiting for these photos to arrive from Ontario so I could show you."

Lily gazed at the first picture, astonished. She was not in love with Rupert, but she instantly fell head over heels in love with the Old Manse in New Hopewell.

"It was modeled after an old manse in Auchterarder, Perthshire, Scotland," Rupert rushed on, noting her pleased reaction. "It has Georgian era features, large windows and perfect symmetry."

"Yes, yes, I can see that."

"The kitchen has a genuine, original double Belfast sink and an Aga cooker."

"Aga cooker?"

Rupert shrugged. "And," he hurried on, "there is a dining room, of course, and a living room and…this is funny," he chuckled, "there's a room called a snug."

"Snug?"

"We would call it a den in Canada, I suppose. Or a family room. They call it a snug in Scotland." Lily smiled. "Upstairs, four bedrooms. Two baths. It will make us a truly splendid home," he added. "The church members are extremely proud of the Old Manse. They want nothing changed."

Lily stared at the photo of the house, taken from the edge of the front lawn. She could see a manicured flower garden with pink climbing roses clinging to a pergola. On the right of the photo, she saw a long outdoor table with eight chairs nestled into a stone patio. But the house…it took her breath away.

"It's a superb example of a Georgian home," she told Rupert, her head tilted, gazing at the photo, turning it around. With a tremor in her voice, she added, "The Georgian Era in architecture lasted from 1714 to 1830, you see, right through the reigns of the King Georges, starting with George I and ending with the death of George IV in 1830. This style was popular for a long time in both Great Britain and North America. No wonder it had a revival in Canada around 1910 and is still popular in the building of grand family homes." Lily was remembering one of her escape visits to Winnipeg, where she spent a happy day wandering through a neighbourhood called Wolseley, photographing beautiful, grand, Georgian, single-family houses stretching along the north side of the Assiniboine River, south of Portage Avenue. "Perfect symmetry," she said, holding out the photo for Rupert to see, almost forgetting that he stood close enough to touch her. "Perfect window placement, five upstairs, four down, two on either side of the front door. The windows must be multi-paned, of course. A hipped roof, and under the eaves you can see the dentils. Great ornamentation. But the front door! Can you believe this front door? It's panelled with a transom window overtop."

Lily paused, pressing her hand against her chest as if to still her beating heart. Rupert noticed this and smiled, noting that a flush had moved from her neck up into her cheeks. He passed her another photo. "The front hall from inside."

This time, Lily gasped. It was painted a soft, golden hue with crisp white wainscotting. The curving staircase with its dark, moulded dowels and shining banister were offset by an elegant dark oak side table holding a gold ceramic vase of daffodils. A long woolen carpet runner led to the glass-panelled front door, which stood under an arched doorframe. Lily could see herself walking slowly toward that doorway, not rushing, merely savouring every minute that it took her to greet her unseen guest. "I can imagine Scarlett O'Hara sweeping down that staircase," she said, and Rupert laughed.

When she turned to hand the photos back to him, she saw that he was smiling at her, his eyes shining with hope. "It is an exquisite house," she began, "and I could never have imagined being able to live in such a grand place, not even in my wildest dreams."

"Then, it's settled!" Rupert broke in. "Now we can set a date for the wedding. My best friend here in Emerson is the Lutheran minister. I know he'd be willing to do a wedding on short notice. We'll just have a few people—your mother, a couple of witnesses. Then we'll be set to go."

It was more difficult than she imagined leaving behind her mother, her home, her Aunt Sofiya, her friend Cathy, the familiar streets of Emerson, and even her long-time canary singers. She wondered if it would be easier if she knew what her life was going to be like. Some mornings she woke in a cold sweat, realizing that this precipitous decision to marry and move to Ontario was not really her decision at all. Everything seemed far easier for Rupert. Feeling a prickle of resentment, Lily reminded herself that not only had he put this plan into action but, in addition, his roots in Emerson were short; there had not been time to build lasting relationships. It was not a wrench for him to leave. She could also see that Rupert knew more-or-less what his life would be like in New Hopewell. He would settle into a new congregation, but the old familiar patterns of ministry would be a continuation, a variation, of his previous life. But what could she expect? What would their life together be like? Would she find herself compared to Elodie?

When he asked if she would help him pack the contents of his manse in Emerson, she replied, "I shall leave that to you." She could not bear to think of having to sort out Elodie's belongings, perhaps discard her needlepoint, find bundles of perfumed letters, maybe even have to dispose of a medicine chest of expired medications. She imagined Elodie's nightgown hanging primly on the back of the bathroom door beside Rupert's robe.

It would take them twenty hours to drive from Emerson to New Hopewell. On the first day of travel, there were long stretches of time to talk and think. She began to worry aloud about her new role. "Is there some type of manual on how to be a good minister's wife?"

Rupert laughed and said, "Just be yourself. That's enough."

After they had rolled along through mile after mile of the endless forest of northwestern Ontario, she tried again. "If there *was* a manual about marrying a minister, would there have to be two parts? One for what is expected of a wife? But something completely different might be expected of a husband if his wife were the minister?" She had begun to suspect that a male spouse of a minister would have far fewer societal and church expectations placed upon him.

"Lily," he said, patting her hand, "don't worry your pretty little head about these things. It will all be fine."

• • •

It had surprised her, on their first night together, that Rupert had been exuberant, even enchanted by what he referred to as her calm beauty. "You are both peaceful and exciting," he told her as he gently caressed her cheek, then slid his hand slowly down her neck, bending to softly kiss the hollow of her throat before reaching down to caress the roundness of her breast. He put his mouth to her nipple, breathing out, "Lovely." She could feel his stiff erection by her side, but still he took his time, a patient, thoughtful lover, stroking, touching, until it felt as if each nerve in her body was alive with longing.

The following day she was overwhelmed by his many small acts of devotion and tenderness—the way he gently brushed aside her hair so he could see her face, the way he held her hand as they hurried through the rain for a meal in a roadside diner, and after stopping at a motel for the night, the way he folded her into his arms, gently kissed her, and urged her to have a long soaking bath after their lengthy and tiring car ride while he promised to put a bottle of white wine on ice. It was a surprise to her, when she emerged from her bath, pink and flushed, refreshed after hours of travel, to find that she eagerly looked forward to another night of making love with Rupert.

On the third day, they both sighed in relief at the sight of the rolling Northumberland hills. They turned off the busy 401 highway, south toward the lake. Their car windows were lowered, catching the summer breeze, and Lily exclaimed, "I can smell the lake." They rolled past a brewery and a farmer's market with bushel baskets overflowing with beans, corn and harvest apples. They gazed in amusement at a herd of alpacas roaming in the pasture of a farm field. On the wide main street of New Hopewell, they noticed a bakery café, a new supermarket, an art gallery, and a square park with a pretty gazebo and mature trees.

"This will be a very agreeable place to live," Rupert said. "It's three times larger than Emerson."

Lily stared out the car window, wondering if she would ever get used to living here, wondering if the house she saw in the photos would be as splendid and breathtaking as she imagined. When they rounded the corner, searching for the address they had been given, Lily's breath caught in her throat, and her heart pounded. Set back from the street, serene, comfortable, solid and symmetrical, the house was exactly as she had seen in the photo.

"We're home," Rupert said, smiling at her, noting the endearing pink flush that had risen into her cheeks.

CHAPTER 11

In the time that followed, there were many things that delighted them about the house and property, and there were some things that made them laugh. Someone—probably a handyman from the church with too many planks of wood taking up space in his shed—had built a privacy wall between the south edge of the manse laneway and a row of aging spruce trees on the neighbouring property. "Most people build a discreet fence," Rupert chuckled, but this one towered over their heads. They privately joked about it, referring to it as the "Berlin Wall." It was only in the months ahead that they came to learn why the fence had been built.

On the morning that the moving van arrived, they had been standing beside the wall, watching as men wearing overalls carried in furniture and boxes sealed with packing tape, when they heard a voice call out, "Well, howdy, neighbours." They turned in unison to see a woman emerging from the far end of the wall. She was short and stocky, her bright red hair kinky and beginning to thread with white. "Name's Dolly Inkpen," she said. "I'd be your neighbour next door, so I am." She held an orange casserole dish clutched in oversized oven mitts pockmarked with burns.

"Pleased to meet you, Dolly," Rupert replied, bowing slightly. Lily raised her hand in a little wave as it was impossible to offer a handshake.

"I saw dat moving van this morning and I thought, for sure, I should fire up a scoff. I said to myself, 'Dolly, my dear, they'll be wanting some taken up. There won't be no time for the missus to fix sumpin tonight.'"

"That is terribly kind of you," Rupert said in his clergy voice. "Shall I…?" He reached toward the casserole.

"Oh, Lardy, no. It's terrible hot. I just took it out of the cooker. I'll just lodge it on da bridge." She stepped around them and set the casserole on the side porch.

That had been their introduction to their neighbour, Dolly Inkpen. She had been born and raised in Newfoundland but had found her way to Nova Scotia as an adult and lived there for twenty years before moving to New Hopewell to live in a small rundown cottage next door to the Old Manse.

After they had lived in the Old Manse for a month, Rupert made an announcement. "When I was married to Elodie and we lived in Vancouver, we always entertained on Sunday evenings. I'd like to continue that tradition, now that we've moved into the fall season."

"Entertained? What does that mean?"

"Oh, something simple. Sunday night dinner. We'll rotate through the congregation, starting with the church leadership, of course. Fall is a busy time in church life. The groups all start to meet again after the summer break, and then we start the move toward Advent and Christmas. What was it that Elodie used to serve? A standing rib roast, medium rare, Yorkshire puddings, some gravy, roast potatoes and green beans with almonds and beurre blanc. A trifle pudding for dessert is nice. A dinner is a good way to build relationships with the people in the congregation, to help them feel at home with us."

Lily felt moisture begin to pool in her armpits and behind her knees. Yorkshire pudding? Standing rib roast? Beurre blanc?

Before the doorbell rang announcing their first guests, Lily stood in the kitchen pressing a cold dishcloth to her brow, listening as the Yorkshires sputtered and smoked in the Aga cooker, an old monster which seemed to have erratic heat. Why could she not have a shining, stainless steel range?

Why had she not insisted on Ukrainian food, which would have been easier for her to prepare? The roast beef sat draped under foil, resting on the counter. When she lifted the cover, she gasped. The roast sat in a pool of bloody juice. She whisked out the Yorkshires, which promptly collapsed in on themselves, a pale mound of dough glistening with oil. She thrust the roast back into the oven.

When Rupert called out to her, Lily rubbed her sweating palms against the side of her dress and entered the hallway to greet their guests. Mr. Cruikshank, Rupert had told her, was the Chair of the Board of Managers and a prominent businessman in town. Mrs. Cruikshank was the local high school principal. After taking their coats, Rupert, who looked both casual and dignified in his crisp khaki pants and navy blue sweater with a hint of white shirt and tie at his neck, gestured toward the living room. "Please. Find yourself a comfortable chair."

Mr. Cruikshank stepped into the room, but Mrs. Cruikshank turned to Lily and said, "Nonsense. There must be things I can do to help with dinner." She took Lily by the arm as if she were the host and Lily the guest and bustled her into the kitchen.

Lily knew that Rupert would be busy offering drinks. He had a surefire method, he once told her. There are Presbyterians who don't—drink, that is—and there are Presbyterians who do, and never the twain shall meet, he explained. It's a mistake to come right out and offer alcohol to a teetotaller because they would be offended. "So," he said, rather smugly, "I always say, 'May I offer you a glass of ginger ale or a sip of sherry before dinner?' If they go for the ginger ale, I know the lay of the land. If they opt for sherry, and," he declared, "if it's a man, I smile and say, 'I can do one better than that. I've got a very fine, old Lagavulin languishing in the cupboard. Ice or neat?'"

"Dreadful business, this," Mrs. Cruikshank exclaimed as they stood in front of the steaming stove. "Expecting you to do a formal dinner when you've just moved in, and you a new bride, too! Men!"

Lily exhaled and leaned forward. "This has been a nightmare," she confessed. "The Yorkshires are an oily mess and the roast is back in the oven swimming in blood. I'm just not used to cooking this way."

Mrs. Cruikshank laughed and patted her arm. "My dear, I'll give you a hand. I'm a whiz with gravy. It covers a multitude of sins. The men will never notice. You have an extra apron? Here, I brought an apple pie for dessert—from the grocery store. Who's got time to bake?"

After dinner was over, Mr. Cruikshank turned to Lily. "You're very quiet." Then turning to Rupert, he smiled and asked, "Is she always this quiet?"

"It's one of the things I love about Lily. She has a gentle, quiet soul."

"Well!" Mrs. Cruickshank declared, turning to address Lily. "You be on guard against letting this congregation gobble you up. You're your own person and you should be respected in your own right and not just because of your role as 'the minister's wife.'" She used her fingers to create quotation marks around the end of her statement. "You remember that book by Virginia Wolfe—*A Room of One's Own*?"

Lily tilted her head and gave a little shrug. "Vaguely."

"She said that women must have their own money and a room of their own if they are to be confident, creative and strong in themselves."

"But surely," Rupert interrupted, "Lily has all those things already. Why," he chuckled, "she has the household money and there are three extra rooms upstairs." He flung his arm upward. "Take your pick, my dear."

Mrs. Cruikshank leaned toward him. "That's not quite what I meant. Lily must be her own person."

"Of course. Of course. No one could argue with that."

CHAPTER 12

In the months that followed, as they ventured out of the manse on various errands and missions of mercy, Lily and Rupert endured a barrage of interruptions, tales, rumours and gossip, all coming from their neighbour, Dolly. Her most beloved rant—which occurred sometimes daily—was her litany of hatred against the Berlin Wall. She wanted it down. Some night, she warned them, if they heard a chainsaw at midnight, they would know that it was her, taking down the despicable fence. It had only been put up, she declared, because of the sensibilities of a previous minister who thought her little cottage too unsightly for his delicate wife to see. But it was Mr. Cruikshank who admitted to Rupert and Lily that their predecessors had asked for the fence to be erected in an attempt to stop Dolly from visiting, to end the litany of frightening stories that she loved to share.

When Lily and Rupert only nodded and displayed dismissive interest in Dolly's grievance, she had changed tactics. When Dolly heard their side door open, she hurried out her own back door, stood behind the wall and shouted over pleasantries, or advice, or complaints. If they couldn't see her, she reckoned, they would come to understand that the wretched wall was a severe detriment to neighbourliness.

• • •

Throughout the autumn months, Lily found herself bombarded with requests. Would she attend the Women's Missionary Society on the second Tuesday of each month? Could she please come to help at the Ladies' Aid Society functions? They had a large church bazaar every Christmas season and it was all-hands-on-deck. Did she knit? Or could she contribute to the bake table? Butter tarts, Dutch apple pie and carrot cake with cream cheese icing sold quickly. When church members learned that she had been a church organist and choir director, there was a request for her to direct the children's choir. The last director had left in a huff, they said, which meant, in Lily's mind, that the children were incorrigible. There was even an inquiry as to whether she would consider joining the untrained weary staff as a Sunday school teacher. There was a shortage of teachers this year and no one, absolutely no one, wanted to take on the teenage class.

As if this was not enough stress in her new life, Rupert added another request. "Lily, my dear," he said one night on a rare occasion when they were home together, "I'm wondering, since you have the free time, if you might consider taking on a project that has great significance to me."

"Project?"

"I had a most interesting time in a mission appointment in northern Alberta when I was newly ordained. Honestly, the stories, you wouldn't believe them. Elodie kept journals and she loved to jot down all the crazy, wonderful things that happened in those years. We were there only four years, but, Lily, it was incredible—the moose that someone had shot, then hung the carcass to age in the old, unused church entry, the boarders we took in from other countries, the children who had to live with us when their parents were accused of abuse, the unpassable roads when it rained, and the snow…there was never a month without some snow, even in July. Yes! I remember building a snowman in July. Ah," he sighed, "those were interesting years and I believe they should be preserved and shared with others. Which brings me to my request… You're good with typing. Would you read Elodie's journals and type them up? Then I could read them through, craft them into a proper story and polish the manuscript for publishing."

He glanced over at Lily, expecting a nod, a smile, a small shrug, but instead she said, "I have some things to clean up in the kitchen."

• • •

On the day after their seventh Sunday night dinner, Lily, wearing her winter jacket, for there was now snow drifting in from the shores of Lake Ontario, and standing on a wooden outdoor clothesline stand, struggled to line up the edges of a cold, wet, damask tablecloth—a wedding gift from her mother—when a fierce gust of wind grabbed the tablecloth and wrapped it snuggly around her body.

"What!" she exclaimed as she struggled to free herself, fearful that the cloth might become soiled again. She had rubbed for a half hour to remove a gravy stain and three knobs of red candle wax that had dripped onto the cloth at last night's dinner. Now, shivering, she felt the tablecloth clinging to her body, an icy, unwanted shroud. Trembling, she blew on her fingers and turned slowly, taking care to unwrap the cloth from her shoulders without letting it touch the ground. She was preparing to pin the tablecloth back on the line when, from nowhere, it seemed, she heard a voice say, "You must leave Rupert to find yourself."

"What?" she cried again, this time her voice cracking with alarm. The declaration was precise, distinct. She heard the words clearly, as if someone was standing beside her. She twisted around, glaring across the laneway, searching for her neighbour, Dolly. Surely, she wouldn't dare to shout out such an outrageous message on a blustery Monday morning. Lily was indignant. She shook her head to clear her thoughts, took a deep breath and turned back to her laundry basket. But before she could attach the second wooden clothespin, she heard the voice again: "You must leave Rupert to find yourself."

Over the years, Lily had learned the fine art of maintaining peace with choir members and her mother. She was able to bite her tongue or turn the other cheek, but this voice with its uninvited and disturbing message upset her. She would put a stop to Dolly's disruptive, interfering behaviour, and she needed to do it now. Dolly was far too intrusive in their lives. She set the laundry basket on a bench and hurried down the steps of the clothesline stand, heading toward the laneway. She strode to the end of the wall and glared into Dolly's backyard, her jaw clenched, her stomach knotted.

But Dolly's backyard was empty. There was no sign of the woman, nor were there fresh imprints on the soft, wet snow, no sign that anyone had been out the back door all morning. Standing at the end of the fence, clutching her jacket around her, Lily peered into Dolly's yard and realized, with an icy stab of fear, that her neighbour had not shouted out the disturbing message. It had come from some other place, and she began to tremble.

CHAPTER 13

Even though living in a beautiful Georgian house was a constant pleasure, as the days crept into weeks, Lily felt a sinking despair. Her head was filled with lists of expectations. In addition to the church demands, there was the cleaning of a large house, laundry, shopping, cooking, and the dreaded Sunday night dinners. Rupert, being a traditional man, liked three hot meals a day. Lily rarely had a moment to herself.

In the back of her mind, she remembered Elodie's diaries, the account of Rupert's early days in ministry. She would need to make a start, but anxiety gripped her belly. Each time she picked up another of the red diaries, full of their spidery notations, she felt the ghost of Rupert's former wife looking over her shoulder. To add to her angst, she didn't find the journals at all interesting, and she couldn't imagine why anyone else would either.

At each dinner party, she may have looked slim and sophisticated, even demurely mysterious, wearing a sleek black sheath, her silky chestnut hair coiled behind her head, but inside she felt like a small, defenseless child, lost, with no one to help her. She would have to try harder.

Toward Advent, Lily received a call from the president of the Ladies' Aid, an imperious woman, Mrs. Hardy. "Our group is gathering this Tuesday to decorate the church for the Christmas season. Would you bring along a dozen raisin bran muffins for our morning coffee?"

When she arrived at the appointed time, she could see that the women had come early and had already hauled out large boxes of greenery, silver balls, giant red bows, even a Christmas tree and strings of lights for the side wing of the church. Everyone seemed to know her role. One woman was on a step ladder, draping a garland over the back door. Another woman held the ladder. A third person was arranging a series of identical wreaths along the back of the choir loft while her assistant had the task of plumping up the crushed foliage and handing along the wreaths. Three people—who clearly knew what they were doing—were assembling the artificial Christmas tree, declaring, as they worked, how wonderfully lifelike it looked, even after all these years. Two women, who took pride in their liturgical knowledge and artistic talent, were decorating the space around the communion table. This year, the table was dressed with a dazzling, embossed white cloth—symbolizing purity, they announced—and at the two ends of the table stood tall candelabras, each holding three candles, which represented the Trinity. In front of the gracefully draped cloth was a two-tiered arrangement of seven poinsettias—red, of course, to presage the blood of Christ. The number seven, they explained, had special biblical significance; it expressed fullness and completeness. The entire bank of flowers was ringed with a tastefully coiled silver cloth, which seemed to have no significance at all except to look pretty and finish off the scene. The candles, they warned, were to be battery operated. "We don't want the fire department visiting us on Christmas Eve," someone declared.

Overwhelmed and confused by the activity, Lily finally found the courage to ask how she could help. "Oh, my dear, it would be helpful if you could get the glass and plastic balls sorted out." The red glass ones were to go on the church windowsills but the blue plastic ones went with the silver bows into the Sunday school rooms. "The children are not so apt to throw them around if they realize that they can't smash the plastic ones to bits."

When she had finished this small task, Lily wandered from group to group, murmuring words of encouragement and appreciation. "Shall I put on the kettle for tea?" she inquired.

"Oh, of course," someone responded, rushing past with an armful of fresh boughs.

Lily set out the muffins, made the tea, brewed coffee, poured cream and milk into little crystal jugs, then returned to the sanctuary. Should she tell the women that refreshments were ready? Did they need a break? "Do you break for refreshments soon?" she inquired.

"Oh, no dear, not until we're all done. And there's the church hall yet to do."

"Is there something I can do to help with that?"

"We always gather up all the bits and pieces not used in the sanctuary windowsills, but here…" The woman handed Lily a cluster of pinecones, balls and a small glittery Christmas tree. "You can start decorating one of the basement windowsills."

Lily wandered down the steps and did her best to artistically arrange her little scene. Then, sighing, she returned to the church kitchen and dumped the cooled tea down the stainless-steel sink, poured out the stagnant coffee, covered the muffins with a tea towel. She filled the kettle again, ready to make fresh tea, scooped fresh coffee grinds back into the urn, ready to be switched on, then sat down to wait.

Later, when the women had finished the hall and Sunday school rooms and had gathered to enjoy their hot beverage and snack over conversation—why could she not understand what they were talking about?—Lily sat quietly, smiling and nodding, until it seemed time to start tidying up. Would she ever come to understand what was expected of her? Were the church women as uncomfortable with her as she was with them? It seemed as if they were talking over her, around her. Would she ever learn their ways? After they had started to gather for refreshments, she had been amazed to see the women dig in their tote bags and produce plastic-lidded containers full of date squares, chocolate chip cookies, banana bread. They had not needed her raisin bran muffins after all. This was just the way they had always done things. It was Lily—the new preacher's wife—who was out of step.

It was only when she had washed the cups and gathered her muffin tin—only one muffin had been eaten—that she noticed the basement windowsill that she had set up. Someone had rearranged it, moving around her little Christmas tree and re-clustering the balls, making it match the others.

Lily walked home through the grey, cold day, tired and discouraged. She had no energy to prepare a lunch for Rupert, so she set out a plate of muffins, cheese and grapes in the little kitchen alcove where they often ate their breakfast. She ignored his look of surprise when she called him for lunch. "I've had a busy morning," she explained, pouring him a steaming mug of tea.

After lunch, Rupert often took a nap. It kept up his energy for his evening meetings, he told her. When they had first moved in and had settled into a routine, he urged her to join him, but she soon discovered that Rupert did not have napping in mind at all. "There is something quite wonderful about being in bed with a beautiful woman at one o'clock in the afternoon when all the other men in town are hard at work," he laughed. Lily put an end to joining him for nap time. It wasn't that she wouldn't enjoy it. It was simply a matter of fearing that a parishioner might come to their front door, wanting him for something. How would it look if his car was in the driveway but there was no answer at the door? Worse still, what if Rupert, in his abandonment—men being so inexplicably comfortable about these things—answered the door in a state of disarray, his shirttails out, his hair tousled, or even—heaven forbid—wearing his pajama bottoms hastily tugged on?

In the early afternoon of the day of the church decorating, when Rupert had ascended the beautiful curved stairway for his nap, she almost gave in. Her bones were weary, her spirit dim. A nap would surely refresh her body and soul. But as she was clearing away the last of the lunch dishes, she heard a boisterous knocking, not at the front door but from the side porch. Dolly Inkpen stood on the doorstep, the now familiar orange casserole dish in her hands.

"Afternoon, missus. Thought you and the preacher might like a nice vegetable stew and doughboys for yur supper. It's such a mauzy day."

"Hello, Dolly. That's very kind of you. Won't you come in?" Lily said, eyeing the dish, wondering if she dared take it. Had it come straight from the stovetop? "I'll put on the kettle," she said, hoping that her voice had some semblance of welcome, because she didn't feel very hospitable. She had experienced too many irritating encounters with the woman. Nevertheless, Dolly had brought them a dish for dinner. I shall have to summon some gratitude, she chided herself.

Although she exuded remarkable confidence when she was outdoors, Dolly looked out of place and anxious on the occasions when she was invited inside the Old Manse. Today, she seemed particularly ill at ease. "Come into the kitchen," Lily urged, indicating that Dolly should sit at the round pine table in the alcove. But it wasn't until Dolly had her hands wrapped around a mug of tea that she seemed to relax.

"I'll be bringing you over a Figgy Duff closer ta Christmas," she confided to Lily as she helped herself to a muffin on which she had slathered a thick layer of butter. "These would be fine with bakeapple jam," she declared. "Maybe when I bring da Figgy Duff, you'd like some jam-jams, too."

"Please," Lily smiled, raising her hand in a gesture of mock protest. "You spoil us." The truth was, Rupert was suspicious of Dolly's cooking, which meant that Lily, out of obligation, tried a nibble and then recycled it in the composter. Flooded now with guilt—for she was sure that Dolly meant well and, judging by the state of her property, lived on limited resources—Lily tried to begin a new conversation. "So, tell me, what is the news around town?"

"Well, you see missus…"

"Dolly," Lily broke in, "I've told you so many times. You don't have to call me missus. My name's Lily. Please call me Lily and I shall call you Dolly."

"Okay, missus. It's just that I'm used to it. Mind now, I didn't call in jist to bring you some good home cookin'. I come to tell you that I've been seeing her again. I haven't seen her now for nigh on two years so I was that surprised, so I was, to see her every night last week."

"Dolly, what on earth are you talking about?"

"Charlotte, of course."

"Charlotte?" Something cold seemed to waft into the kitchen and Lily swung around, wondering if Rupert had wakened and, hearing Dolly's voice in the kitchen, had crept out the front door. She wrapped her arms around her body.

"Oh, ya don't need to be afrightened of her. She never means no harm. It's just a little unsettling at times when you think she's finally quieted down. But don't you worry. You'll never be in danger. Not with our Charlotte."

"What are you talking about, Dolly?" Lily heard the annoyance in her own voice.

"Those good church people didn't tell you?"

"Tell me what?"

"About Charlotte. You've a ghost living here wit you in the Old Manse."

Lily wondered if her face turned ashen. She felt suddenly a little light-headed. "A ghost," she said quietly.

"As I said, I hadn't seen her for a coupla years. My bedroom window looks acrost at your upstairs hall." Lily made a mental note to warn Rupert to wear his bathrobe when he passed down the hall between their bedroom and the bathroom. "At night she walks around in a long white nightgown and a little cap on her head. She's always carrying a candle in a brown candlestick. She's not mean or scary, our Charlotte, just restless and unhappy. She's lookin' for sumpin."

"Dolly, this is nonsense."

"Oh, no, missus. Ya don't believe in the spirits? After all my years in Newfoundland and Nova Scotia, I know there is something in that spirit world. You and the preacher believes in miracles, don't ja? Miracles and the spirit world are kinda related." Lily wondered if this was a new ruse Dolly had devised to stir up trouble and irritate her. "I only came over to tell you not to worry. If ya hears doors opening and shutting on their own, or if you hears some-un rocking in the rockin' chair in the guest room, don't fret none. It'd only be Charlotte. She sometimes takes things away for a while, but don't worry, she always puts them back."

For a moment, Lily was speechless. Finally, she blurted out, "What makes you think there's a ghost in this house? Who told you this?" She stopped herself from saying, "Who told you this nonsense?"

"I seen it with me own eyes, I did. I've lived next door for fifteen years and I'd talked to lotsa preachers and their missuses who use ta live here. They don't stay long, most of 'em."

"Particularly not after you tell them that they are living with a ghost," Lily exclaimed.

"One of 'em, the third before you," Dolly continued, "she got so a-scared, she and the kids and the preacher moved into the church basement until he could find another place to live."

CHAPTER 14

It took Lily several days to share with Rupert what Dolly had told her, but she realized that she couldn't keep worrying about ghosts. She had to talk things over with her husband, for now she had become aware of some strange happenings.

The day after Dolly's visit, she had set aside an hour to type some of Elodie's journal. She turned on her computer, pulled out the dreaded red notebook from a drawer, opened it and reached for her mouse. Although her laptop had a touchpad to control the cursor, she had never become accustomed to it, preferring to use an external mouse. Where had it gone? It always sat on a little rubberized pad to the right of her laptop, but now the mouse was nowhere to be seen. Perhaps, she reasoned, Rupert had used her laptop, checking on her progress. She searched all the drawers in the desk. Sighing, she turned to her work, but only fifteen minutes later, she shut down her computer in frustration. The touchpad felt awkward and slowed her down. She would try again the next day.

When she returned to her task in the extra bedroom, which she now referred to as "Lily's office" and in which she had hung a sign saying "Staff only," she was surprised to find the mouse sitting precisely in the middle of her rubberized pad. "Rupert," she sighed. Then, feeling a tinge of disloyalty, she settled herself again at the computer, but when she opened the drawer where she kept the journal, she found it empty. She felt a sudden chill and heard a soft sound that could have been slipper-shod feet. "Crazy!" she called out. She waited. She could hear nothing.

It was only later in the day, when she walked down the basement stairs to retrieve a laundry basket, that she was flooded with dread. This is utter nonsense, she told herself. I will speak to Rupert about this and we will never let that woman, Dolly, into this house again.

Friday night was a time when Rupert rarely had commitments—unless there was a wedding rehearsal, which was seldom. Rupert had told her that twenty-five percent of the people of New Hopewell were between the ages of sixty-five and seventy-nine. "That will probably reflect our congregation, too," he added, but Lily noted early on that there seemed to be a disproportionally higher number of people with white hair in the congregation. At the time, Lily felt a pang of disappointment. There would be lots of funerals but few weddings. It had surprised her when Rupert told her—how many other secrets did she not know about being a minister's wife?—that in traditional households where the clergy wife does not have her own career and income, the gratuity or wedding fee for the clergy was passed on as a gift to his wife. It was for her little purse of "mad money."

Because there were so few wedding rehearsals, Friday night had become their special time together. Lily prepared hors d'oeuvres and learned to make martinis in a shaker, setting them to chill in the refrigerator while she prepared the garnishes—olives for her, a twist of lemon for Rupert. In the afternoon, she created simple but elegant dinners—lobster and shrimp lasagna or creamed chicken in crisp puffed-pastry shells. The table was set in the dining room, the dinner warmed in the old Aga cooker, and candles sat on the sideboard, ready, along with some mellow jazz, for ambiance. Everything was ready so she and Rupert could enjoy conversation and cocktails in their "snug," as they now laughingly called it, before moving to the dining room.

After she had taken two sips of her icy martini, she found the courage to tell Rupert about Dolly's visit and her strange tale of Charlotte, the ghost. Rupert threw back his head and roared with laughter. He slapped his hand against his thigh and said, "That's the best story I've heard all year." Immediately, Lily relaxed. Rupert reinforced her own disbelief. The whole thing was nonsense.

"It reminds me of a story someone told me about Trinity Anglican Church in Liverpool, a little community on Nova Scotia's south shore. The building is very old, so it's bound to have a few creaks and groans. They say that the ghostly presence of a long-ago church member is often felt, but the ghost became more active after they added a new part on to the church—a kitchen, a meeting room, offices and washrooms."

"Perhaps she was just a traditionalist who didn't like change," Lily suggested.

Rupert laughed. "My friend told me that there were stories of unusual sounds in the church and of things being moved around. There were footsteps in the sanctuary when no one could possibly have been upstairs, as all the doors were locked, and when a brave parishioner went to investigate, the sanctuary was empty. There were reports of objects going missing—the communion chalice, the pulpit Bible—then, next day they would be back in place again. The church had a collection of five chalices and it was common over the years that one would always be missing. Then, eventually it would turn up. Now here's a weird one, Lily. You'll enjoy this. Parishioners reported hearing organ or piano music when there was no logical explanation at all."

This time Lily didn't laugh. She was remembering an occasion in her former church in Emerson when a piece of music—her favourite prelude—had disappeared. Then, weeks later, it miraculously appeared again on her organ music stand.

"The members of Trinity Church took to calling their ghost Mrs. Smith," Rupert told her, "simply because it seemed to suit her. They came to believe that the ghost is a past organist because so many of the pranks are musical. The people at Trinity don't find it upsetting. In fact, they say they feel at ease and comforted by the ghost. They claim that they never feel alone at church. There's always another person in the building."

Rupert laughed again, but Lily pulled a comforter around her shoulders. She felt a sudden chill. She was remembering the last moments of Dolly's visit. Her neighbour had lingered briefly at the side door. Then, from her pocket she pulled a hairpin, and reaching up, she stuck it into the corner of the door casing. "There," she declared. "That will keep out evil. A wicked ghost or witch will never pass by a hairpin. You'd be smart to put one at your front door, too, and at the back door into the basement."

Without asking, Rupert had volunteered her for yet another task. In the New Year, the church in New Hopewell would celebrate its 170th anniversary as a congregation. "I want to do this up right," he told her. "This church was officially opened in June. Why not make the entire month of June a time of celebration, some musical events, guest speakers, workshops on visioning? It's a great opportunity to celebrate our history and help us reflect on where we should head in the future." Mrs. Cruikshank, the high school principal—did Lily remember her?—had been a history teacher before becoming a principal. She had agreed to write a history of the congregation, full of accurate details but written in a storytelling style to encourage more people to read it. He hoped that Lily would work with her on this project, perhaps type up the manuscript?

Although she had initially been annoyed with Rupert for volunteering her without asking, she accepted readily, for she remembered Mrs. Cruikshank's kind assistance at her first dinner party. The two women agreed to meet on Tuesday evening to talk about the project. Mrs. Cruikshank had already written a chapter on the first decade.

Although she felt timid about it, Lily suggested a title for the book, *Building a Church*. It would have a double meaning, she explained. Not only did the physical structure change over the years but the body of believers grew and changed, too. The cover would feature a detailed line drawing of the church as it now was. Then, inside, the line drawings would start out with a mere frame and a handful of people, and as the chapters progressed and each part of the church history developed, more detail would be added to the line drawings until the present day when the artist would be asked to somehow depict a part that is yet to be built. It would be a visual reminder that churches—both the buildings and the people—are always growing and changing.

"I like it!" Mrs. Cruikshank enthused. "Your talents are wasted, my dear. I'll leave you with my first chapter. You can take your time reading it and let me know what you think."

Rupert was not due home for an hour, so after Mrs. Cruikshank left, Lily headed down the hall toward the living room, the manuscript tucked under her arm. As she neared the room, which took her past the front door, she glanced up, as she so often did. Yes, she could see it. Despite her scorn for Dolly's story and disparaging the existence of haunting spirits, she had quietly but firmly stuck a hairpin in the casing of both the front and basement doors. She turned into the living room, curled up in her favourite chair, pulled a blanket around her knees, and opened the manuscript to read.

> *Put yourself into this story. The year is 1853. You and your family have arrived by boat at a wharf near Quebec City. Oh! what a long and arduous crossing, crowded in with others for nine weeks, enduring seasickness, stomach-turning foul smells, rancid water and wretched food. When your ship finally docks at Quebec City, at least there is fresh air.*
>
> *But there is no time to rest or linger. Everyone has warned you about winter. You have to arrive at your final destination in time to plant some potatoes, carrots and cabbage to tide you through the long winter ahead. Almost immediately, you climb onboard a smaller ship, this time heading up the more peaceful waters of the St. Lawrence River. Finally, you arrive, landing at the dock of a small community called New Hopewell on the shores of Lake Ontario. You feel bewildered, hopeful, excited, scared. This strange and densely wooded land feels like the end of the world, and you are suddenly homesick for your family and country left behind. You realize, with a painful ache in your heart, that you will never see them again. You want to cry, but you straighten your shoulders. There is work to be done.*

Mrs. Cruikshank's story invited readers to build a log shelter, begin to clear more land behind the small shed that is intended to house a cow and pig, maybe a team of oxen, then plant the root vegetables needed for the long winter ahead. She asks you to imagine how your neighbours—some of them Anishinaabe and Haudenosaunee Peoples—helped you learn many things: how to spear fish, forage for wild mushrooms, weave baskets, hunt deer. And from other settlers you learn how to shear a sheep, spin wool, churn butter, make a batch of bread each morning and keep alive the yeast. Then, she said, imagine that your neighbours of Scottish and Irish descent begin to talk about missing their Presbyterian church in the homeland. If they worked hard, pooled their resources, could they sponsor a Presbyterian minister from Scotland who would care for their spiritual needs, provide moral support, help them build a community life and educate their children? But where would he live? Did it not make sense to build a home that would be so splendid that it would attract the finest quality of minister? It would, of course, need to be a stone house, for that is surely what a Scottish minister would expect. They could gather for worship in the manse and later, when they had more resources, they would build a church. Someone who had come from Perthshire in Scotland made a drawing of the old manse he remembered from his youth. They agreed to build their manse based on that drawing. Although smaller than the manse in Scotland, this Georgian house in the new world was an unusual and much talked about mansion in a village of humble log farm shelters. It was barely completed when the first minister arrived. The Reverend Henry Chalmers was considered a great preacher and came from a prominent and respected family. His older brother had been the first moderator of the Free Church in Scotland, in a time that was sometimes called *The Disruption of 1843*. In the fall of 1854, after long weeks of travel across the Atlantic Ocean, Henry Chalmers, accompanied by his wife, Charlotte, stepped into the new manse.

CHAPTER 15

Lily woke the next morning, determined to contact Mrs. Cruikshank, eager to know if she knew anything more about Charlotte, the wife of the first minister. But this did not happen.

At mid-morning, she heard the now-familiar clank of the mailbox lid. Strolling toward the front of the house, she recalled how, when Rupert first showed her the photo of the hall, she imagined herself doing just this: leisurely making her way down the long, carpeted hallway, past the elegant curving stairway, past the burnished oak hall side table, past the living room, to the front door. Careful now not to look up at the hairpin in the doorway, she unlocked the front door and reached into the mailbox.

At once, she recognized the writing on a large manila envelope. Aunt Sofiya. Eager for news from home, she shut the front door firmly and ripped open the seal.

> *My dearest Lily: How we miss you here in Emerson but I hope you have found happiness—perhaps even love—in your new life in Ontario.*
>
> *This letter will be a terrible shock, I'm afraid. How I dreaded receiving letters like this from back home in the old country. I thought about phoning you but somehow a letter feels like a gentler*

way to pass along sad news. I'm sorry to tell you that your mother, who had always been well, died suddenly of a heart attack last Tuesday. If it is of any comfort to you, she did not linger or suffer at the end. She simply curled up in her bed after she had her breakfast and when I came to the door for our morning coffee, I called out for her. I could see her dishes still on the table but when I rushed up to her bedroom, I could see that she was gone.

I am heartbroken for she was like a dear sister to me. It is strange but I sometimes wonder if people have a feeling that death is near. Just a few months ago she had given me an envelope that contained instructions for what she wanted at the time of her death. She wanted no funeral. You know that your mother never liked people to make a fuss over her. She asked to be buried in Gretna in the cemetery where her parents and grandparents are.

All she asked of those of us who knew her was that we should light a candle every day for a week, think of her and remember our blessings. And if we had time, we could make a Kyiv cake to share with someone.

I'm sorry to have to tell you this sad news and I'm sure that your new husband will be comforting. There's one more thing. Your mother gave me a private letter. She wanted me to give it to you after her death, so I am honouring her wishes. The letter is in an envelope which is included in this packet.

Blessings on you, darling Lily.

Love, Aunt Sofiya

Groping her way down the hall, Lily collapsed into a chair in the snug and began to sob. It was a terrible shock, and as she cried, gasping for breath, guilt consumed her. How had she so casually and carelessly left behind her mother and her Aunt Sofiya? How had she abandoned her dearest and only close friend, Cathy? She had deserted her faithful choir, too, while at the same time leaving them without a minister.

She reread the letter, wishing that Aunt Sofiya had telephoned with such important and tragic news. Then Lily realized that Aunt Sofiya—and her mother, too, when alive—would have considered this the height of extravagance to make a long-distance phone call all the way from Manitoba to the neighbouring province of Ontario. She was of the generation that believed that long-distance calls were expensive, an extravagance. A letter was the appropriate and best way to convey sad news, just as they had always done in the olden days.

She held the personal letter from her mother in her hand, turning it one way, then another. She did not have the courage to open it. She tucked it into the book she had been reading, promising herself that she would read it when she felt stronger.

Each night at dinner, Lily lit a candle in memory of her mother, and Rupert, in his protracted pre-dinner grace, thanked God for the blessing of the woman who had produced and nurtured such a beautiful and loving daughter. This small daily ritual seemed too little, too insignificant, but she could not think of anything else to do. One afternoon, she took time to make the delectable Kyiv cake but could not think of anyone with whom she would like to share it. She certainly wouldn't invite the Ladies' Aid or the Women's Missionary Society in for cake and tea. She definitely wouldn't invite Dolly Inkpen over for a morning break. In the end, she and Rupert ate it by themselves.

Several days passed. She could not find courage to open the letter. Then, one day, as she listened to the CBC radio news, she heard a horrifying account of the war in Ukraine and the heroic efforts that mothers were making to maintain for their children a life that was as hopeful and normal as possible, given the constant danger and terror. "Lily," she chided herself, "get a grip. Other people face grave dangers every hour and respond with enormous bravery. It's a small thing to read a letter from your deceased mother." But, when she had read it, and reread it, folding the letter in disbelief, then opening it again to ponder the incredible revelation, she knew that it would take more than mere valiant pluck to follow through on her mother's request.

She waited until Rupert had finished his dinner. "I have something to show you," she said. "I received a letter written by my mother. She asked Aunt

Sofiya to forward it to me after her death." She handed the letter to Rupert and watched his eye movements as he read from the top to the bottom, then returned to the top for a second read.

Finally, he carefully folded the letter and set it on the table. "Well, that's a shocker. Quite incredible. You knew nothing about this?"

"Nothing at all. I had no idea." She felt as if she might cry and hastily withdrew her hand so Rupert wouldn't reach out and touch her. In the past, when she was hurt or bewildered, she could maintain her stoic composure until someone reached out to hug her. Then she would break down. She didn't want to do that in front of Rupert.

"Will you do it?" he inquired gently.

"I don't see how I possibly can."

"Still, Lily…the money…"

"There's no need to rush into anything. We didn't know about this situation last week. Today we do. There's no need to spring into action."

She reached out for the letter and took it into the snug, where she tucked it into her book. But when Rupert had gone out for his evening meeting, she could not resist the urge to read it again.

Dear Lily,

By the time you read this letter you will know that your old mother has gone on to her great reward or her eternal punishment, whichever is the case. As you are my only child, I have left my entire estate to you, not that our old house is worth much. You may remember that after your father's untimely death, you and I lived on his scanty pension. What you probably don't know is that I had a considerable bank account which I kept in Gretna. This was money inherited from my parents when they sold their farm. You may wonder why I didn't dip into that to make our life a little more comfortable. The truth is, I didn't want you to be spoiled. It never hurts people to struggle a little for what they get in life.

Lily stopped reading as resentment, despair and amazement swept over her. She could barely breathe. Her mother had $500,000 in a bank account in a nearby town. Lily imagined what she might have done, had she been able to enroll in university and study architecture. Why had her mother denied her this future when she knew how much it meant to her? But then, she began to wonder, had she ever clearly expressed to her mother her greatest and deepest desires? Had she, in self-protection, simply swallowed her private hurt and disappointment until it became like a hard stone in her belly?

I have instructed my lawyer to forward half this investment ($250,000) to you immediately and later you will receive the money from the sale of the house. The remaining $250,000 of the investment depends on you. This may be a shock to you, but you are an adopted child. Your father and I were not able to have children of our own and when we found that you were available for adoption at only eight days old, we felt very lucky. What we didn't know at the time was that your birth mother, who was unmarried—had twin girls. Your twin sister was adopted by a family in Toronto, we were told later, but I know nothing else about her and her whereabouts.

It is my dying wish to have you reunited with your sister, and my request to you is that you begin a search to find her. It is also my dying wish that $250,000 of my estate should go to her. It would create a bond between you, I think. I have heard that twins, when separated as infants, have a longing to connect, that they feel incomplete, that they feel there is something always missing. Perhaps this is why you were so shy and unsure of yourself growing up. You needed your sister. If, after a concerted effort over the next two years, you are not able to locate your sister, I have instructed the lawyer that her share, $250,000 of the estate, will be forwarded to you.

Your mother, Krystyna

CHAPTER 16

For a week, Lily woke and slept, cooked and swept, did the shopping and washed the dishes, but when she looked back on her day, there was nothing she could remember. It was as if she was walking in a dense and chilling fog. Her mind refused to acknowledge that she had lost her mother, that she was an adopted child, that she was in all likelihood not even Ukrainian, that she had a twin sister somewhere, and, most incredibly, that she was a person with her own money. It was overwhelming.

When Mrs. Cruikshank arrived promptly at seven to work on chapters two and three of their project, it was a welcome distraction. She stomped the snow from her boots, shrugged off her coat and declared, "That's a bitter wind, Lily."

"Let me hang your coat, Mrs. Cruikshank."

"Lily, listen to me. You have *got* to stop calling me Mrs. Cruikshank. My name is Margaret. Not Marg or Maggie or Meg or Peggy. Just Margaret. Now then, let's get down to work, shall we?" They had barely settled at the dining room table, their papers scattered in front of them, when Margaret turned her head to one side and said, "Now Lily, I've become an astute judge of character over the years. Heaven knows, if I can figure out teenagers, I should have a PhD in people-ology. I can see that something is wrong. Spit it out. What's troubling you?"

Overwhelmed and confused, Lily began to cry, clutching her hands together in her lap, folding and unfolding a handkerchief. Margaret waited patiently until Lily composed herself, and then Lily told her everything: the contents of the letter, her feelings of resentment and exhaustion with church and home responsibilities, even Dolly's upsetting story of Charlotte the ghost. "Oh, my," Margaret murmured. "Oh, my, my, my." There was a long pause while both women wondered if proceeding with a church history booklet was possible. "I don't usually suggest this," Margaret said finally, "but under the circumstances, I do believe the occasion calls for a good nip of scotch. Where does that husband of yours keep his secret stash?"

They retired to the snug to sip their Scotch, both confessing that they really didn't like the taste. "It tastes like an ashtray," Margaret declared.

"Or the lining of a mouldy barrel."

Lily wondered if she could summon the courage to ask Margaret about Charlotte, the wife of the first minister. Margaret, in turn, was thinking about a rumour she had heard about Rupert and why he had left his Vancouver church so suddenly. Rumours, she almost said aloud, the scotch loosening her tongue. This town thrives on rumours and tales.

"I've been wondering," Lily began, "if you know anything at all about the wife of the first minister. Her name was Charlotte, I believe."

"Not much, I'm afraid, but there was talk that she was an unhappy person. More than unhappy, really. A depressed, restless and morose person. It's my understanding that her marriage was somehow not satisfactory. People said that she came to believe that she had to leave her husband, Henry, in order to find herself." Lily pressed her fist against her mouth, remembering the day when the cold, wet, tablecloth had wrapped itself around her. "But, of course, Charlotte didn't leave him. Where would she go? And what would become of her? She left behind a life of ease and servants to come here. I'm sure she wondered what she had been thinking about."

"But sometimes you don't always know what you are getting into, and sometimes you feel as if you have no choice."

"True, true." Margaret took another sip of scotch. "There was a story about her child," she said. "They had only one baby and he died when he was an infant. They say she never got over that."

"Oh, dear."

"You know the patio at the front of the house? When they were excavating to lay the stone base for the new patio, they unearthed a tiny grave made of cement."

Lily gasped. "You don't mean the child is buried right outside the front door?"

Margaret shrugged. "They did things like that back then. The contractor recommended that the most respectful thing would be to simply cover the grave again with stone and let it rest in peace."

Lily shivered but then protested, "Surely that can't be true. Was cement even invented then, back in the mid-1800s?"

"Cement has a long history." Lily could hear that Margaret had switched into her history-teaching voice. "There were reports in Syria and Jordan of cement being used for concrete floors and underground cisterns in BCE. And, of course, the Romans used concrete in construction from 300 BC to 476 AD. In Great Britain there is an account of a British engineer in 1828 using Portland cement to repair the Thames Tunnel. So, to your point, could there have been cement for a tiny coffin back in the mid-1800s in Ontario? Absolutely. After all, if it was your only child, you wouldn't want wild animals digging up its tiny carcass."

"Oh, that is quite horrible." Lily shuddered.

"Sorry. Sorry. It's the scotch."

"Do you believe it then, Dolly's story? That the restless ghost of Charlotte walks the halls of this house searching for her lost child, looking for happiness?"

Margaret's booming laughter filled the room. "Lily Kaltyk, this world is full of strange and wonderful and sometimes scary things that are ever-so-real. But there is absolutely no indication at all that spirits from long ago roam among us. That Dolly..." She shook her head, smiling.

Lily leaned back, smiling too, flooded with relief.

After Margaret had gone, Lily collapsed into a chair, fatigued and spent, but she also felt a stirring of hopefulness, a sense of relief. She realized that in Margaret she had found an open, honest, straightforward ally. She had someone to whom she could turn. She understood that any advice Margaret would give her would be direct and frank. Margaret would tell her the truth. She was, Lily realized, an older, brusque version of her dear friend Cathy.

The following day, feeling a new optimism and sense of purpose, Lily woke early, ready to take on the tasks of the morning, but when Rupert arrived home for lunch, she could see that he had a small, black tape recorder tucked under his arm. "The women borrowed it from the church nursery," he said by way of explanation. "They still use this old technology with the toddlers. I've had a request from one of the women's groups, I can't remember which one." He handed the tape recorder to Lily, who set it down on the hall side table, looking baffled. "The secretary of the group was unable to attend the meeting yesterday," he continued. Lily realized, with a start, that she had completely forgotten about the women's meeting. It had been her second time to forget. "They made a recording of their meeting and wondered if the church secretary might transcribe the important bits and those would become their minutes for the next meeting." Lily looked at her husband, then at the tape recorder. "The church secretary is quite overwhelmed at the moment, getting the announcements ready for Sunday's bulletin. I wondered if you would consider doing this small task?"

This has got to stop, Lily declared in her mind. This has simply got to stop. But instead of voicing this, she turned to the kitchen, saying, "Lunch is ready."

Still angry and resentful in the afternoon, Lily decided to get this additional burden off her to-do list. She settled herself in front of the computer, plugged in the tape recorder and pressed play. Someone—an overly anxious person who didn't really trust that a little black machine could tape their conversation—had started the recording before the meeting. Lily settled back into her chair, crossed her arms and waited for the pre-meeting chatter to end.

"Did you ever...and those skin-tight dresses she wears! And high heels. It just doesn't seem quite right to come prancing into church in high heels." Lily recognized the voice of Mrs. Hardy.

"Should we wait another five minutes? She isn't usually this late."

"I say we go ahead without her and she can join in when she arrives. I don't understand why she can't be on time. What has she got to look after?"

"I know I'm old fashioned, but when I got married it was just assumed that you would take your husband's name. It's the right thing to do. Besides, what kind of a name is Kaltyk?"

Lily jumped to her feet, gasping. They were talking about her! And it was not kindly talk. She folded her arms tightly around her body and sank back into her chair, her face flushed with anger and embarrassment. I've tried, she thought forlornly, but these women don't like me any more than I like them. She snapped open the cassette holder, yanked out the cassette and, using a pencil, began pulling out the tape, twisting and tearing at it. Racing down the elegant curving stairway, she plunked the ravelled tape on the hall side table where Rupert was sure to find it. She could already hear him murmur, "Old technology. Oh well, not having minutes from a meeting isn't the end of the world."

CHAPTER 17

The following evening, Lily was in the snug watching television when the front door opened. She heard Rupert remove his overcoat and head down the hall toward her. "You're home early," she remarked, muting her show.

"I don't think they needed me at that meeting," he sighed. Perhaps, she considered, he, too, found some of the church meetings difficult. "Besides," he said, "I have something on my mind."

"Mmm?"

"I've been wondering if you have given any more thought to that business of finding your twin sister?"

Lily hesitated, not feeling ready to share the steps she had taken. It felt like a private matter. "A bit," she confessed, finally. "I've done a search in Canada Birth Records but came up with nothing. Nothing for either me or her." She didn't admit that she was also considering signing on to a website that offered—almost guaranteed—sibling reunions. Her efforts, to date, had been tedious and frustrating, and the process grew increasingly complex.

"Is there any way I can help with that?" Rupert offered.

"Oh, no, but thanks. It's my responsibility." And, she nearly added, my personal quest.

"If I can be of any help, please let me know," he added, in a rather formal tone of voice.

"Of course."

"And," he said, clearing his throat, "have you heard from the lawyer about the $250,000?"

"No. I expect to hear when the house is sold. Selling a house in a small town takes time."

"Oh yes, of course."

After a brief silence, Rupert said, "There is one more thing." Reaching into the inside breast pocket of his sports jacket, he pulled out a letter. "From my sister in Montreal."

"You have a sister? In Montreal? You've never mentioned that."

Rupert had an odd look on his face. Was it embarrassment? Shame? "We aren't close," he said abruptly. "She was born twelve years after me. My parents were older, tired of parenting, I'm sure. She was a strong-willed child and when she was in her teens, she ran wild. Got into drugs, alcohol, partying. Finally, she ran away at seventeen and I've heard very little from her over the years. She has obviously kept track of me, though," he said, waving the letter, "especially when she needs something."

"What does she say?"

"It's her nemesis," he grumbled. "She has a teenage son. I didn't know I had a nephew. He's causing her a great deal of grief. She can't do a thing with him. That is retribution, considering all the pain she caused my parents."

"What does she think you can do about it?"

"That's the thing, Lily. She's asking if the boy—his name is Brendan—might come and live with us for a while. She's under the delusion that living with a clergyman might straighten out her errant son."

"Live with us?" Lily felt as though she might have shouted the words, but in reality, they came out in a raspy voice, like a croak. "What will you say?" she demanded. "What will you tell her?"

Rupert sighed. "Of course, I'll say that it's fine. Maybe there is some small way we can help the lad. He is family, after all."

• • •

When Margaret came by again—they were restarting their work on the church history—Lily could hardly wait for her to take off her coat before blurting out the dreadful news that Rupert's troubled nephew would be moving in with them.

"That's a lot to ask of you both, but look on the bright side, Lily. With a responsibility like that, you can pull back on your church duties. Not that they really are your duties. You're just a bit too polite to say no to all the demands people put on you."

"Do you think so? Do you think people ask too much?"

Margaret snorted. "You wouldn't catch me doing half those things."

Lily slumped in discouragement, then shuffled out the pages of chapter two. "The truth is, I know nothing, absolutely nothing about teenage boys, let alone one who is wild and troubled."

"Surely you remember boys from high school. You're not that old," Margaret teased. Lily shook her head, for she had not dated much in high school. Nor had she the courage to go to the wild bush parties that everyone talked about on Monday mornings. As a child, she had even been too timid to do what the boys loved to do—walk in the ditches wearing rubber boots, seeing who would walk with the water up to the top of their boots but not get their feet wet. She could not even watch when the boys played on the train overpass in Emerson. No, she didn't understand boys at all.

"When I was young, I didn't even babysit," Lily confessed. "I can hardly remember what kids are like, let alone a teenager who is acting out." But even as she said that, she began to wonder if her experience working with the school choir children in Emerson might be somewhat helpful in understanding this new situation with Brendan.

"Will you enroll him in our high school?"

"I'm not sure. We haven't got that far yet. He arrives next week, so we'll have to see how things go."

"If it's any consolation, I have a wonderful vice principal. He's a big softie in real life, but he knows how to turn on the tough guy act when he's with unruly kids—especially boys. He could be a big help with the nephew."

Lily sighed. "That's good to know."

"Now then, let's buckle down and get this chapter two done."

• • •

Mid-morning the following day, Lily heard the unmistakable clink of the front door mailbox. She propped the vacuum cleaner against the kitchen door and hurried down the hall. There was a flyer for pizza and a package forwarded from Aunt Sofiya, from the University of Manitoba Architecture department. Her hands trembled as she ripped open the packet and unfolded the cover letter. *Ms. Kaltyk*, it read, *we are pleased to inform you that additional space has opened up in our first-year architecture program for this coming fall. We regret that we were unable to consider your application of last year, but if you are interested at this time, please return the enclosed application form as soon as possible.*

Oh, great, Lily thought bitterly. Rotten timing. I no longer live a one-hour bus trip into Winnipeg. She was about to stuff the letter back in the envelope when she noticed a shiny brochure. Because the University of Manitoba did not offer this program, the cover letter informed her, they were pleased to share this innovative initiative offered by the University of Toronto. *Considering a career in architecture?* the brochure asked. The St. George Campus of the Faculty of Architecture, Landscape and Design in Toronto, often referred to as the Daniels Building, had received a government grant to run a pilot project. Three members of the faculty—two on the teaching staff and the third an administrator—had been selected to work with applicants who wanted to be considered in their school. The staff would meet monthly with each applicant selected. They would assign appropriate reading and provide an opportunity for independent study, then meet again the following month, at which time the student would make a presentation on their research. The staff promised feedback, direction, and most of all, discernment. They were particularly interested in applicants with diverse backgrounds who could "think outside the box." Mature students were welcome to apply. This was an excellent way, the brochure claimed, for people to assess whether or not architecture was an appropriate career path, and it also gave the staff an opportunity to discover people with specific architectural skills.

Taking a deep breath, Lily noted with concern that the registration deadline was a week away, only a day after Brendan's pending arrival. Out of the question, she thought, stuffing the brochure away.

Sleep did not come easily that night. Lily lay awake worrying about how they might manage their life with a teenage boy. She tried to push from her mind the opportunities that the glossy brochure had opened. Then she felt adrenalin pump through her body and her excitement grew as she considered the possibility of taking steps to fulfill a long-time personal dream. Afraid that she would waken Rupert with her tossing and turning, she crept out of bed and tiptoed into the room that she had prepared for Brendan. Settling into the rocking chair, she switched on the bedside lamp and read the brochure over and over. Never in her entire life had she sensed herself so drawn to something. She felt such a conviction that this program was made for her. How could she possibly make this happen? Did she dare to do it?

CHAPTER 18

Brendan planned to sleep on the bus all the way from Montreal to New Hopewell. He had been out most of the night, making final contacts with night customers. He felt an urgency to have some quick and ready cash for whatever craziness lay ahead. Two weeks, I'll stick it out for two weeks, he told himself, just to get everyone off my back, and then I'm heading west. Who knows, maybe two weeks in a sleepy little dump like New Hopewell has possibilities, maybe there is even an underbelly of excitement in town. There would probably be little competition from other dealers, not like Montreal. The local cops would already have their finger on every user and dealer in town, maybe even know them by name. Two weeks was a perfect schedule, he reasoned. Too little time for the police to get on to him and begin their hassle, and just enough time to make firm connections in the local high school. Besides, he grinned, what a perfect cover. Nephew of the local bigwig Presbyterian minister.

Brendan had maintained a strong, angry front with his mother, but in truth he was somewhat relieved to get out of Montreal. At first, becoming a drug dealer was exhilarating, but in the past few months he had begun to feel the burden of being always in demand. His phone rang at all hours, texts flew in and out. He had to make deliveries in the most unsavoury parts of town. Lately, he had taken to carrying a good bone-handled knife with a strong six-inch blade.

When he first started, his best markets were the unofficial smoke pits at high schools. It was easy. All he had to do was take a city bus to the high school, then walk around the block until he found the smoking area. Every school had one. He decided early on to deal only weed and amphetamine. The criminal element in the hard drug trade scared him. Selling to school kids made him a reasonable income, but one evening when he was out riding around on his motorcross bike, he spotted a 24-hour bowling alley that had video games and machines for candy and pop. It amazed him that teenagers had so much cash. He watched as teens slipped coins into machines, then sidled up to them and made them an offer. It gave him courage to try other venues: outside convenience stores where youth clustered to drink energy beverages, restaurant staff exits with tired dishwashers coming off a late-night shift, behind grocery stores where overnight stockers took their smoke breaks, houses lit up at 4 a.m. with heavy metal music blaring.

In the whole scheme of drug dealing, he was small fry. He knew that. Nevertheless, someone had tipped off the police to the fact that his main customers were underaged teens. On more than one occasion he found himself uncomfortably close to being stopped and searched. He blamed his mother, for his teachers had long ago given up on him. When his mom emerged from her own haze of weed and from her latest disaster of a cowboy boyfriend, she began to notice him, see that he rarely went to school, stayed out most of the night, always had money. She tried screaming and swearing at him, warning of the disaster that lay ahead. He had no doubt at all that his mother had called the cops on him, to teach him a lesson. And now this…being sent off as if he was a naughty child, having to live under the supervision of an uncle he had never met, chilling out with the nerds in Nerdsville. It was all too much. He went back to sleep.

When Brendan stepped off the bus, both Lily and Rupert were nervous. Rupert reacted by becoming stiff and formal. Lily found herself struggling for words. She had been too tense to eat breakfast. The teen looked around, a battered army tote slung over one shoulder. Lily wondered if he was as uneasy about this as they were.

What a study in contrasts, she thought, clutching her handbag to her breast. Rupert had worn a tweed blazer, tailored dress pants and a brown sweater over a classic white shirt. Brendan, on the other hand, favoured baggy denims with a chain looping from the back pocket and an oversized black hoodie. He had a tattoo of a wolf on his neck and three spiked earrings in his left earlobe.

Lily felt as if she could hardly breathe. Margaret's advice, when they last met, rushed into her mind. "Remember, Lily, male teens are just boys grown big and trying to figure out what it means to grow into a man."

The days that followed were a nightmare. Brendan didn't get out of bed until after lunchtime. Lily crept around the house, not wanting him to waken. She dreaded having to talk with him when he left his room. She was afraid to turn on the vacuum or even the radio. When he did get up, he seemed unable to figure out what to do with himself. He slouched in the snug eating potato chips and watching sitcoms on TV, and then, later in the afternoon, he left the house.

"But where does he go?" Rupert demanded at dinner.

Lily shrugged. "He just disappears. I have no idea."

Rupert chewed carefully, then set down his fork. "He needs to be in school. Or get a job," he declared. "I'll have a word with him, if I can find him."

In the end, it was Lily who talked with Brendan. "Where do you go when you go out, Brendan?"

"Nowhere. There's no place to go in this dump."

Lily took a deep breath. "Your Uncle Rupert and I were wondering if you need something to fill your time. Perhaps you would like to enroll in high school, or maybe Uncle Rupert could help you find a job."

"A job?"

"Yes, you know, in a shop or cooking burgers and fries."

"Me? Slinging burgers?"

Suddenly, Lily was flooded with irritation. "You have until tomorrow to make up your mind," she told him. "You have a choice. School or a job."

When he sullenly mumbled that he guessed school was better than flipping burgers, it was Lily who took him to the high school and introduced him to Margaret. “I’m Principal Cruikshank, Brendan. We’re pleased to have you here and hope you’ll have an easy adjustment. But I have to tell you,” she said brusquely, “we run a tight ship. Let me introduce you to my vice principal. He can be a big help to students.”

CHAPTER 19

On the third day of Brendan's enrollment in high school, Lily sat at her computer, transcribing more pages of Elodie's diary. She flipped to the end of the journal, wishing that this project was complete. It sapped her energy, and while she didn't admit this to Rupert, she found it all quite uninteresting. She sighed and bent back to her work but was startled when her phone rang.

"Lily?" She recognized Margaret's voice at once. "I'm afraid we have a bit of a situation here."

"Brendan?" Lily pressed her hand against her heart, hoping to still the panic which had risen from her stomach.

Brendan, Margaret informed her, had been quick to find what they referred to as "the smokers' pit," an area just off the school property and around the corner on a side street. "Of course, we do everything we can to discourage this gathering," Margaret went on. "There is always the danger of illicit drugs, skipping classes, smoking pot, maybe even alcohol. My vice principal takes a stroll out there a few times a day to scatter the kids, but it doesn't take any time at all until they regather. Today, though, when he went out to do his patrol, there was only a police car, a town worker and a street cleaner…you know, one of those cart-like machines with the brushes on the bottom that clean up along the curb?"

Lily exhaled. Where was this going?

"The town worker was giving a report to the police officer. It seems that he had stopped his machine for a minute and was using a broom and shovel to remove debris from a storm drain when one of the boys at the smokers' pit jumped on the street cleaner, put it into gear and started to drive it down the street." Despite the seriousness of this prank, Margaret chuckled. "The worker chased after him and soon caught up. Those machines aren't exactly built for the Indy 500. The boy jumped off the machine just before it made a crash landing into a fire hydrant. The description of the kid was quite clear—baggy jeans, black hoodie, wolf tattoo on his neck and spiked earrings. We called Brendan to the office and had a stern word with him, of course, but I'm afraid we have no choice but to suspend him from school for two weeks. The rest of the students need to understand that this type of behaviour is unacceptable. Can you come and pick him up?"

"No," Lily asserted. "I don't drive. Tell him to walk home."

"There are some things that must change," Rupert stated in a loud, firm voice. Brendan sat slumped in his chair, his face sullen and defiant. He wasn't used to being treated like a child. "First of all, if you leave this house, you must tell me or Lily where you are going and when you will be back. Secondly, you will not sit around the house for two weeks doing nothing. Lily will make you a list of chores that can be done here. Thirdly, you must agree to meet us in the dining room for dinner every night at six. That's how civilized people live. Do I make myself perfectly clear, Brendan?" When the boy didn't answer, Rupert shouted, "Brendan, is this clear to you?"

The days that followed were long and unpleasant for Lily, full of anxiety and uncertainty. She was afraid to tell Rupert that Brendan had resumed his former habit of sleeping until the afternoon, but letting him sleep was easier for her than keeping him busy with make-work tasks. On the second day, brooding and ill-tempered after he had washed and dried the lunch dishes, then vacuumed the hall carpet, he slumped down in the snug and switched on the television, but before long, he rose and began to pace. "I'm going out for a while," he told Lily.

"Where? And when will you be back?"

"Can't a guy just go out for a walk?" he barked.

Their evening meals, too, had become a nightmare.

"What did you do today?" Rupert inquired.

"Nothin'."

"You must have done something," Rupert insisted. "Didn't Lily make you a list?"

"Yeah. I did a bit."

"More shepherd's pie?" Lily offered, but Brendan shook his head. Planning meals that appealed to both of them was a challenge. Rupert favoured traditional British food, but Brendan had grown up on pizza, macaroni and cheese, quesadillas and poutine. Should she make two separate meals to ease the tension?

Lily set Brendan the task of sweeping the side porch, but she had discovered, to her annoyance, that he had a passive aggressive attitude when assigned a task. He swept the porch in a somewhat adequate fashion, but left the broom outside, leaning against the wall. Lily stepped out to see if he was finished but was surprised to see him walking down the driveway. When he reached the end of the Berlin Wall, he turned into Dolly's backyard. Sighing, Lily retrieved the broom and headed back into the house to put it in the closet.

Dinner that evening was a compromise. Lasagna. For the first time in their marriage, Rupert declined a second helping, while Brendan accepted another hearty slice. Lily passed the bowl of Caesar salad to Rupert but both paused mid-air, shocked, when Brendan began to speak. It was the first time that he had contributed to the conversation at the dinner table.

"I met your neighbour next door," he said, stuffing lasagna into his mouth.

"Dolly? You met Dolly Inkpen?"

"Yeah, she's really cool."

"Cool?"

"I think she's a witch or something."

"Oh, I hardly think so."

"She knows the coolest stuff about ghosts and spirits. Today she told me about a place on the south end of Nova Scotia. There was this old guy—

a drunk—who hung himself in a barn. In the olden days, people who killed themselves weren't allowed to be buried in the cemetery, so they dug a hole and buried him under the street. Then, a second guy—a soldier—got a Dear John letter from his girlfriend so he shot himself in the head and was buried under the street, too."

"Really, Brendan, this is hardly suitable conversation for dinnertime," Rupert interrupted, glancing at Lily, noticing that she seemed flushed and upset.

"I thought it was cool, those stories that Dolly Inkpen knows. She said the spirits of people who commit suicide are restless and want to roam around bothering people. So, that's why they buried them under the street. They thought that the noise from the street traffic would make the spirits stay down there."

Rupert set down his salad fork and pushed away his plate. "Lily, my dear, I wonder if there is any dessert?"

After dinner, Lily urged Rupert to take the newspaper into the snug for some rest before his evening meeting. Brendan, too, she pushed toward the hall, suggesting that he call home, have a chat with his mother. He left the kitchen and headed to his bedroom. She could see that he had no intention of calling home, but she didn't care. She needed some time alone. She needed time to tidy up from dinner and to make a plan. Most of all, she needed a sliver of space to think something through.

Since Brendan's arrival, Lily and Rupert had not had time nor inclination for a long, slow amorous Friday evening, so when Rupert arrived home after his meeting, he was surprised to find her in their bedroom. She had taken a bath, changed into a lacy nightdress and brushed out her hair after dabbing some perfume behind her ears. She had a favour to ask, and she thought this might be the most effective path.

Their bedroom was commodious, large enough to accommodate a seating area with two wingback chairs and a small antique pie crust table nestled between them. On this table, Lily had placed an ice bucket and a bottle of chardonnay beside two red-stemmed glasses.

"This is a lovely surprise!" Rupert exclaimed, easing shut the door.

After he had sipped some wine, told her about his meeting and taken off his shoes, she began. "Rupert, I'm wondering about something."

"Mmm…?"

"I'd like to go away for a few days. Take the train into Toronto. I've had a bit of a lead about my sister. I've been in touch with an agency and they think they may be able to help."

"Ah. That sounds promising."

"I did some research. I can be in Toronto in a couple of hours, maybe less. The problem is…I would need to stay in the city for two or three days, take a hotel, while I follow through on the information. There's the expense of it all. I don't have my own money yet and…"

"Oh, of course! You will need money for your travel and hotel and meals. I'll go to the bank tomorrow and make a withdrawal, and I can lend you my credit card as a backup. How much do you think you'll need?"

"There's Brendan, too, of course…"

"Nonsense, Lily. He can look after himself. It will be good for him."

Later, before she had drifted off to sleep, she was amazed at how easy it had been. She had thought it all through so carefully but had still dreaded the conversation with Rupert, feeling the shame of having to ask for money. Had she been manipulative? Or, perhaps, she considered, smiling, it was merely being strategic.

She felt a tingle of shame, for she had not been honest with Rupert. She was going to Toronto not in search of her lost twin sister at all. She was going to Toronto for an interview with three people at the Daniels Building. Her stomach knotted in anxiety and excitement. How would she ever find her way from Union Station to the St. George Campus Faculty of Architecture at One Spadina Crescent?

CHAPTER 20

Philip Karpen was going through a mid-life crisis, he told his friend and colleague, Evelyn. He had always had a flair for the dramatic, so he expressed it this way: "Evelyn, my friend, I am going through a full-blown elaborate and ornate purple-blue funk." He was thinking of taking a year off, maybe do some travel abroad, he confessed.

Evelyn knew that Philip's twin sons were leaving for university in a few months and that his wife had a busy practice as a family doctor. Perhaps, she considered, he worries about how his life might change now. "Alone? You'd go alone?" Evelyn inquired, her voice full of motherly concern.

"That's just it," he sighed. "I don't really want to travel alone. In fact, I don't really know if I want to travel at all. Some days I want a cabin in the woods. Some days I think about switching careers altogether. Try my hand at something entirely different."

"Good grief, Philip! Get a grip. You are one of the most progressive thinkers here at our school. What would the field of architecture do without your ingenuity, passion and drive? Everyone acknowledges that you are the country's leading expert on Canadian architecture. You can't just turn your back on that. We need you in our field." It was the closest she had ever come to scolding him.

"Maybe I just need to start jogging or go on some crazy macro diet," he muttered. "My wife is always telling me that I could lose a pound or two."

"You remembered that we have another interview this afternoon?"

"Oh, damn," Philip replied, beginning to pace up and down the room. "I'll be so glad when these things are over. I know I agreed to do them with you and Suzanne, but they have been a royal pain in the butt. I can't believe that I was ever the age of most of those kids we've interviewed. How can they be so indecisive about life? How do they have the nerve to apply to this program when they know diddly squat about architecture?"

"Now, now. The concept behind this project is great, and if we can help steer a handful of creative, hard-working, innovative candidates into the field, it will be worth it. It saves us from having to weed out the inappropriate ones later. You know how difficult that process can be. The problem is," she sighed, "the candidates just haven't been that strong. Alas, I'm not too hopeful about today either." She pulled out a file folder. "An older wannabe student, Lily Kaltyk from New Hopewell, who doesn't seem to have had much of a career."

Philip groaned in response. "I'll grab a bite to eat and see you back here at one."

When the train finally slowed for Union Station, Lily's anxiety soared. She knew that she had to take a subway to reach the university, but the subway map showed that she was at the bottom of a big U. Which train should she take? The one heading to the right or the train on the left? How could she manage through the turnstile with a weighty suitcase? She paused, pressed against a tiled wall, fearful that she might hyperventilate. As her breathing slowly eased, she remembered Margaret's advice—although she had given it on an entirely different matter. "When you don't know something, all you need to do is ask. You would be surprised at how many people are pleased to offer help."

People were rushing past her, but then she spotted an old man, wearing a cloth hat, shambling along. "Excuse me," she said. "I'm new to the city. I'm wondering which way I would take the subway to get to the University of Toronto."

"Oh, glad to help you out, miss. You take this loop here, off to the left. There are four stops close to the university—Queen's Park, Museum, St. George and Spadina. Just get out at the one that is closest to where you want to go." Lily had no idea which stop was closest to One Spadina Crescent, but she thanked the man.

She struggled down the steps with her bag, and when she saw a young mother grappling with a baby stroller, she said, "Excuse me, I'm wondering if you can tell me how much it costs to ride on the subway?"

When she finally arrived at the Daniels Building, sweaty, uncomfortable and confused, she glanced at the instruction sheet she had been given. "Excuse me," she called out to a passing student. "Can you tell me where I would find meeting room 204?"

Lily paused outside the door. She was ten minutes late. Taking two deep breaths, she tapped on the door, then twisted the knob and stepped inside. "Oh! We were afraid that you were a no-show," a woman said, "but glad you found us. Come in and make yourself comfortable. Suzanne just put on a pot of coffee, but there are cold drinks if you prefer." Three people were looking at her—a smiling, middle-aged woman who introduced herself as Evelyn, a young slim woman with a brisk way of speaking whose name was Suzanne, and a man who said casually, "Hi. I'm Philip."

"You look a little frazzled," Suzanne said. "Did you have trouble finding us?"

"This is my first time in Toronto and I didn't know where I was going," Lily stammered. "I asked a man at Union Station for advice on where to get off the subway but I obviously picked the wrong stop."

"Poor thing," Evelyn said in a soothing voice. "Take a few minutes to regain your composure, then we'll get to know each other. Perhaps you'd like to stow that bag by the doorway." Lily blushed in embarrassment. Why had she not planned to first check into her hotel so she could leave her bag there? Why had she not thought to take a cab to One Spadina Crescent?

When they had settled at a round table, their beverages in front of them, Evelyn began. "I seem to have been volun-told that I would be the official spokesperson, so why don't I tell you a little more about the purpose of our pilot project." Evelyn explained in more detail what Lily had read in the brochure. "Before we proceed, do you have any questions for us?"

"No."

"Then why don't you begin, Philip?"

"Tell us a little about yourself, Lily, and why it is that you are interested in this program."

Lily blushed again. What could she possibly say that wouldn't sound ridiculous? That she had harboured a grudge for years against her high school guidance teacher for steering her away from architecture? That her mother had hidden from her the fact that she had been wealthy enough to send her to university but never told her? That she had lied to her husband about the reason for going to Toronto? That she couldn't wait to get away from a troublesome teenager for whom she felt no affection? Her voice was frozen. She could think of nothing to say.

"Perhaps you're considering a second career?" he prodded. "The others were straight out of high school."

Lily nodded and swallowed. "Yes. A second career. I was a music teacher before." Looking down at her hands clutched together in her lap, she agonized about how to proceed, how to overcome the terrible shyness that was paralyzing her.

"Ah!" Evelyn exclaimed with more enthusiasm than was merited in the situation, hoping to put Lily at ease. "We spend a substantial amount of time in this school considering how architecture is an art but also a discipline as well as a business. Modern architecture, even architecture of the past, had to have all three of these components. They really can't be separated. Perhaps you found this to be true of your life as a music teacher, Lily? You must have a certain aptitude for music, an ear as they say, but you also had to practice for long hours and you had to earn enough at your art to put food on the table."

Lily glanced at Philip and saw that he had shut the file folder with her name on it. Suzanne, too, had crossed her arms and leaned back as if she were biding her time until the interview was over.

"It's an interesting consideration," Lily murmured, "...the interplay of art, discipline and business. I remember reading that here in the city in 1899, when that group of young architects met and formed themselves into the Toronto Architectural Eighteen Club, they came to believe that architecture is an art, but they were also astute enough to recognize that establishing a professional club helped them hone their discipline and skills. They were practical enough, too, to realize that if they didn't get commissions, they could not survive." Lily felt her shyness receding and her voice growing stronger. She reminded herself that she certainly had an informed opinion on this subject. "I would think that great contemporary architects like Mies van der Rohe and Frank Gehry would consider themselves artists, but they also worked extremely hard at their craft and they paid attention to the business elements of their work."

She glanced at the women and back to Philip. He was now sitting up straight, alert, gazing at her, his mouth gaping slightly. Suzanne uncrossed her arms and pursed her lips before glancing sideways at Evelyn and Philip.

"So, Lily," Philip asked, "is there a particular aspect of architecture that is of most interest to you?"

"Oh, yes," she enthused. "I have long been interested in Canadian historical architecture, and because we are such a young country, I am fascinated with how architectural styles were imported, then adapted in the Canadian framework. Certainly, Eden Smith, the architect who founded the Eighteen Club, was profoundly affected by the Arts and Crafts movement, but after his arrival here in Canada, even his knowledge and interest in this style was shaped by his experience of the Canadian landscape. When he was growing up in England, he could not have envisioned the vastness of Canada, the boundless forests and immense rivers and lakes, the rocks of the Canadian Shield. I do believe there is some justification, like the architectural historian William Westfall noted—although he was referring to church-building in the late 1800s—that architects may have considered their craft an art, but they were shaping a Canadian adaptation when they refashioned the Gothic into an Ontario style. Some have even suggested that these artistic compromises may be called 'the Canadian style.'" She paused, looking off across the room, "Oh, I do hope that while I'm here in Toronto I'll have time to see Eden Smith's house on Indian Road. I understand that it features a half-timbered cross-gable, quite unusual."

"So…you're interested in the contextual aspect of architecture, Lily?"

"Oh, absolutely. All art forms are created within a context. Why wouldn't it be the same in architecture? When you look at St. John's, Newfoundland, for instance, the buildings and hardscape are profoundly different, in most part, from Quebec City or Calgary or Vancouver. Since there are different needs across this broad country, different types of climates and different resources, the style and form of both public and private structures must fit with the landscape and the needs of the people. Of course, there are other factors—like cost or a builder's personal taste or a client's preference or even the availability of regional resources like stone and brick."

Lily could hear that her voice was strong, but she paused, worried that her ideas, while clear in her mind, may have come out in a profusion of verbiage. She took a deep breath and felt a flush move into her cheeks. Evelyn, Suzanne and Philip were all staring at her. "I'm sorry. I got a little carried away," she murmured, gathering her handbag toward her lap.

"No, no, please," Philip said, continuing to gaze at her. "It's just…well, you have certainly been a surprise, Lily. Quite different from anyone else we have interviewed." The women nodded in agreement.

They asked her a few more questions. Did she have a particular area of interest? Domestic architecture? Public buildings? Churches? To which she responded, "I'm interested in all of these areas, and while I'm not particularly interested in military architecture, I do hope to find time to tour Fort York. I think it is quite amazing that the British built eighteen buildings between 1813 and 1815 and that the Toronto Historical Board has restored eight of them."

"Are there other buildings you are hoping to see in Toronto?" Philip asked, smiling.

"Oh, I have an enormous list," she enthused. "Far too many to see in a few days." She pulled a notebook from her handbag. "I'd love to see The Grange, the original home of D'Arcy Boulton, and the Sir William Campbell House, which has been moved, I understand. Such wonderful examples of an embellished variant of the Georgian style. And there's Colborne Lodge in High Park, the summer home of the Toronto architect John G. Howard. There are several churches I'd love to see, too. St. James Anglican, such a great example of Gothic Revival. And then I'd like to see old Osgoode Hall. That Palladian Georgian style was used so often for public buildings." She flipped a page. "I am the first to admit that there's a huge gap in my knowledge base regarding modern architecture, so I would love to study Massey College and Toronto City Hall. Then there's Santiago Caltrava's arcade and Daniel Libeskind's crystal addition to the Royal Ontario Museum..."

"Whoa, Lily!" Philip laughed, throwing up his hands in mock horror. "You may need a lifetime to work through that list."

"Yes," she answered. "I may need a lifetime."

"I'm afraid our hour is up, Lily," Evelyn explained.

"Of course." She began to rise, having already forgotten to ask when she would hear back from them.

"One moment, please." Philip raised his hand, then leaned toward her and said, "Lily, tomorrow is not a teaching day for me. I'm wondering if you would accept an offer from me to act as your personal chauffeur and guide so we can see some of those places on your list? I'd love to introduce you to the architecture of Toronto." Evelyn and Suzanne looked surprised, smiling indulgently at Philip. "I'll pick you up at nine o'clock tomorrow morning. Where are you staying?"

CHAPTER 21

When she stepped off the elevator into the hotel lobby at nine in the morning, there was a man standing by the front door, his back to her. Was it Philip? She wasn't sure. He was taller than she remembered and had thick brown hair, combed straight back, twisting into gentle curls at the nape of his neck. He wore casual, rumpled pants and a dress shirt with the sleeves rolled up. He turned, jiggling car keys. "Lily! Right on time! Let's get started. This will be a fun day."

"Oh, I know," she breathed. She had been too excited and nervous to have breakfast or even a coffee.

He swung out of the parking lot and turned south. "I know you have your list, but I can't resist starting with my personal favourite. This was, by far, the most creative, imaginative, exciting project I've ever worked on." Lily could hear the exhilaration in his voice. "I had a small part in a much larger scheme. I've a passion for merging old and new while maintaining the integrity of the original. We were able to repurpose original material and blend it with new and modern materials as well as green technologies."

He stopped in front of a kiosk that read *Welcome to The Distillery Historic District*. Lily looked out at a red brick avenue where people strolled among café tables topped with green umbrellas. There were large, old-new, brick buildings as far as the eye could see.

"Amazing," she breathed.

Philip laughed in delight. "Thirteen acres, ten streets, forty-seven buildings. The restoration opened like this in 2002. It started out as a wind-powered flour mill in 1832 and when the owners, Gooderham and Worts, added a distillery in 1837, their business really took off. It flourished and developed into the biggest distillery in the world. They became the largest corporate taxpayers in Canada. Let's get parked and we can have a good walkabout."

The sun warmed their skin as they strolled from building to building. All had been beautifully restored and now hummed with people shopping, strolling and chatting. Others sat quietly dreaming on benches or sipping a cappuccino while using their laptop at a café table. Philip paused often to point out details, his passion making him vivacious and animated. "Such architectural cohesion in the building design, craftmanship, construction, and in the palette of materials and colours. In my opinion, it is the finest collection of Victorian industrial buildings in Canada. Look here, Lily. Do you see the continuous articulated facades? The pitched roofs and decorative cupolas. Look at the parapets on those buildings. I love the Italianate detailing on the round arches, those segmented windows and the corbelled brickwork. They say," he added with a laugh, "that the windows in the Still House were designed to blow outward in case of an explosion. Sheer and utter genius." He pointed out the overhead pipes and bridges that ran between buildings, facilitating the movement of materials and people.

They moved from street to street, passing a shop called *Bergo Designs*, which featured sleek contemporary home decor. They strolled past stores displaying exciting men's and women's fashions. A shop called *Distill* offered ceramics while *Corktown Designs* promised one-of-a-kind jewellery. Philip pointed out the *Young Centre for the Performing Arts*, restaurants with exotic names like *El Catrin Destileria* and *Adrina Bar and Tapas*. He paused in front of intriguing street sculptures, naming them one by one—*It, Still Dancing, Love Locks, Big Heart*—and told her a little about each artist.

"It is such a dramatic fusion of the new and old," Lily observed

"Exactly!" Philip exclaimed. "The developers were a visionary lot. I was very lucky to work with them."

"Perhaps they were lucky to have you agree to help," Lily smiled.

"My dear lady, you do flatter me so. Now, it's time to take a break. We'll stop at Balzac's Coffee Shop. They not only have great coffee but also decadent snacks…mmm… Their dark chocolate espresso cookie is to die for." He tucked her hand under his arm, flung out his other arm and said, in a mock- gallant manner, "Après toi, madame."

When they reached the front of the coffee shop, Lily stopped. "What was this building before?"

"The Pump House for the distillery," Philip laughed. "Can you imagine building a humble pump house with such elaborate brick detailing?" He pointed toward the peaked roof. "There was always a need for water on site for cooling, washing and brewing. And there was always the risk of fire, so this beautiful little building would have hummed along 24/7. Now, it pumps out java. It has evolved into a two-storey Grand Parisian-style café."

"Listen to this," Lily said when they had settled under a yellow umbrella at a bistro table on the patio. She opened a brochure: *"Our vision was to combine the romance and relaxing atmosphere of European walking and patio districts with the hip, cool dynamic of an area like New York City's SoHo or Chelsea, where creative minds get together and you feel as if anything could happen."*

"Well, yes! That's exactly what we were going for. And all the while it's also like stepping back into an era of windmills, horse-drawn carts and sailing ships."

The rest of the day was a blur of activity, moving from one moment of excitement to another, but before heading north, Philip had pulled up in front of St. Lawrence Market and stopped, moving his car seat back so Lily could have a good view. "This building both intrigues me with its history and makes me sad."

"Why is that?"

"This area was first set aside as a public market in 1803 in York, as Toronto was called then. It would have been a small community at that time. There were some structures, but it wasn't until 1820 that a permanent market building went up. Then in 1831 it was replaced with the first

St. Lawrence Market North building. There was a great fire in 1849 and a new building went up in 1851. Then the market expanded using part of the former city hall of Toronto to create St. Lawrence Market South. Then in the early 1900s a new matching building replaced the north building. This was superseded with another new building in 1968, before you were born," he added with a smile. "Then in 2016, that north building was demolished to make way for this." Philip swept his hand toward the façade of the market.

"How do you know all this?"

"It's my business, Lily. I could give you a boring lecture on every historical building in Toronto. How else do I earn my paycheck?"

"I'm more than a little overwhelmed," she said, then added, "to be given a private tour by such an expert."

He glanced over at her, grinning, trying to discern if she was teasing him, but she was gazing through the front windshield of the car, looking thoughtful and serene.

"Lily, you have no idea what a gift this day has been to me. This day has just shouted to me—Philip Karpen, you can't turn your back on something you love so much. It is totally wonderful to spend a day with someone who reminded me of this and who shares my passion for architecture. You are quite an extraordinary person. I've never met a lay person who is as knowledgeable about Canadian architecture. And what's more…you care. You really care!"

Lily felt suddenly embarrassed and shy. "You didn't tell me why you find the St. Lawrence Market sad," she said, to deflect the conversation away from herself.

"So many of our historic buildings are gone. Just disappeared because… well, for a lot of complex reasons. St. Lawrence Market is one example of that. Build, tear down, build, tear down. I don't know if you've travelled to Europe, but before he died, I took my dad back to visit the town where he grew up—Berezhany in western Ukraine. It's not a big place, about 17,000 people, and was founded in 1375. In the mid-1600s it was sacked and pillaged, then rebuilt. Honestly, Lily, the buildings there—both the public and the private ones—are solid, sturdy, ornate, beautiful. It was like stepping back a couple of centuries. I almost expected Sergei Prokofiev to come strolling out through a front door and down the stone steps, a music score tucked under his arm. You don't find people in Europe demolishing and rebuilding those lovely old buildings with the same zest that we have for this in Canada. There have been entirely too many wonderful buildings destroyed for convenience and greed and 'progress,' especially here in Toronto."

"You're…Ukrainian?"

"Well, sure. Second generation. That surprise you? You with a name like Kaltyk?"

"Your name. Karpen. It doesn't sound Ukrainian."

"When my dad first arrived, someone advised him to shorten his name from Karpenko to Karpen. It would make it easier to get a job in this city."

"Did it?"

"There are certain prejudices that die hard. His accent was a dead giveaway," Philip laughed.

At the end of the day, Philip drove Lily back to her hotel. "I'll see you safely to the lobby."

"Oh, no, no, please. You've done so much already."

"It's a gentleman thing. I can't just dump you out on the curb."

When they got to the little alcove beside the elevator, Philip turned to face her. "Lily, I can truly say that today has been beautiful for me. I will cherish it as one of the happiest days of my life."

Lily tilted her head to one side, looking up at him, thinking back through all the things she had learned about him in only one day. "Really? Right up there with your marriage to a beautiful doctor? The birth of twin sons? Right up there with the day you received the Governor General's medal in architecture?"

"Right up there, Lily," he said, lifting her chin. He bent to kiss her softly on the lips, but when she slid her arms around him, he kissed her with all the fire and passion that he usually reserved for lovely old buildings.

CHAPTER 22

On her first day home, she wandered from room to room, trying to coax her body and mind back into the space where they had been before. It was mid-morning and Rupert was out. Brendan was also missing. The door to his bedroom stood open and she could see a confusion of clothes lying around the room, and there was a sour smell that she couldn't identify. Had he encountered a skunk?

She walked down the stairs, not feeling at all like Scarlett O'Hara, then leaned on the kitchen counter waiting for the kettle to boil. After stepping out the side door, she settled into a porch chair, clutching a mug of hot tea, thinking about Toronto. She heard chatting and laughter and realized it was coming from Dolly Inkpen's backyard. Brendan. She would recognize his voice anywhere. She couldn't hear what they were saying, but the situation baffled her—a salty, superstitious, older woman and an unruly, undisciplined teenager. How was it that they had befriended each other? Or was something else going on right under her nose?

Unable to settle to any task in the afternoon, she decided to make cabbage rolls. She had done no Ukrainian cooking since her marriage. Why do I cook to suit Rupert's and Brendan's tastes? she demanded of herself. She longed for the comfort of her own food, the familiar tastes and smells of her childhood.

She and Rupert had settled into their seats in the dining room when Brendan rushed in and flopped into a chair. "What's this crap?" he exclaimed.

"Young man, watch yourself," Rupert snapped. "I demand that you apologize to Lily. She probably spent all afternoon preparing our dinner."

"Sorry, Lily," he mumbled, not looking at her.

"They're cabbage rolls," she explained. "Probably the most popular dish among Ukrainian people. I grew up on them."

"Try them," Rupert urged.

She tried not to watch as Brendan took his fork and knife and unfolded the cabbage leaf, trying to separate the ground beef filling from the tomato sauce. She reached over and gave Rupert a large spoonful, but he, too, ate more slowly than usual.

"You must tell us about your time in Toronto, Lily." He cut off a small piece of cabbage roll and chewed for a long time.

"I'm afraid there's not much to report. It was a challenge to find my way around the city, but I met some wonderful people and we made a start." She hesitated, then added, "I will need to go back in a month's time."

"Oh, of course. You must keep on this." He turned to Brendan. "And you, young man? What are your plans for tomorrow?"

Rupert didn't want to confess to Lily that he had done absolutely nothing to supervise Brendan while she was away. He had no idea how the boy had spent his days. Lily, too, was awash with guilt. She had been evasive, even untruthful, about her time in Toronto. A snippet of a poem from her high school days rushed into her mind: *Oh, what a tangled web we weave, when first we practice to deceive.* Sir Walter Scott. It was only later, as she recalled their conversation, that she realized that Rupert was really not all that interested in her activities. Some wives might find that hurtful, she considered, but the flip side was that it gave her rather enormous freedom.

Before switching off the bed lamp, Lily plumped her pillow and leaned back against the headboard. "Rupert, there's something I want to ask you."

"Mmm…?"

She told him about Dolly and Brendan spending time together. "This is the second time I've noticed it. Do you think there's any harm in it? Is something crazy going on?"

"Oh, I sincerely doubt it. They're just two lost souls who enjoy hanging out together."

"You think so? They're a very unlikely pair."

"Time for sleep. Sufficient unto the day is the trouble thereof."

Lily sighed and rolled over. She wondered if Rupert was thinking of the same thing that was unsettling her mind. At dinner, after she had reluctantly suggested to Brendan that he make himself a peanut butter sandwich, he returned to the table and began telling them a story that he learned from Dolly.

"You know that famous Peggy's Cove in Nova Scotia that all the tourists go see? Dolly told me why it's called Peggy's Cove. A young woman washed ashore after a shipwreck in St. Margaret's Bay. Still alive. She was wearing a cornflower-blue dress and couldn't remember her real name, probly 'cause she had a trauma. Maybe lost her family out there in the ocean. The people who rescued her called her Peggy because of St. Margaret's Bay, see? She was very pretty and a young fisherman met her and was gob-struck. He just had to marry her and kept trying to cheer her up. He climbed up on some slippery rocks where the Peggy's Cove lighthouse is now and did a fancy Irish jig for her, but he slipped and fell on the rocks, split his head open and died. Peggy's heart was broken again, so she stepped off the rocks and into the crashing waves and drowned herself. To this day, her ghost wanders around the cove still dressed in the cornflower-blue dress. If you go to the lighthouse at night, you'd be sure to see her. Cool, huh?"

When Brendan had finished his story and sandwich, Lily said, "You seem to be spending a lot of time listening to Dolly's stories." Brendan had been boyishly lighthearted as he told his story, but now he looked sullen and withdrawn. He stood up and clomped from the room, his untied running shoes slapping against the hardwood floor.

Rupert hadn't seemed to notice. He covered her hand with his. "It's great to have you home, Lily. Can I help you clean up the kitchen?"

CHAPTER 23

The next morning at breakfast, Rupert suggested that he take a day off, stay home and do some odd jobs around the house. He would get Brendan up and moving, maybe show him how to use the lawn mower.

"Oh, really, no, Rupert. That isn't necessary." Lily spoke with more authority than usual. Having found a centre of stability within herself, she was determined to begin working on the architecture project for Evelyn, Suzanne and Philip. "Besides," she rushed on, "I need to get Brendan to sort out his room. It's a disaster and I want to teach him how to use the washing machine and dryer."

"You're sure?" Did she detect a look of relief on his face? Looking after a recalcitrant teenager had been arduous for both of them.

"Absolutely. Maybe I'll have time in the next couple of days to get back at the journals, too."

"That would be good," he murmured.

"There's something I forgot to mention. It slipped my mind. When I was at the train station getting my ticket for Toronto, I had a conversation with the ticket agent. He comes to our church once in a while, I think. He told me that he had met Brendan. He distinctly remembered the wolf tattoo. Apparently, Brendan went into the train station recently and inquired about the cheapest way to get to Vancouver."

Rupert showed little interest in the information, shrugging it off as harmless. As he was leaving the house, he called back, "You did remember the Women's Missionary Society meeting today, Lily?" She felt her shoulders sag.

Things did not go well for her at the meeting. The women were polite to her, but early in the meeting, Lily made a blunder. The president, Mrs. Hardy, announced that it was time for the roll call. Instead of answering "here" or "present," the women were to tell the others what food they most missed from their childhood.

There was a long silence while the president shuffled to the correct page in her notebook. Lily blurted out, "I really miss my mother's borscht."

Mrs. Hardy looked at her in surprise. "Mrs. Cameron, it's not your *turn*. You have to wait your turn like everyone else. We go in alphabetical order."

Lily flushed in embarrassment. She glanced at the other women, but they were all looking at Mrs. Hardy, waiting for their names to be called. Her eyes searched the room and settled on a wall plaque across the hall. She stared at it until her cheeks cooled. She felt an almost uncontrollable urge to stand up and walk out but was too self-conscious and shy to do that. Instead, she folded her hands, glanced at her watch and calculated how many minutes it would be until she could politely excuse herself.

When it was Lily's turn, Mrs. Hardy said, "Now then, Mrs. Cameron, tell us about that strange food your mother used to make."

Lily's phone began ringing as she walked into the house. She recognized Margaret's voice at once. Perhaps she wanted to arrange an evening for working on chapter four?

"Lily, is Rupert home?"

"Not yet. I expect him around five."

"It's urgent that I speak with you both. Can I drop by at five? I'll be bringing my vice principal along. Can you arrange for Brendan to be there, too?"

"Brendan?" Lily felt her stomach knot.

• • •

They arrived at the same time, Margaret, Rupert, the vice principal. Lily had not had time to give Rupert a heads-up. He looked baffled and worried.

"No Brendan?" Margaret inquired.

"I can't find him anywhere," Lily replied. She didn't want to admit that most days she didn't know where he was or what he was doing but that he always showed up at six o'clock for dinner, to appease them, she thought.

"I'll get straight to the point. We've had another incident. A serious one. Perhaps you'd like to start," she said, nodding to the vice principal.

"Sure. This afternoon I was doing my regular scaring thing around the corner from the school property where the kids hang out to smoke. When I approached, the kids all scattered, which is not all that unusual, but not before I noticed the unmistakable earthy, skunky smell of marijuana. I was able to grab one boy and when we questioned him in the office, he confessed that some kid had been coming around every day selling weed. We asked the name of the seller and he didn't know, but he said he had a wolf tattoo on his neck and skull earrings."

"We do have a set of protocols to follow," Margaret continued. "If staff see illegal or disruptive activity, they are obliged to report it to me, and in turn, I am obliged to report the incident to the parents. In this case, there are some unusual circumstances. Do I have this straight? There is no father in Brendan's life and his mother is in Montreal but found herself unable to control him, which is why he was sent to you?"

"Yes," Rupert said, looking down. "My sister. I'm afraid she should never have been a parent."

"Do you have legal custody of Brendan, or is it just a family agreement?"

"We thought we might be able to help the boy a bit, but this has gone beyond us. There's no legal arrangement."

"Let's see what we can do," Margaret said brusquely. "Brendan will need to be involved in the solution, long term, but in the meantime, here is our bottom line as school administrators. We take into account the particular student and circumstances, the nature and severity of the behaviour and the impact on school climate. In this incident, we consider it a very serious offense to sell cannabis to underage teens who are our students. We know that the incident took place off school property, but nevertheless, it involved our students, kids who return to math class and science labs and gym. The entire student body needs to know and understand that this will not be tolerated. Brendan has already been suspended for two weeks, but I hope you understand that now we have no choice but to expel him. We simply can't have someone loitering around our school property making drugs available to our students." Lily and Rupert nodded in understanding. "This gives you a dilemma, though," she continued in a gentler tone. "Brendan is heading down a wrong path and he needs intervention and help. This is not simply 'unacceptable behaviour.' This young man is seriously drifting into criminal activity. Have you any idea at all where he is getting his product?"

"None," Rupert replied, and Lily shook her head.

"Have you noticed the people he hangs out with? Friends who might be influencing him?"

Again, both Lily and Rupert shook their heads, and Lily said, "He goes out a lot and he's very secretive about it. The only person I've seen him hang out with lately is our neighbour, Dolly Inkpen."

"Dolly Inkpen!" Despite the seriousness of the conversation, Margaret laughed. "That is the most unlikely pair I could ever imagine. A teenager acting out in a serious way and the town eccentric who sees ghosts and goblins around each corner."

"Exactly."

"Where do we go from here, Margaret?" Rupert's face was drawn with anxiety and frustration. If Lily had been sitting closer, she might have taken his hand.

"As I see it, the ball is definitely in your court. I can give you the names of counsellors and agencies who we know and trust. They can help sort out with you and Brendan the possible reasons why he is selling pot and, no doubt, using it himself. Maybe it's his misguided way to fit in, to belong. Some kids just get in over their head and go along with what others are doing. It's entirely possible, too, that kids have anxiety or depression which they try to hide, then turn to drugs for self-medication. Maybe they struggle with self-esteem, and smoking pot gives them more confidence. And there are others who are just plain bored and looking for excitement. They get a kick out of buying and hiding drugs and sneaking around. It's complicated. That's why professional help is needed."

"What happens if Brendan refuses to go with us for help?"

Margaret sighed. "That is a worry and a very real possibility. Kids often feel they can handle these situations by themselves. If he does refuse, I suggest that you go without him. The agencies we recommend can suggest how best to help Brendan, even with something as fundamental as how to have a good conversation with him."

"I feel terrible about this," Rupert admitted. "I feel that we've really let the boy down."

"Don't be too hard on yourself. Brendan is a product of his upbringing and his own poor choices. You can't be expected to change him overnight, but you must have conversations with him. It's important to think through how you are going to react. He needs to understand the gravity of the situation. You must stay calm but firm. Ultimately, Brendan needs to hear and know that you love him despite his mistakes."

Lily sat gazing down at her twisted hands. She could not raise her eyes to look at Rupert, but she knew that she certainly did not love Brendan. In fact, she resented that he had been catapulted into her marriage and became one more thing that she had to look after. How could she go on pretending to be concerned when what she secretly hoped is that he had enough money to get on a train, if not to Vancouver, then some place far away where she would never have to see him again.

CHAPTER 24

Brendan did not come home that night. Perhaps, Lily considered, he had intuited that something was up or had come home and spotted the principal's car in their driveway, then fled. The following morning, when there was still no sign of the boy, she decided to gather his dirty clothes into the laundry basket and haul them into the basement. Throughout the day, she washed, dried, folded and set neat piles into the dresser drawers in his bedroom.

By mid-afternoon, she had become restless, impatient with herself. What am I doing? she demanded. I have a fascinating project to prepare and I'm wandering around the house like a lost soul, worrying about a kid who needs to grow up. She climbed the stairs to her office, turned on her laptop and opened a PowerPoint file.

In the Daniels Building, after Evelyn had announced that their hour was up, she had asked Lily if she could identify an area of research that intrigued her. "In a month's time, we invite you to return and make a presentation on a topic of your choice," she told Lily, "but if you can't think of a topic, Philip, Suzanne and I could assign one." It was the first indication that the group had, by some tacit agreement, accepted Lily into the program.

"Oh, I'd like to choose my own," Lily blurted out. "For some time, I've been wanting to research the Georgian revival movement in Canada. I know, for instance, that the Georgian style was used widely in Upper and Lower Canada in the mid-1800s because it expressed solidity, establishment and order, and those were values of both the British immigrants and the American United Empire Loyalists who came north following the American War of Independence. But what I've been wondering is whether the Georgian revival movement was evident all across Canada. Somehow, I can't imagine examples of it in Saskatchewan or Alberta, for instance, but I don't know that. I'd like to research that."

Philip, she noticed, had begun to scribble something rapidly in her file folder. "Terrific topic, Lily. Great idea. We look forward to hearing what you discover."

Lily gathered up the breakfast plates and returned the strawberry jam to the refrigerator. "Rupert, I'm wondering if we should contact the police?"

"Police?" He looked up from the morning paper and set down his mug of tea.

"Should we report Brendan missing?"

"Oh, I'm sure he'll show up when he's hungry...or when he runs out of clothes. Let's give it a few more days."

"I'm not sure that's wise," she muttered. The truth was, Lily was having trouble focusing on preparing her architecture project. Although she resented the boy, she also felt responsible. Somehow, it didn't seem right to ignore the fact that he was missing. "Could you not call your sister in Montreal and see if he has returned there?"

"And admit that we've lost him? No, let's give it another day. If we still haven't heard from him, we'll report him missing tomorrow. Maybe I could make an inquiry at the train station. See if he bought a ticket out of town."

Having finished her housework and shopping, Lily climbed the stairs, determined to start her project. She paused in the doorway of Brendan's room, wishing now that he was back so her mind would be at ease. If he returned, she vowed she would no longer comment on the state of his room or urge him to do his laundry or ask him to do chores.

She was about to turn toward her office when she noticed something. Brendan's brown toiletry bag always sat on top of his dresser, but now it was gone. She stepped into the room and tugged open the top drawer where she had stacked his folded T-shirts. The drawer was half empty. She pulled out the big drawer at the bottom where there were jeans and hoodies. It, too, was half empty. She shut the drawers and hurried to the closet. His big army tote bag was still there.

Lily slumped on the bed in relief. At least she knew that Brendan was alive and nearby. But where was he staying? Even more creepy to her, when had he sneaked into the house to get his things?

Lily sat waiting for her laptop to boot when the phone rang. It was a voice she didn't recognize, a woman who introduced herself as the program chair of the Women's Missionary Society. Would Lily consent to come to their meeting in two weeks and speak to their group?

"Speak?" Lily pressed her hand against her heart.

"Our scheduled speaker cancelled," the woman explained, "so we said, 'Wouldn't it be nice to have the minister's wife take our program?'"

"But what would I speak about? I don't know anything much about mission work."

"Oh, you just take your pick of topics. Anything will do."

When she had hung up, a wave of anger washed over her. Would these people never stop pestering her? After all, she fumed, this was Rupert's work. Why hadn't they asked him?

She stormed down to the kitchen, determined to have a firm word with Rupert when he returned for lunch, but as she worked in the kitchen, she began to see that she might turn this speaking engagement into an advantage. She could research and make a PowerPoint presentation on the historical significance of the architecture of local churches. Not only would this be of interest to her, but it would also give her an opportunity to practice her PowerPoint skills for her presentation at the Daniels Building in Toronto. There was one problem, though. She needed to have Rupert drive her to towns around New Hopewell and wait while she took photos and explored the detailing of each building.

"Of course, we could do that on Saturday afternoon," he said after she had asked. "It would give me a chance to do something that I've been neglecting ever since we arrived—a bit of bird watching. I've been hoping to spot some of the late warbler migration, maybe see a Blackpoll or Bay-breasted, or spot some piping plovers. But honestly, Lily, don't you think it's time that you learned to drive a car yourself?"

"Oh, Rupert! I couldn't really," she protested, thinking of his immaculate, shiny Audi. "What if I put a ding in your fender? Or bumped into a curb?"

"I see your point. Well, perhaps we could find a driving school and you could learn in their car. Why don't you make some calls about that this afternoon?"

Five days passed and there was still no sight of Brendan. Lily had informed Rupert about the clothes and toiletry bag. He, too, seemed relieved but equally puzzled. In the afternoon, as Lily was setting out the garbage for pick-up at the end of the driveway, she was sure that she caught a whiff of marijuana. She was positive that it was coming from Dolly Inkpen's backyard. Was it possible that Brendan was staying with her? She would ask Rupert at dinner.

"Oh, I think that is highly unlikely, Lily. Why would she? Dolly doesn't have a lot of money judging from the state of her property. Why would she take in a troubled teenager and hide him right next door to his own home? No. Improbable and impossible."

"Could you just knock on her door and inquire?" Lily pleaded, but Rupert had passed his plate, indicating that he would like a second helping of steak and kidney pie.

The following morning, restless and unable to concentrate on either her Women's Missionary speech or her Toronto architecture project, Lily walked to the end of the driveway to retrieve the empty garbage pails. On an impulse, she set them down on the lawn, went to the front door of Dolly Inkpen's cottage, climbed the crumbling cement steps and knocked loudly on the door. There was no answer, but Lily heard stirring inside the house, so she knocked again. The door eased open, then shut. She could hear someone removing a chain and the door slid open a little wider.

"Oh, it's you, missus."

"Hello, Dolly. How are you?"

"Oh, this is it, ducky."

"Dolly, I'm wondering if I might come in for a minute. I have something to ask you."

"Oh, I don't think that will work till now. I'm busy, ya see."

Lily hesitated, and Dolly looked back over her shoulder, causing the door to swing open. Lily gawked in amazement and shock. The front door opened directly into the kitchen and there was a living room to the right. The table in the kitchen was littered with clutter: leftover pancakes, a thermos, piles of papers and letters, a hot sauce bottle, a roll of paper towel, a wallet, a bottle of ketchup, a blue vase holding a dead flower. The counters, too, were covered with bottles of oil, a spray can, boxes of corn starch, a small fan, a metal ornament in the shape of a kitten. The cupboard doors hung open displaying a muddle of tins and boxes. There were pots and fry pans on top of the stove, and for some inexplicable reason, the bottom freezer door of the refrigerator was propped open. On the floor were dozens of cardboard boxes and shopping bags overflowing with books, newspapers, towels, plastic bags, but a small path had been kept clear to move from the front door to the sink. The living room was almost as cluttered with empty soda bottles, a tattered red quilt, half-eaten pizza slices, papers and books scattered on the floor. The unmistakable smell of marijuana hung in the air.

Lily realized she was gaping and closed her mouth. "I'm sorry to bother you, Dolly. Perhaps you'd like to drop in for a cup of tea later today."

"Well, we'll see, missus. I'm terrible busy these days."

In the middle of the night, Lily woke with a start. Had it been a dream? She was sure that she heard the click of the back door. She crept out into the hall, then remembered something that Dolly Inkpen had told her. From her upstairs window, Dolly could see Charlotte the ghost walking in the hallway of the Old Manse. If Dolly can see into our hallway, Lily considered, then I should be able to see into the bedroom window over Dolly's kitchen.

It was no surprise when a moment later a light appeared in the bedroom across the driveway. There was a single bulb suspended from the ceiling and a small, disheveled bed crammed against the wall. The floor and chair were strewn with a jumble of clothes, a backpack, sneakers. Then Lily quite clearly saw Brendan walking toward the bed, wearing only pajama bottoms and scratching his belly with one hand. In the other arm, he carried a stack of clean T-shirts.

CHAPTER 25

"In conclusion," Lily said, as she turned to the last of her PowerPoint slides, "I confess that I had not expected my perspective on architecture to become so altered by this research. I began at a simple point: I truly just love the symmetry, solidity and beauty of a Georgian-style house. At the beginning, I believed that architectural styles are standard bearers, that they reflect a set of beliefs and expectations. The national railway—our Canadian ribbon of steel—linked the east coast of Canada to the west in 1881. With the resulting increased interaction and better communication, we might then expect some uniformity in beliefs, practices and styles as we travel across the 5,500 kilometres we call Canada; we might expect to find Georgian homes in all ten provinces. I also asked myself, is there a uniquely Canadian aspect to Georgian-style homes, some distinguishing and uniting features that express our journey from colony to nation after inheriting this style from Great Britain? What I discovered is that the architecture of this country is much more fluid than rock, brick, concrete and wood.

"The surprise for me, as I moved from province to province, was the discovery that architecture is more organic, more adaptive, more varied to a particular region. Yes, there are examples of Georgian-style houses in each of the provinces, but they vary considerably. We can illustrate this from opposite coast provinces in Canada—Newfoundland on the east coast and British Columbia on the west.

"In Newfoundland, we looked at the restored Ashbourne Longhouse in Twillingate, built by a sea captain and merchant, a man who no doubt longed for his British Georgian-style home. Handsome as it was, the Ashbourne house with its large rooms and high ceilings was not practical in a province that contends with icy winters, ocean gales, short summers and abundant rain. Instead, the Salt Box style, named for its resemblance to the boxes of salt that were sent to Newfoundland to preserve their great shipments of cod, and the Biscuit Box style from 1870 to 1960 were more suitable for warmth, for withstanding the elements, and for cozy kitchen parties favoured by the people of that province. In other words, we do find Georgian-style homes in Newfoundland, but the lasting and best architecture for homes is a dynamic mix that expresses the culture of the island people, the natural resources available to them for construction, and, of course, reflects the physical environment in which the structure must survive.

"Similarly, in British Columbia there are also fine existing examples of Georgian-style homes. When we looked at Dunlop House in Saanich, we found a home with many of the standard Georgian features: the projecting entrance supported by pillars, symmetrical bays, the low-rise hipped roof with bell cast eaves and generous overhangs and modillions. But we also notice that the architect, Samuel Maclure, borrowed elements from the Arts and Crafts and Tudor Revival styles, which he had seen in the United States. Physically cut off from the rest of Canada, in many ways, because of the vast range of Rocky Mountains, it seems natural that architects in British Columbia would look south to their American neighbours for inspiration and design ideas.

"As I moved through the provinces, I was amazed to see how architecture, the hardscape we create, could mimic the environment and express values and opinions and personal preferences. But also, since Canadians are above all a pragmatic people, the architecture of Canada makes good use of natural resources like rock and wood. If one lives in a heavily forested land, why not make full use of lumber in construction? Since we live in a land where our four seasons are so very different from each other, why not use glass to help us stay connected to nature? As an aside, a good example of the connection between the land and a building is found at the University of Lethbridge, Alberta, where the University Hall is described as a hymn to the horizon, its genius lying in its revelation that the prairies are not flat but undulating.

"Many buildings bear the imprint, or at least the influence, of certain architectural styles. Some are faithful to a single style, almost slavishly so. But this exploration of the Georgian-style homes of Canada informs us that adaptive variations are possible, even expected. It then becomes the responsibility of the student of architectural history to understand the basic characteristics of a specific architectural style in order to observe other add-ons more critically or with more understanding and appreciation.

"Thank you for giving me the opportunity to do this project."

Lily placed her laser pointer on the table and sat down. She felt drained, exhausted. Evelyn and Suzanne were looking at her, smiling, but Philip was looking at his file folder, writing some notes, frowning.

"I'm afraid I went a little over my time limit." Lily glanced at her watch.

"Not at all," Evelyn responded. "I loved the attention to detail and your enthusiasm for this subject. I must say, though, that I feel quite tired, having taken a 35-minute flight across Canada." Evelyn and Suzanne laughed. "I've jotted a few questions, and I know that Suzanne and Philip will have some, too. Suzanne, why don't you start?"

After fielding a question about the impact of Indigenous architects, Lily admitted that she had not encountered a current Indigenous architect who used Georgian Revival design, but she had come across a renowned Albertan Métis, Douglas Cardinal, who had designed St. Albert Place in Alberta so that it seemed a sculptural imitation of the Sturgeon River that flows nearby. That had impressed her and reminded her of the connection between land and buildings.

Evelyn asked questions on the sourcing of local materials, a particular interest of hers. Lily explained that while local architecture expressed a spirit of place, in a new land like Canada where there were many tasks, people had to think outside the box. "As I said before, Canadians are quite pragmatic. If they find themselves in a region where there is yellow clay, they use it to make yellow brick for buildings. In one article," she added, "I read a funny quote: 'Even a Scot, an unwavering fan of stone, will build a house of wood in a region without a quarry!'" All three women laughed.

"I have another question," Suzanne said. "Did you find the vocabulary of this discipline overwhelming? Did you learn any new words that stuck with you?"

"I admit that it will take me a lifetime to learn the vocabulary—all those pediments, modillions, balustrades and cornices. I had to make myself a glossary and I referred to it over and over. It was overwhelming," Lily laughed. "One of my favourite words I learned, one that I promise never to drop at a cocktail party, is 'palimpsest.'" All three women laughed again, but Philip's head snapped up. The mood in the room shifted, and Lily suddenly became very nervous. She realized that Philip had not made a comment, nor had he asked a question or even looked at her.

"So, what does it mean, then, this new word 'palimpsest'?" he asked.

Lily felt herself blush, and she took a deep breath to calm herself. "Palimpsest," she started slowly, "is a term that describes when something is reused or altered but the structure still bears visible traces of its earlier form."

"Ah. Sorta like the historic distillery district here in Toronto?"

Lily nodded. "Or like the blended landscape of French and English buildings in Quebec City."

Philip passed her a folded sheet of paper. "I've made a few notes for you to consider," he said. "Perhaps you would like to read them later, when you have recovered from this ordeal."

When Lily returned to her hotel room, she sat down on the edge of the bed, kicked off her shoes and unfolded Philip's paper. There were no comments or questions at all. Instead, he had written, *May I take you out to dinner tonight at six? Call me if you are in a hotel different from last time.* He had signed his name and underneath was his cell number.

CHAPTER 26

When Philip came to pick her up, he had dressed in fresh clothes and a sports jacket. Both were quiet as they drove to the restaurant. They settled at a table and began to study the menu. Why had he still said nothing? His opinion was so important to her. Overcome with anxiety and feeling depressed, Lily could not figure out what to order.

"You like steak?" Philip asked. When she nodded, he ordered two meals of filet mignon, medium-rare. "That okay, Lily?" She nodded again. "You must be tired."

"Yes, a bit."

Still he said nothing about her presentation. When their meals arrived and he had taken a few bites, he suddenly set down his knife and fork. "Lily, I want to tell you that was one of the most smashing presentations I've ever heard from a student. If there was an undergraduate award for best presentation of the year, you'd have it, ten times over."

"Really?"

"Yes! You didn't realize it? That it was good?"

"Frankly, I didn't know. I only knew that I was terribly interested in the topic and it gave me so much pleasure to do the research and organize my thoughts and reactions."

"That's what I especially loved about it. Your passion and interest in architecture shone through, your research was solid, your conclusions were more than insightful, some of them were downright brilliant. Your knowledge about the world of architectural historical design and your drive astound me. I wish I had more students like you. I sat there watching you make your points and I thought, 'My God, that is one smart, committed and beautiful woman.'"

"Philip!" she exclaimed, overwhelmed by his enthusiasm. It was her turn to set down her fork and knife. "There's something I don't understand. If you thought so highly of my presentation, why did you not say something when the others were asking questions? I was almost sick with worry and I'm sure that Evelyn and Suzanne wondered why you were so silent."

"I'm sorry, Lily. I apologize. I apologize profusely. I am so filled with remorse that if I weren't afraid of getting the knees of my pants dirty, I would kneel down on the floor of this restaurant and beg for your forgiveness." Although Lily laughed, Philip's expression was serious. "I have a confession. I couldn't look at you at the end because I was afraid that I was going to cry and make a fool of myself."

"Cry? You, Philip?"

"You were so beautiful and articulate, so eager to learn, so caring about the same types of things that I love. It moved me in a way that I haven't felt for a long time. I felt like bawling like a baby."

This time she did not protest when he walked her to the elevator in the hotel. They stood together in silence, and when she touched his arm and said, "Would you like to come up to my room?" he smiled.

Later, the thing that she would remember most was how very easy it had been to talk to him.

"You will apply for entry for the fall, won't you, Lily?" When she didn't answer, he said, "Why the sigh?"

"My life has become complicated, as if it no longer belongs to me." She found herself telling him about her precipitous and somewhat disingenuous decision to marry Rupert, more as an escape from her old life than a commitment to a new one. She described her angst about not fitting in with the church women's groups, and he roared with laughter as she described the fiasco of decorating the church for Christmas. She did a fine imitation of Dolly Inkpen and gave a more serious account of Brendan and his problems, confessing that after two weeks he was still hiding out with Dolly and sneaking into the Old Manse at night. When she began to tell him about the disconcerting letter from Aunt Sofiya and her mother's startling revelations, she became angry. "What kind of a mother would do that?" she demanded of him. "Deny her only child the opportunity to go to university when she had the financial means to make it happen? And why did she never tell me that I was adopted and that somewhere out there I have a twin sister. My mother's dead and gone but I'd like to shake her!"

Philip stroked her arm. "Ukrainian moms," he murmured. "Family means everything to them. She must have had her reasons."

"She told me in the letter that she didn't want me to be spoiled, that it doesn't hurt people to struggle for what they want in life."

He laced his fingers through hers and kissed her bare shoulder. "Well, maybe she was right."

"Oh, I doubt it, Philip. I think she was so filled with pity for her own hardships and losses in life that she couldn't move beyond that. It would have been too much for her to see me happy." She hated the bitter tone of her voice.

"Tell me, Lily, do you love your husband?"

"What a crazy question. Do you love your wife?"

"Yes. Yes, I do. But there are many points about which we differ, and lately we seem to be a bit estranged from each other."

"Rupert once told me that he considered love highly overrated in marriage. There are so many other things that bind people together in a relationship—shared interests, good times, laughter."

"Good sex?"

"That too."

"Will you do it, Lily? Enroll in our program in the fall?"

"I really don't know, Philip. I need to go back home and straighten out some things." He pulled her toward him and kissed the top of her head.

"The truth is, I can't bear to think of you as my professor, my teacher," she confessed, as she pulled away.

"Then don't. I can easily arrange for you to have classes with other professors."

"Let me see how things go back in New Hopewell."

They were silent for a long time.

"Lily, do you always put everyone else's needs ahead of your own?"

She couldn't answer. "I'm not sure," she mumbled finally. "It's such a long, ingrained habit. I feel guilty and selfish if I put myself first."

"But Lily! That is not being selfish. Putting yourself first is self-care. You can care for yourself and still be responsive and compassionate to others." They lapsed into silence again. Then Philip propped himself up on one elbow, leaning eagerly toward her. "I've just had the most wonderful, totally fantastic, crazy idea. Wanna hear it?"

At ten o'clock Philip gathered his things and said, "I've got to go. Have a great sleep, Lily. You deserve it."

But she did not have a great sleep. Not only did she relive and relish every minute of their time together, but she stayed awake long into the night imagining, reshaping and redefining the crazy scheme that he had suggested to her. For the first time in her life, she felt not only alive but totally daring. Expressing her views and findings about Georgian-styled Canadian homes had birthed a new confidence within her. But could she actually pull off the daring stunt that Philip had suggested? Could she find that much courage?

CHAPTER 27

Rupert was feeling grumpy and out of sorts. He plugged in the kettle to boil water for his morning tea. When Lily was away, he missed her, not just because of meals and companionship. He longed for her gentle, serene ways. Her comportment calmed him. Elodie, he realized with a start, had not soothed him. She prodded and jibed and always wanted more—a house in a more upscale neighbourhood, a fancier car, new furniture, meals out in the finest restaurants. He had colluded in this, for he had come to desire the finer things in life, too. There were times when his ministerial stipend could not match their lifestyle, but Elodie didn't seem to notice that. It had made him anxious, worried that his insistence on an annual raise might anger his Board. It was demeaning to have to keep asking year after year.

Not only had Lily been in Toronto for three days, but the business of Brendan weighed on his mind as well. It had now been three weeks. They knew where he was—staying with Dolly Inkpen—but when Rupert had attempted to make contact, Dolly had firmly refused to let him in the door. He didn't want to resort to calling the police. How would it look to have a scene on his street? What would people say if they saw a cruiser parked in the driveway of the Old Manse?

• • •

When his cell rang, he was delighted to hear Lily's voice. She seemed in a rush. "Rupert," she said, "a couple of things have come up and I hope you will understand."

"Certainly, my dear. What is it?"

"I've had a call from the lawyer in Emerson. He asked me to sign some papers on the sale of my mother's house. We could do this electronically, of course, but I would like to fly back to Manitoba, spend a little time with Aunt Sofiya and Cathy, have one last look at our old house and visit my mother's grave."

"Oh! When will you do that?"

"I looked at flights and booked one for noon today."

She didn't admit to Rupert that the lawyer *had* called but only to ask for her personal bank account information so he could transfer the $250,000 from her mother's estate. She admitted that she only had a joint account with her husband in New Hopewell, that she had closed her personal account in Emerson before she left.

"I strongly advise, in cases like this, that the money go directly to the personal account of the recipient," the lawyer advised. "Could you open an account in your own name?"

"Of course. I'm currently in Toronto. I'll open one today here in the city."

Rupert seemed surprised and taken aback to hear about Lily's flight to Winnipeg, but he was shocked to hear her second piece of news.

"Rupert, I've located my twin sister. It has been quite a whirlwind the last couple of days. She's here in Toronto to visit some friends but is flying back to Los Angeles at the end of the week. That's where she lives. She knows that I have to go to Winnipeg, but she's wondering if she can come out to New Hopewell to meet you and see where I live. Then, she promised, she could fly back later in the year for a visit with both of us."

Rupert was stunned, finding this piece of news difficult to take in. "She's coming today?"

"Yes, this afternoon. She has her own rental car. Don't worry about that. What is today? Everything has been such a blur. Wednesday? Yes, she leaves on Friday from the Toronto airport. It will be a fleeting visit to New Hopewell. Just make sure the guest room is ready. Oh…one more thing, Rupert…

so it doesn't come as a surprise. We are identical twins. I imagine she might remind you of me, in appearance at least. We're quite different in personality."

"But, Lily, have you forgotten? You were supposed to be the guest speaker tomorrow for the Women's Missionary Society. Your presentation on old churches in the area?"

"Oh! Oh, dear me. I'm sure they will understand that there's a great deal going on in my life at the moment."

"I doubt that," Rupert grumbled, "but perhaps I could pass on to Mrs. Hardy an article that she could read for the program."

After Lily said goodbye, she realized that she had been honest about forgetting the meeting, but then she smiled. Perfect, she thought, perfect timing.

Rupert pulled into the driveway, returning home for the evening, when a car swung into the driveway behind him. It screeched to a stop. Obviously, this was a terrible driver. After he had crawled out of his car, he stood watching as an unkempt woman jumped out of a rental car. It was clearly Lily's twin sister—same slim build, identical colouring, similar thick chestnut hair, but in this case, it was wild and windblown. She must have been driving with the windows down. She reached in and snapped off her tunes. She had been listening to heavy metal.

The woman whipped off her sunglasses. "You have gotta be Rupert. That white thing at your neck is a dead giveaway."

Rupert reached up and touched his clerical collar. "I can see that you're Lily's sister. You look quite a bit alike. You are…?"

"Lulu." She snapped her gum and gave him a friendly slap on the back.

"Lulu?"

"It's a nickname. My parents had a weird sick sense of humour. They labelled me Luella. What kind of parents call a cute, innocent baby Luella? Not even in California. As soon as I could talk, I gave myself a nickname and Lulu stuck. You wanna give me a hand with this bag, Rupe?"

She needed a good stiff drink to relax, she announced, then would he drive her around town so she could see for herself where Lily lived?

Rupert obliged, but within an hour he was exhausted by her irreverent commentary, her interruptions, her gum snapping. She had a way, however, of encouraging him to disclose things. In that short car ride, she found out all the details of the dilemma with Brendan. They were returning to the Old Manse with a pizza box—he had offered to take her out to dinner but she had declined, saying that she preferred pizza—when she announced that after they had eaten, she was going next door to straighten things out with Dolly Inkpen and Brendan.

"Oh, I don't think that's a good idea," Rupert said.

"Nonsense, Rupe. Got any paper towels we can put this pizza on? Any beer in that fridge? Ah…" She inhaled as she opened the box. "My favourite. Kale, anchovies and black olives."

"That was perfect," Lulu declared, rising from the table and crumpling the uneaten crusts into a ball of paper towels. "I'm off to bring Brendan home. You wanna come?"

Rupert shook his head and stared into his mug of tea. He had declined the offer of a slice of pizza—it looked too weird to him. He told her that he had muffins with the women at the church in the afternoon and was not hungry.

"Suit yourself, big boy. Wish me luck."

When Dolly Inkpen removed the chain and eased open her front door, she stood staring at Lulu, her mouth open.

"Missus?"

"Missus? What's this missus crap? My name's Lulu and I am the twin sister of Lily next door."

For once, Dolly Inkpen was at a loss for words. "You do look alike. Sorta," she stuttered, taking in Lulu's jeans that were ripped at the knees, her tight crop top shirt which revealed her belly button, the gold medallion that hung into her cleavage.

"I've come for Brendan. I've come to take him home. You get upstairs and tell that boy to get his sweet ass down here, and fast. If I don't see him in one minute, I'm coming up for him. That is, if I can find my way through this mess without breaking my bloody neck. Why the hell don't you clean up, Dolly Inkpen? Off! Off you go. Tell him that my patience is running thin."

Seconds later, Brendan came running downstairs. "Brendan," Lulu snapped, "this garbage pit is not your home. Your home is over there," she gestured to the west, "where your uncle and Lily have been worried sick. I'm going to give you one minute to cross that driveway and get up to your room. If that doesn't happen, I'm calling the cops."

Brendan looked from one woman to the other, wide-eyed and frightened, then ran down Dolly's crumbling steps, up the driveway of the Old Manse and in the back door.

"I'll be back for his clothes in a half hour," Lulu told Dolly. "Round them up, and if it's all dirty laundry, there is going to be hell to pay."

CHAPTER 28

Rupert escaped from the house early in the morning. He did not want another encounter with Lulu. He would have tea and toast downtown at Hopewell Diner. "She may be Lily's sister," he fumed to himself, "but she is a complete disaster. I shall insist that Lily never invite her back again. She gets everything and everyone in an uproar."

He had not seen Brendan the previous evening, only heard the boy rush in the back door and race up the stairs, taking them two at a time. Soon after, he heard the back door open again and the sound of dragging. Lulu was tugging in two stuffed garbage bags. She plunked them at the bottom of the elegant stairway and screamed up into the hallway. "And don't even think about sleeping in tomorrow, ya little punk. You have a mountain of stinky laundry to do." She turned back toward the living room where Rupert was staring at her over the top of his newspaper. "Well, Rupe, I'm all tuckered out," she yawned. "All this activity and country air. I'm off to bed. See you in the morning."

Because Lily couldn't be there to provide the program, Rupert had given Mrs. Hardy a fine article on mysticism in African culture and how it had informed and transformed the missionary endeavors of south-central

Africa. She had seemed most appreciative but told him she was deeply disappointed that Mrs. Cameron would not be the guest speaker. "You might have supposed that we were a priority," she pointed out.

"Perhaps she will speak to your group in the near future," Rupert murmured before hurrying off.

The meeting was called to order sharply at two p.m. Mrs. Hardy liked to run a tight ship, everyone agreed. They had barely begun the thought for the day and started the Bible reading when they heard a commotion in the little kitchenette off the meeting room.

"Hey! Anyone know where the cream is? I can't stand that powdered creamer stuff. It's worse than imitation sugar."

Startled, the women all stared toward the kitchenette. The room grew very silent. Then Lulu entered the meeting room, wearing the same torn jeans, the crop top shirt and the heavy medallion that she had worn the day before.

"Hi, ladies!" she called out, settling down with her mug of coffee at the head of the table in the spot reserved for the guest speaker. "Name's Lulu and if I bear an uncanny resemblance to Lily Kaltyk, that's 'cause I'm her identical twin sister, but we were separated at birth. Our Mom got into a spot of trouble in her teens…you know the thing I mean," she said, winking. "Had us, then had to give us up for adoption. Bet that sort of thing never happened around here with any of you ladies, huh?" She laughed and paused to take a slurp of coffee. "Oh, do carry on. Don't let me interfere. Lily told me that she couldn't be here, so I offered to come in her place. Carry on, carry on," she said with an impatient wave of her hand.

Mrs. Hardy cleared her throat and prepared to continue reading, but she was now flustered and had lost her place. Flipping open her Bible, she began reading from 1 Chronicles instead of 1 Corinthians.

> *Over the king's treasuries was Azmaveth, son of Adiel. Over the treasuries in the country, in the cities, in the villages and in the towers, was Jonathan son of Uzziah. Over those who did the work of the field tilling the soil was Ezri son of Chelub. Over the vineyards was Shimei the Ramathiete. Over the produce of the vineyards for the wine cellars was Zabdi the Shiphmite. Over the olive and the sycamore trees…*

"Bwaa-ha-ha," Lulu roared. "You ladies got nothing better to do than listen to a chronology of job descriptions from four thousand years ago?"

Mrs. Hardy slammed shut the Bible and said in a loud voice, "Really! This is too much. Marybelle, will you please escort Miss Lulu to the door. She is an unwelcome guest at our meeting."

"You're throwing me out into the street?" Lulu laughed. She glanced around the table at the faces of ten worried, anxious women. "I don't get it," she said. "Why do you let this bossy woman bully you?" No one answered. They looked nervously sideways at each other. "I asked a reasonable question," Lulu continued. "Why do you let yourself be bullied like this?"

Finally, one woman spoke up timidly. "I guess we don't see it as bullying." She looked down at her hands. Was she being disloyal? "We're just used to the way things are, I guess."

"Well," Lulu exclaimed, "may I suggest that you find something more useful to do with your time—look around you. I've only been in your town twenty-four hours. I saw low-income moms hanging out in the park pushing their babies in tattered buggies. I saw a homeless man begging in front of the grocery store. I saw a donation box for the food bank empty except for a few tins of beans while people with steaks and ice cream and boxes of fresh fruit just walked by with their shopping carts. Why don't you lovely ladies look outside and see how you could make a real difference?"

The women around the table sat frozen. Mrs. Hardy was stunned into silence.

"Now, if you'll excuse me, I have business elsewhere." Lulu stood up, walked into the kitchenette, rinsed out her coffee mug and set it upside down on a clean tea towel. Then she left.

CHAPTER 29

"Lily, it's wonderful to have you home." In an uncharacteristic public display of affection, Rupert wrapped his arms around her at the train station. When they were almost home, he said, "This may be a surprise. Brendan is home."

"Really? How did that happen?"

"I have to give your sister credit," he said, his voice twinged with sarcasm. "She has a gift for making things happen."

When Lily took her suitcase upstairs and passed Brendan's room, she could see that he had returned to the Old Manse but nothing had changed. On the bed was a jumble of laundered T-shirts waiting to be folded. His clothes and shoes from the previous days covered the floor and his bed was unmade. From the room came the musky skunk smell of marijuana. Brendan was, of course, missing.

Sighing, she turned to her own bedroom, stripped off her clothes, wrapped herself in a terry cloth robe, walked down the hall and began to run a deep, hot bubble bath. When she had submerged herself in the warm frothy bubbles, she began to make a mental list of all the things she wanted to do the next day. At the top of her list was an appointment with the driving agency. Tomorrow, she vowed, she would make time to practice her driving. Although she had passed her driving test and received a driver's license, she knew she needed more experience. Would she ever feel confident behind the wheel?

• • •

Rupert had, mercifully, stopped asking Lily about her progress on transcribing the red journals. Instead, he inquired as to whether they might resume their romantic Friday nights. He loved that special time with her, he explained, and if Brendan happened to be in the house, they would give him money to hang out at the burger joint downtown.

When they were nibbling hors d'oeuvres in front of the fireplace, Lily turned to him, speaking quickly before she lost her courage. "Rupert, I want to stop doing those Sunday night church-people dinners."

"Stop? Stop our lovely prime rib roast dinners? Whatever for, Lily? They are so wonderful, and everyone seems to really like them."

"They are too much for me."

"Oh." He looked baffled. "But our Friday night romantic evenings are not too much for you?"

"No, I enjoy them."

He put his arm around her. It had been as simple as that. The last of the Yorkshire pudding disasters.

"Ah," Rupert sighed, setting aside his bowl. They had eaten beef ragu with pappardelle, topped with fresh parmesan and basil, and were now content to gaze into the fire in the snug while candles twinkled on the mantel and soft music played in the background. "I don't tell you often enough how much I appreciate you and miss you when you go away."

"Perhaps I should go away more often," she teased. He kissed her lightly on the cheek.

"That sister of yours," he laughed. "It's a very good argument for nurture versus nature. If she hadn't looked so much like you, I would never have believed you were twins. You are gentle, kind, loving, giving, considerate, and your sister is brash, rude, bossy, determined. Did you hear how she managed to get Brendan home? And did you hear that she was like a bull in a china shop at the women's meeting in the church hall?"

Lily laughed half-heartedly. "I can't be responsible for that. She obviously had a very different upbringing from me, much more opportunity to become daring, and she no doubt had experiences that broadened her viewpoint. I just can't imagine what my life would have been like in Emerson if I had behaved like that. My mother would never have allowed it. My Ukrainian community would have been shocked, and my teachers... well..."

"Now that you've found out that you were adopted, have you ever wondered if you really are Ukrainian at all?"

Lily sat in silence, twirling her near empty wine glass. "It has crossed my mind several times since I received that letter from my mother. Tell me, Rupert, have you ever wondered if you really are Christian at all?"

"Lily! I'm shocked. What kind of a question is that?"

"Okay, maybe I didn't ask it correctly. Don't you ever wonder if you had been born Jewish if you would be a rabbi? Or if you were born into a Muslim family, would you be an imam?"

"The way I look at it is like this: everyone has to believe in something in life. Even non-religious people believe in something that glues their life together."

"My point was not to question your faith. I'm just trying to figure out if it matters at all if I'm Ukrainian-Canadian. After all, I have to be something. If I can be physically adopted into a family, why not be culturally adopted into a group with great traditions and make it my own?"

"Enough of this deep philosophy on our romantic night. Tell me, do you have anything on tomorrow? Any special plans?"

"Just a little shopping. There are a few things I need to pick up."

"Mmm...that reminds me, have you heard yet from the lawyer about the money from your mother's estate?"

"It's a little early for things to be settled."

"Unfortunately for you, now that you've found your sister, you'll have to share half your inheritance with her."

"That was my mother's wish."

"Pity, really, don't you think? After all, what did your sister do to deserve it? Your mother didn't even know her. Who knows? She may have been adopted into a wealthy family and $250,000 is nothing to her."

Lily looked off into the corner, worried that she was blushing, hoping that if Rupert noticed, he would think that she was flushed from the fire and wine. She still sensed it was too early to tell Rupert that her portion of $250,000 was already earning interest in her private bank account in Toronto. Somehow, she intuited that she needed to be careful.

He squeezed her hand. "Think of what we can do now, Lily. There was a poster in the window of the travel agency on Main Street advertising a two-week all-inclusive cruise to the Baltics. It's only $38,000. Or we could upgrade our car and drive to Prince Edward Island, spend a month in a lovely little cottage by the ocean. Or fly to the Bahamas or Cuba. Go sailing in the British Virgin Islands? Have you ever wanted to experience the Caribbean, Lily?"

Lily felt suddenly very tired, discouraged and frightened. How could she explain to Rupert that this precious and unexpected gift, in her understanding, was hers and hers alone? How could she tell him of her new burning desire to enter into architectural studies and to live by herself in a studio condo in Toronto?

CHAPTER 30

They had settled in the dining room for Saturday night dinner. "Wanna hear a good one?" Brendan crammed a forkful of shepherd's pie into his mouth. "Back in the 50s, there were these four guys in Dartmouth, Nova Scotia. They got this idea to build a raft from telephone poles. Then they built a little plywood cabin on it for shelter and headed out to sea. They took two kittens because one of them had read that cats can predict storms, see? They sailed across the Atlantic Ocean and landed in Falmouth, England, eighty-eight days later. Guess who invited them to dinner? The Queen. Then a dude called the Duke of Bedford met up with them. He wanted to adopt the kittens."

"Really, Brendan, where do you get these preposterous stories?" Rupert demanded.

"I don't see why they can't be true," Brendan muttered, suddenly sullen.

Lily asked Brendan if he was ready for dessert. "I made a Kyiv cake. It was one of my mother's specialties."

Brendan's mood shifted as he shovelled Kyiv cake into his mouth. "I heard another good one. Dunno where this was, some place in Nova Scotia. Some miners were working in a pit—the deepest pit in North America—when there was an earthquake and the mine collapsed. One hundred and seventy-four miners were trapped underground. There was a mongo rescue effort and they saved one hundred of the men. On day ten, one of the last seven survivors was a dude called Maurice Ruddick. He was an African-Canadian who everybody called 'The Singing Miner' 'cause he sang and composed songs. He had a broken leg, but he kept singing underground as they were waiting to be rescued, to keep up spirits, like." Brendan held out his plate for another slice of cake. "When the Governor of Georgia heard this story, he offered the last seven rescued miners a free vacation with his family on some posh tourist island off Georgia, but when the Governor found out that Ruddick was Black, he didn't want to invite him. So, the other miners refused the vacation because they didn't think that was fair, but Ruddick insisted they go. He didn't want them to miss out on this rad vacation. Cool story, huh?"

"Very cool story, Brendan," Lily murmured, cutting a slice of Kyiv cake for Rupert. There was only one possible explanation for where the boy was getting these fantastic and weird stories. He was back to visiting with Dolly Inkpen. Lily had been puzzling over who was supplying the teenager with marijuana. Could it be Dolly?

When Rupert had gone out, Lily retreated to her office, hoping to get started on her second architectural assignment. Evelyn and Suzanne, then later Philip, had urged her to choose her own topic again, explaining that they trusted her judgement and they believed that when students pick their own area of research, they are more enthusiastic and thorough in their investigation.

Several options rushed into her mind. Which should she choose? Perhaps she could profile four influential Canadian architects—one from each century from the 18th to the 21st. It would be fascinating to observe how their concepts and practices shifted through the years. Or should she concentrate on some of the issues facing modern architects? With rising costs, how do they handle budget restrictions? How do they incorporate sustainability and green structure into their plans? How do they keep projects on track and manage diverse teams? Having just read a biography of Canada's influential west coast artist Emily Carr, Lily wondered if it might be fascinating to juxtapose the life story of a visual artist with the biography of a contemporary who was an architect. Would she find parallels or similarities in these two worlds? Was there interplay between these two disciplines?

Lily rose from her desk, stretched and began to pace, hoping for some clarity in her decision. As she walked into the hall, she saw that there was a light on in Brendan's bedroom and that his door was ajar. She paused, her hand on the doorframe, a wave of resentment washing over her. She and Rupert had discussed the issue of getting Brendan to go for counselling. Rupert had agreed to discuss this with Brendan, but that had been a week ago and nothing had happened. This boy is not my responsibility, she fumed, but after a moment she began to realize that Brendan was, in Margaret's words, just a boy trying to figure out how to be a man. I must have courage, she scolded herself. After all, how difficult is it to have a simple straightforward conversation with a teenager?

She knocked lightly on his door. "Brendan? May I come in?"

He had been lying on his bed, looking at his phone, which he turned upside down. "Yeah."

Lily settled herself on the edge of the rocking chair, then took a deep breath and slid back into the support of the cushion, reminding herself to relax. "I've been wondering how things have been going for you lately."

"Okay."

"You're not bored or unhappy?"

"Sometimes."

"Your Uncle Rupert and I...well, we wonder sometimes if you should have more things to do." Brendan shrugged. Lily resisted her instinct to ask him to sit up while she talked with him. She looked off across the room. It helped to imagine him as a small boy wearing a hockey jersey or a baseball cap, short pants, scratches on his legs, his hair buzzed off for the summer.

"When you got into trouble at school..."

"Not that again," he groaned, shifting on the bed.

Lily waited. How should she proceed? "Principal Cruikshank and the vice principal both recommended a counsellor who might—"

"No."

"No? We could try. Your Uncle Rupert and I would go with you..."

"No!"

Lily felt a wave of anger surge through her belly, up into her chest. The boy was incorrigible and exasperating. An old adage surfaced in her mind: you can lead a horse to water but you can't make it drink. How could anything be different if he didn't want to change? She sighed and began again. "I know that you were staying with Dolly Inkpen and that you still go back to visit her."

"Yeah, so?"

"So, I'm sort of wondering if Dolly is supplying you with marijuana?"

"Dolly," he snorted. "That's a good one. She doesn't even smoke or drink."

"Then where are you getting marijuana?" When Brendan didn't answer, she continued. "I'm not totally dumb, Brendan. I can smell it on your clothes and in this room. You're underage. So, I'm asking again, who is your supplier?"

Brendan rolled over on his bed, his back partially to her. "Are you done yet?"

Lily sighed. She would just leave, walk out of this room and not care, go back to pondering her architecture project. But something made her ask, "What is it that you like about Dolly Inkpen? In my opinion, she's a bit nutsy, and her house is a pigsty."

"She's cool," Brendan erupted, "a lot more cool than you or stupid Uncle Rupert or my loser mom."

"Your Uncle Rupert—"

"And," Brendan said, swinging his legs over the side of the bed and sitting up to glare at her, "she's the only person in my life who likes me just the way I am. She's always happy to see me and talk to me. She doesn't give me twenty bucks to buy a burger and tell me to get lost."

Later, when she narrated an edited version of this interaction to Rupert, Lily confessed that the conversation had been difficult for her, that she was not sure she had handled it well. "In a way, though, it helped me change my attitude a bit. Brendan is rude and inconsiderate, flirting with some dangerous life choices. But how would it feel if everyone in *my* life—

except some loony old woman next door—thought the worst of me? We may not like how Brendan is right now, but what he needs is what every human being needs. He needs to be loved and accepted."

Lily realized that, for the first time, she had not added in her own mind, "He needs to be loved and accepted by someone else, but not me."

CHAPTER 31

After Rupert had finished Sunday worship, he returned home, tired and cold. "I think I'm coming down with something. I don't feel well at all."

"Oh dear," Lily said, taking his coat, then gently pushing him toward the stairway. "Pull on your pajamas and crawl into bed. I'll bring you some hot lemon and a couple of painkillers. You need to sleep."

The next morning, Lily crept down into the kitchen and prepared a tray with a pot of weak tea and a plate of crackers. She carried them back up to the bedroom and saw that Rupert had been up but then crawled under the covers again. "The best place for me for a day or two is right here. Lily, could you do me a favour? Go over to the church and pick up the laptop from my office? I might as well use my time to think through my message for next week."

Monday mornings were slow in the church office. Sometimes Rupert took the day off to rest and relax. The church secretary, without the pressure that built as the week moved toward Sunday, often came in late, having taken time to stop at the café to pick up a coffee and donut for herself and the church treasurer, a jovial, retired man who came in to tally the offerings from the day before. It didn't surprise Lily to arrive at nine thirty and find the office empty.

She used Rupert's key to let herself in, then shut the door and proceeded into his inner office, sinking down into his tall leather office chair. What would it be like, she wondered, to sit in this chair every morning, making notes for a sermon or chatting with parishioners who would settle into the green suede chairs on the other side of the desk? She imagined him easing the door shut for privacy before listening to the grief of a depressed widow. What types of conversation did he have with his church organist as they planned for worship? Were they different from the ones he'd had with her in Emerson? What would it be like to overhear all the phone conversations—many of them mundane—of the church secretary? To hear the side doorbell ring and listen to the secretary, who was the first line of defense, explain to a homeless person that the church's charitable allotment for the month had already been distributed, knowing that he would be back in a few days to ask again?

Sitting quietly in her husband's big chair, she wondered why she had never taken time before to think of what his daily routine was like. It's the human condition, she pondered. We are all so self-focused that it is hard for us to step into another's shoes, to feel both the joys and frustrations that come with every vocation. Or did Rupert think of this as a job? And why was some work "jobs" while others were "vocations"? Was some work more worthy than others? Had it not been the great reformer Martin Luther who said that each person—not just clergy—has a vocation? Our vocation, she seemed to remember, is to do good work.

Voices in the outer office startled her from her reverie. She recognized them immediately as the secretary and church treasurer. After a few pleasantries, she heard the treasurer unlock the small safe where the offerings from the previous day had been stored. Now that most people gave their offerings by e-transfers, there was less cash to count. Nevertheless, it all had to be tallied and entered into the church's financial system, and that was his job.

"Did we have a super over-the-top Sunday yesterday?" the secretary teased.

"The offerings have been good since Rupert came. People seem to like him. It's a crazy thing, don't you think, that people give more if they like the minister?"

"People do vote with their feet and their money," the secretary murmured as she shuffled through some papers.

"Still…whatever happened to the good old concept that we give offering because it reminds us to put our love for God ahead of our love for money?"

The secretary laughed. "My father used to throw in a twenty to 'pay the preacher.' That's what he called it."

"Mmm…" Lily heard the treasurer rip open the manila envelope containing the offerings from the day before.

"I noticed that you've changed your procedure since Rupert came," the secretary said. "You used to gather up the cheques and loose bills and lock them up, then count the money on Monday morning here in the office. But now you and an elder count the offering right after the service before locking it up, and then you and I count it again on Monday morning before you take it for deposit."

"It's a bit of a safeguard. Always good to have a witness and do a double check."

"What do you mean?"

"I'll let you in on a little secret, if you promise not to mention it to anyone."

Lily, overhearing this conversation, held her hand tightly against her mouth, terrified that they would come into Rupert's office and know that she had overheard their conversation.

The treasurer's voice dropped. "I have a friend in Vancouver, and when he heard that Rupert had been called here as our minister, he phoned and gave me a bit of advice."

"Advice? What about?"

"They had been really happy with his ministry, but as the years went by, they began to notice that the loose offering on the collection plate became less and less until it had almost disappeared."

"Perhaps people were using their offering envelopes more? Or perhaps there were fewer visitors?"

"No. That's the thing. The church treasurer began to follow the same practice I now have. He counted the offering after the service, locked it in the cupboard, then recounted it on Monday morning. At first there was just twenty or forty dollars missing, then later it was hundreds. Someone with sticky fingers was helping him or herself to the loose bills."

"Oh dear. That is serious. What happened?"

"The treasurer reported it to Rupert and asked if they should call the police. Rupert thought that would make the church look bad, so he urged against it, but shortly after that, Rupert moved to Emerson, Manitoba. His wife was ill and he wanted a smaller parish so he could care for her, he said."

The secretary gasped. "You don't believe that it was Rupert, do you?"

"Oh, I wouldn't think that a minister would do that, but I suppose we'll never know. Isn't there something in the Bible, though, about not yielding to temptation?"

"Come on. This coffee will get cold. I got us each an apple fritter. Let's take them into the library where there's more room and I can watch you count the offering. Gotta keep an eye on you," she joked.

Lily exhaled and stood up quietly, clutching Rupert's laptop to her chest, then crept into the hall and slipped through the side door to the parking lot.

CHAPTER 32

As the weeks crept toward summer, Lily found herself longing to dig up some soil, plant something around the patio at the front of the house. Previous residents had made a half-hearted attempt to plant beds at the ends of the patio, but these plots were now overgrown with dandelions, crabgrass and other wild growth. Perhaps Rupert would help her dig out the weeds and ready the plot for planting, or perhaps Brendan might help. Then she realized that this was a silly idea. Brendan had never shown any interest in lawn care or plants, and besides, this was not the type of weed that interested him. She had no idea what to plant. One bed was partially shaded by a cedar tree. Would anything grow there? The other bed by the door was in full sun. Should she visit the local garden centre and ask for advice? She hesitated, realizing that in the middle of May, the staff would be too busy at the cash register, ringing through plants for people who knew what they were doing. As she stood leaning on her hoe, she saw movement from the corner of her eye. Dolly Inkpen.

"What's goin' on, then?"

"Good morning, Dolly. I'm thinking of planting something in these flower beds for the summer."

"Eh yeah," she said with an inward breath. "This 'ere white cedar, we had those in N'foundland. Lovely soft needles. In the old days, da natives used to make tea from the needles so's they wouldn't get scurvy. Maybe still do. Don't know. This here tree is happy here, away from the front door and by the downspout of that there roof. These here cedars love the rain, so they do."

"Mmm...you know much about plants, Dolly?"

"Only the ones that I grew in Newfoundland and Nova Scotia. Them's the only gardens I ever had. I'd be plantin' some blue-bead lilies and arctic lupines here under this tree. That's what I grew in Nova Scotia. And over there by the door..." Dolly paused, hesitating so long that Lily thought she had lost her train of thought. Her words seemed frozen in mid-sentence. "Over there by the door, you'd have to be careful, but you could try a N'foundland garden—some harebells, blue flag iris, sea thrift, maybe some sweet peas to grow up a trellis."

Lily nodded without any understanding of whether this was good advice, but there was something intriguing about creating a flower bed of plants from two different provinces. Maybe if she became good at gardening, she could do more beds. What kind of flowers were native to Alberta? And what about Manitoba? Or Prince Edward Island?

Both women glanced up when they saw Brendan coming down the driveway. "What's goin' on, b'y?" The teen shrugged, but he stopped instead of walking past. "Ya find decent work yet, luv?" Dolly inquired. When Brendan shook his head, she said, "Now, me friend, ya don't want to be going on the pogey, specially when you don't even know your fader's name. Ya gots to be your own fader to yourself. Pull up your socks, like." Lily was surprised, even shocked at Dolly's words, sure that Brendan would be offended, but Dolly's voice had been soft and gentle, and when Lily glanced at Brendan, he seemed to nod a little, still not moving away.

"I wouldn't be digging there, though," she said to Lily, pointing to the bed by the front door. "Just pull out them weeds and plants a gentle crop atop."

"Why?" Lily demanded.

"Well, missus, I never askt fur it, but I have the gift of the second sight. That's when you see things in the spirit world where the people are dead. But I also have the gift of forerunning. That's when ya see things in the spirit world about the living. Don't know which is better. I gots em both."

"Oh Dolly, really!" Lily protested, but she could see that Brendan was listening intently. "I don't see why we couldn't dig there. Do you see a problem, Brendan?" she asked, hoping to gain an ally in the conversation.

"Ya see, missus, that's where the baby boy is buried," Dolly persisted. "I seen it myself, with the second sight. Down about three feet. Charlotte's baby. Ya don't want to disturb it."

"That's so cool," Brendan erupted.

"G'way wit ya," Dolly said. "Taint cool at all. We have to be respectful of the dead. When I was on down at Antigonish Harbour, I heared about a man called William who was at the harbour. I heared this story told me by William's niece, who had it from himself just before he died. He sees his fader coming up from the shore half carrying a sick man. He knew this was nothing natural, 'cause he didn't know the man. A year later, William himself took poorly. One day he went to the shore, and was so long away that his fader got anxious and went lookin' for him. He found him lying on the sand: he had a paralytic stroke. The old man drug him home very hard like. William knew then that he himself was the sick man he had seen a year before and that he was going to die. That's why ya have to be careful, dealing with the spirits."

"Cool!" Brendan exclaimed again.

"Oh, it's a terrible thing, having the second sight or the forerunning. I don't know which is more troublin' to the mind...but to have both..." Dolly shook her head, her mouth downturned.

Mid-morning, Lily took a break and settled into a lawn chair at the back of the Old Manse, a glass of lemonade in one hand and the *New Hopewell Gazette* in the other. As she flipped to the second page, she inhaled sharply. Staring her in the face was an article entitled "Places Every Architect Must Visit in Kingston, Ontario." Lily scanned the list: Fort Henry National Historic Site, Cathedral of Saint Mary, Murney Tower, Frontenac County Courthouse, Kingston City Hall, Bellevue House, Confederation Park, Kingston Customs House, Kingston Penitentiary, St. George's Anglican Cathedral, St. Andrew's Presbyterian Church.

Her pulse quickened. Kingston was only an hour's drive away, but she was too frightened to drive there herself. Would Rupert agree to take her?

Perhaps he would be interested to see the historic Presbyterian church? As soon as this idea came to her mind, she realized that he would have no interested in dragging around with her for several days, exploring the old buildings of long-ago Kingston. What she needed, she now saw clearly, was her own car. It had been a struggle for her to learn to drive, but she had been able to pass her driver's license test. Yes, she decided, she needed a car of her own.

When Lily heard the side door bang, she hurried to the kitchen. "Brendan? You have a minute?" He grunted. "There's something on my mind and I could use your help." This time he groaned. "I want to buy a car," she blurted out. "I was wondering if you would come with me and help me choose."

"A car? What do I know about cars? We never had one. Didn't need one in Montreal."

"I understand. It's just that I would feel more confident if someone came with me, helped me pick."

"Why don't you take Uncle Rupert? He has a thing about cars."

"Well, I think that your Uncle Rupert and I have different ideas about cars. He loves a beautiful, posh, high-end vehicle, but I want one that's been around the block a few times. Pardon the pun."

"Naw. I don't know nothing about cars."

"You don't have to. Please come with me. It would give me courage." Brendan turned to walk away, heading toward the staircase. "Would you agree to come with me if I offer to let you learn to drive it? I could pay for your driver's education course."

The salesman was confused. An attractive, tailored forty-year-old woman about to buy her first car seemed to be turning for advice to a punky-looking kid in a black hoodie, a boy who sported spiked earrings and had a wolf tattoo running up his neck. "I don't get it," he said. "Most people want a low-mileage car in good condition, but you're asking me for a low-mileage car with some bangs and dents?"

"Yes. I'm a new driver, you see. And Brendan, here, is going to learn to drive, so we figured we might as well start with a few dings. Then it won't be such a shock if we add a few more." Lily laughed, but the used car salesman did not look amused.

"Do you have a make and model in mind?"

"Dudes at my last school told me that Honda Civics are cool cars," Brendan said. The salesman glanced over at the boy and saw that the woman was nodding.

"Only have one on the lot. A Civic EX, about 52,000 kilometres, engine is 1.5 L Turbo 14, red. We were going to paint. It's got a good scratch on the hood and a dent in the bumper."

"Red is good, don't you think, Brendan? Red is good for courage."

After Lily had taken the car for a test drive, the salesman in the front seat and Brendan in the back, the nervous salesman got his second surprise.

"You want to pay cash for the car? Nobody pays cash for cars anymore. We have a finance department..."

"No. I want to pay cash. Do you want a cashier's cheque from my bank or a wire transfer from my bank to your dealership?"

All that remained now was to think of a plausible way to explain this purchase to Rupert.

CHAPTER 33

Lily was eager to work on her second architecture project. It would be hours of pure pleasure. Even more exciting to her was the prospect of being with Philip again. Buying the car had distracted her, but it also opened new possibilities. She could now travel and explore on her own. Should she do her project on significant buildings in Kingston? She had discovered that Kingston, the "Limestone City," was well known for its preservation of historic buildings that expressed aspects of Canada's evolution as a nation. The location of the early settlement where the mighty St. Lawrence and the smaller Cataraqui rivers flowed into Lake Ontario made this a strategic trading location for Indigenous peoples for thousands of years, but modern Kingston claimed to be a city where history and innovation thrive happily side by side. Philip would love that. In the end, she decided that there was not enough time to explore Kingston and prepare her presentation. She would save that for her third and final presentation in the architectural pilot project.

A letter from her mother's lawyer in Emerson arrived in the morning mail, telling her that he was holding in trust the second allotment of $250,000. In another year, he would be in touch with her to find out if she had located her twin sister. Lily felt a cold sweat break out on her body. She returned to her office and sat down to continue her research, but the letter had frightened her and she could no longer concentrate. She began to pace in the hall, glancing to the south, hoping that Dolly Inkpen wasn't watching. Brendan had again disappeared and she assumed that he had escaped back to the house next door. Perhaps our quiet, sedate life is just too stifling for him, she surmised. She paused in front of his room to pull shut the door—she found the clutter and smell offensive—but then she reconsidered. She would do Brendan's laundry. It would distract her and perhaps things might play out as they had before. He would come home for clean clothes and then, eventually, he himself would return.

The letter from the lawyer had turned her thoughts to Emerson. Maybe she should plant some sunflowers in the patio flower bed. It would be a way to pay respect to her mother. And, she shuddered, if there really was a little cement coffin there, it would honour the life of an infant, snuffed out too soon. Perhaps Charlotte would find this comforting. Lily paused in the middle of folding T-shirts. There is no such thing as a Charlotte ghost. Get a grip, she scolded herself. You're certainly smart enough to not let that silly Dolly Inkpen get under your skin.

Lily set the clean, folded jeans and T-shirts in Brendan's drawers and turned to make his bed. As she was smoothing the sheets, she noticed what she thought to be a magazine tucked under his pillow. Cautiously, she reached for it, shocked to see that it was not a magazine at all but an art design book. Slowly, she opened the first page, then the second, flipping through to the very end. Each page was full of meticulous ink designs. Some were dragons. There were stylized turtles, a raven, a dreamcatcher, an angry sun, and several intriguing versions of clocks surrounded by roses. On the inside cover Brendan had written "My Guide to Drawing Tattoo Designs." Lily sat down on the edge of the bed, staring at the book. She could not make sense of this at all. After a few minutes, she rose, tucked the book back under the pillow and unmade the bed. She didn't want Brendan to think that she had been snooping in his room.

When dinner was over—one of Rupert's favourites, bangers and mash—Lily rose to clear the table.

"Lily, wait a minute, please," he said, putting his hand on her arm. She sank back into her chair and waited. "It's been peaceful, don't you think? Just the two of us on our own again. And it's not as if we need to worry about Brendan, because we now know where he escapes to."

Lily nodded. "I have been wondering, though, if we ought to offer Dolly some money, for his food and lodging."

"Pfff...that would only confirm in both their minds that this arrangement is okay, maybe even permanent, and you know that we can't let that happen."

"I suppose not," Lily conceded. She looked around the table, wondering how long it would take her to clean up so she could return to her project.

"Maybe we should get in touch with that sister of yours. She has a talent for whacking things back into place."

"I don't think that's possible," Lily murmured, looking down. "She seems to have vanished into thin air."

"Vanished? You didn't mention that to me."

"I'm sorry. I didn't want to make it your worry. I'm still working on it."

There was a pause in their conversation. "Lily, there's something else I've been wondering."

"Yes?"

"Well...I guess I've been wondering if you are happy?"

"Happy? Rupert, don't be silly." She looked down into her lap where her hands were clasped tightly together.

"You missed another meeting of the women's group this afternoon. Mrs. Hardy mentioned it to me."

"Oh, really, Rupert," Lily declared, colour rising in her cheeks, "who does that woman think she is? Does she have to monitor every single thing I do?"

Rupert sighed. "Has it ever occurred to you, my dear, that the women of this church—particularly Mrs. Hardy—may actually like and admire you, so they miss you when you don't show up?"

"No. I'm afraid that has never occurred to me. Nor do I believe it." She stood up and banged the dirty dishes on top of each other.

"I'll do that," Rupert said, sighing again.

• • •

On the following day, when Rupert brought home travel brochures from the agency on Main Street, Lily's head was in another space. She had wakened in the night thinking again of her former guidance counsellor, Mr. Stone, and how he had abruptly and swiftly steered her away from studying architecture. "It's too hard for women," he'd said. Maybe he was right, she sighed. Maybe it really was a difficult career path for a woman. That was over twenty years ago. Were things any different now? She didn't know. She remembered that in 2015 when Canada's new Prime Minister, Justin Trudeau, was challenged about his decision to create more gender parity in cabinet and was asked why he had done that, he replied, "Because it's 2015." Many things had changed for women, so perhaps women in architecture had changed, too, since her high school days. She turned eagerly to her computer and began to search. She now knew what her second presentation would be called: *The Problems and Promise of Being a Female Architect Today.*

She began by searching out the number of female professionals in other careers, professions that were demanding, had long training and an internship. How many doctors in Canada were female? When she found out that 40.2 percent were women, she asked the same question about lawyers and found the answer to be 37 percent. But to her surprise and confusion, only 29 percent of Canadian architects were women. Why is this? she demanded of herself. Are there unfair hiring practices? Is there unequal pay for males and females? Is there a climate of protective paternalism, such as Mr. Stone had exhibited? Is there a macho culture and sexism? Is there a lack of female role models? Is there less flexibility in the field for women who want to have children? But if that were the case, why had she read that even female architects without children showed less job satisfaction than their male counterparts? In a journal called *Architectural Review*, Lily read that only 28 percent of women reported overall job satisfaction compared with 41 percent of men. And another curious thing—while the provincial percentages across Canada were consistent, why did the province of Quebec report that almost 39 percent of their architects were female? What was different in Quebec?

It was a confusing but fascinating study, and when she read the obituary for Zaha Hadid, the world-renowned Iraqi-British architect, she began to appreciate the insidious complexity of the problem. Despite winning many design competitions early in her career, most projects did not result in a completed structure. No developer seemed willing to take a risk on building them. She had been blamed for these aborted projects, unfairly attacked for her personality, and had her competence questioned. How belittling it seemed to hear her described as "the queen of the curves."

When Rupert spread out the brochures after dinner, Lily looked up in surprise. The Canary Islands? Moonlight on the Mediterranean? The romantic Danube? "What's this about, Rupert?"

"Well, now that we have a little extra money from your inheritance, I thought perhaps we could treat ourselves to a cruise this summer."

"Oh, I really don't think that would be possible."

"Why not? There will still be lots of money left over."

Lily turned her back, terrified that she would lose control. She felt like screaming. She wanted to yell, "This is my money and I will make the decisions about how it will be used!" It was only after she had finished the dishes, gone for a walk and returned home that she began to think that she had been unfair.

A slow and trembling realization came to her: Rupert was thinking of retirement, leisure and travel at the end of a long career while she was considering a new life and new beginning for herself. In fairness to Rupert, perhaps he deserved a slower pace at this stage of his life. She also realized that he had accepted her unconditionally, providing her with a lifestyle and house that was beyond her wildest dreams. He was a good, kind and patient man, even though his traditional attitudes had been an irritant. Why could she not share her money with him? And why was she hiding from him the fact that she was secretly taking an introduction to architecture course? That she was disingenuous about her quest to locate her twin sister? That she was enormously attracted to another man? That she had received her inheritance long ago and set up a secret bank account in Toronto where her husband couldn't touch it? When she crawled into bed, she was too horrified to sleep, flooded with self-loathing. She was cold and sweaty, her breath ragged and shallow. What had she become?

The bedroom window was open and the first pale fingers of morning sun had set off a chorus of robin calls. Lily stirred, realizing that she had finally fallen into a fitful sleep but now was wakened by the slow and steady rhythm of bird syllables, rising and falling. Cheerily, cheer up, cheer up. Then a pause until the robin began again. She closed her eyes and pulled the sheet over her head. From inside this safe cocoon, she heard Philip's voice, "Lily, do you always put everyone else's needs ahead of your own?"

She pushed back the blanket and hurried down the hall to the bathroom. She knew what she had to do. Brendan had refused to go to a counsellor. She knew they couldn't force him to go against his will. "It's me," she said aloud to herself, gripping the cold edge of the bathroom sink and staring into the mirror at her pale face and tousled hair. I need to get help, she thought. I need help to make some changes for myself.

CHAPTER 34

Lily had no idea how to choose a counsellor. She didn't even know if she should ask for a counsellor or a therapist. Was there a difference? Remembering that Margaret had given her a brochure when they talked of helping Brendan, she looked up the counselling agency and saw that it offered many types of help. She was relieved to find that the centre was in a town east of New Hopewell. It terrified her to think that someone from the church or town might recognize her in the waiting room.

She scanned the descriptions of various types of help offered—marriage and family conflicts, stress, trauma, anxiety, eating disorders—and she also read the bios of the therapists. One reminded her of her old school friend, Cathy, with a similar friendly smile and open gaze, and when she read, "I am here to support your journey to heal and empower yourself," Lily decided to ask for her. No one can fix me, she thought. It's something I have to do for myself, but I don't know how to do it.

Driving on the highway in her red car flooded her with anxiety. Would she ever feel comfortable steering, staying in the middle of the traffic lane and making left turns? By the time she reached the *New Beginnings Counselling Centre*, she was exhausted, perspiring and pale. Why had she thought this was a good idea? She turned off the car and was about to start it again, ready to flee back home, when she saw an ordinary looking young woman swing out of her car and stride toward the front door. If she can do this, so can I, Lily thought. Taking a deep breath, she eased out of the driver's seat.

Her therapist, Ruth, was warm and welcoming. She listened attentively as Lily poured out her troubles, interjecting now and then with questions for clarification. When she said that their hour was nearly over, Lily was surprised.

"You know, Lily, sometimes it takes a few months for people to sort things out and make the decisions that are needed, but sometimes the journey is much faster and shorter. One of the things I like to ask at the end of each session is this: was there something in our time today that was helpful to you and sticks in your mind?"

Lily looked down at her hands knotted tightly together, not knowing how to answer.

"Is there, perhaps, one thing that you would like to work on this week?" Ruth persisted.

Lily raised her head. "I liked when you said that sometimes we find positive interests that become an act of self-rescue. I feel that way about my study of architecture. I lose myself in that world and I love it. It's a world in which I feel confident. This week, I want to give myself permission to just enjoy it. It soothes and comforts me, but it is also stimulating." She paused, frowning. "There is something else that I need to do this week. I need to find a way to explain to Rupert the depth of my love for historic buildings. I have to find some way to help him hear that this is not just a hobby. I feel passionate about this. It is vitally important to me."

Rupert returned for lunch at noon as usual, thinking it strange that Lily's car was gone. She hadn't mentioned an appointment. Perhaps she had gone shopping and got detained. He sat down with the morning paper and waited. When she hadn't returned in a half hour, he began to feel irritated. He wandered into the kitchen and started to pull out drawers in a random fashion. He realized that he left so many of the household duties to Lily that he had no idea where the bread was stored or where to find the butter dish. Opening the refrigerator, he spotted a drawer labelled "cheese," pulled it open, set the block of cheddar on the counter and cut himself a thick slab. Something was wrong. He could sense it. If he were honest with himself, he had realized for some time that something was not right between himself and Lily, but he hadn't been able to face it. He heard the back door open.

"Oh, sorry, Rupert," Lily said, rushing in. "I'm afraid I'm late. Let me make you some lunch." She dropped her purse and jacket on a chair and hurried to a box labelled "bread."

Rupert saw no shopping bags full of celery and ground beef, and she said nothing about where she had been. She busied herself pulling out cold cuts and tomatoes from a container in the fridge and buttering some bread. "There. I'm just going to wash up and we'll have a cup of tea together." She set the sandwich on the little table in the kitchen alcove and hurried upstairs. Rupert sighed, then took his plate into the snug, settling into his favourite chair.

When Lily came down, he could hear her putting on the kettle, then pouring the boiling water into the pot. He heard her open the fridge door to retrieve the milk, put a splash into the bottom of the mugs, then pour the tea. When she entered the snug with their steaming cups, he was holding the travel brochures in his hand but set them down and thanked her. They sat in silence for a few minutes.

"I had hoped that you might be excited about one of these trips," he said finally, glancing at her. She was looking straight ahead into the empty fireplace.

"There's something I need to tell you," she said. "I should have told you this long ago."

"Yes?"

She began to explain her long-ago desire to study architecture and her recent bitterness knowing that her mother had enough money to allow her to pursue a university dream but hadn't offered that. She told Rupert that before she knew him, she had travelled into Winnipeg to explore the study of architecture, and then she told him about her acceptance this past year into the experimental pre-architecture program at the University of Toronto.

"When I went into Toronto for three days last month, I was busy with architecture things—exploring and learning. And I have to go back to

Toronto for another three days next week. My final presentation is in July." She couldn't find the courage to tell him what she wanted to do in the fall—enroll full time and buy a condo in Toronto.

"Well, goodness, Lily. I knew most of that. I've known for some time that you are very knowledgeable and interested in architecture. I just didn't know about this experimental program. I don't see any reason for you to have kept that a secret from me. After all, everyone deserves a hobby."

"Don't you see, Rupert?" Lily cried out. "This is not a hobby. It's a career path."

Rupert laughed. "Really, Lily? At your age? At our stage of life? When we could be going on a beautiful cruise and enjoying some of the fruits of our labour?"

Lily rose and walked blindly into the kitchen, set her mug into the sink, then turned into the back hall and opened the door to the porch. She needed time to regain her composure, but there in front of her stood Dolly Inkpen, ready to knock on the door.

"Dolly! I can't talk right now. I'm in a rush."

"It's terrible important, missus. It's about the young lad, Brendan. I tot you should know. He was out all night, doing whatever. He's a good lad, that un, but sometimes he doesn't know his arse from a tea kettle. He kept lookin' out the window all morning, and when he saw you pull in at twelve tirty, he grabbed his ole duffle bag, jumped in your car and drove off. Ya may regret givin' him them drivin' lessons, missus."

Lily gasped. Rushing out into the driveway, she saw that her car was gone. "Where do you think he went, Dolly? And why did he take his duffle bag?"

"No idea, missus." Dolly shook her head, her mouth turned down in a mournful expression. "And der's anuder ting. That there Charlotte is restless. She's roaming the halls like crazy. Something has her wound up. Sometin's not right."

CHAPTER 35

Lily was angry. She stomped back into the house. "Rupert," she shouted, "that nephew of yours has taken my car without permission."

Both were upset by the situation, but neither could figure out what to do. Should they call the police? Would that further alienate them from Brendan? If he hadn't told Dolly—who he trusted—where he was going, was he engaged in some dangerous or illegal activity? Rupert suggested that Lily call Margaret and ask her opinion on how to proceed, but when she did that, the secretary said that Margaret was out of town at a principal's conference and wouldn't return until late evening.

"Let's wait a bit," Rupert suggested. "Heaven knows, we don't need a scandal. When he gets hungry and needs a bed for the night, he'll be back."

Lily was not at all convinced that this was true. She was still angry. Not only had Brendan taken her car without permission, he had also stolen her peace of mind.

In the afternoon, unable to focus on her women in architecture project, she went to the lakefront for a walk along the boardwalk that followed the shoreline. There were benches at intervals, and when Lily had walked until she could no longer feel the rage gnawing inside, she sat down, clasped her hands tightly together and stared off across the expanse of Lake Ontario's grey-green waters.

She remembered what her therapist, Ruth, had taught her about yoga deep breathing, and when she had inhaled and exhaled deeply through her nose, she asked herself where she felt the tension in her body. My stomach, Lily thought. Then she realized that her stomach was clenched as tightly as her hands. In, out, she breathed. She felt her rib cage expand, her belly rise and fall.

What would happen, she wondered, if I just open my hands, turn them face up and let go. Let the breath carry oxygen into my centre. Let the carbon dioxide escape. Her stomach calmed, she felt the muscles between her shoulders soften, even the space between her eyes, her lips, her cheeks, all seemed relaxed. She closed her eyes and listened to the gentle, deep flow of her breath, the lap of the waves on the shore. She had been engaged in church life for decades, but for the first time she wondered if this was how it felt to have God within you and to know that God was also beyond you, willing to take on your troubles, just waiting to be asked.

That evening, Rupert made a preposterous request. "The church organist is going on vacation for a month," he told Lily. "We'll need to make a decision very soon about our own vacation, but I am wondering if we might take our holiday in the month of August and you could play the organ for July. It would be like old times," he said, smiling at her, but she didn't smile back.

Rupert was confused and irritated. The qualities he had once admired and loved about Lily—her quiet, gentle self-sufficiency—had become an irritant. Why could she not make up her mind about a vacation? What was wrong with spending a little of her inheritance on a cruise? And, most annoying of all, having been married for over a year, why did he feel that he didn't really know her at all?

The last thing Lily did before crawling into bed was to look, once again, down from the bedroom window into the driveway. There was only empty blackness where her car usually sat.

"Why did you leave the hall light on?" Rupert asked before switching off his bedside lamp.

"Just in case," Lily responded. She was thinking, but did not say, "Just in case Brendan comes home. Just in case Charlotte gets restless in the dark."

Around two in the morning, Lily woke with a gasp. Had she heard something? The back door? Footsteps in the hall? She felt perspiration gather at the back of her neck and put her hand on her stomach to calm herself. She crept from her bed, eased open the bedroom door and glanced into the dark hole of Brendan's room. Why did it seem as if the grey willow rocking chair was tipping back and forth? She rushed back into the safety of her bedroom, eased the door shut, climbed into bed and burrowed close to Rupert, keeping her cold feet away so she wouldn't wake him. She remembered that Dolly had once said, "When ya sees a rockin' chair tippin' like dat, back and fort, my grandmudder would tell ya it's a sure sign some-uns gonna die."

The robins had stopped their early morning vigil. Lily supposed they had paired off and were now nesting. In the morning, I'll take a stroll through the backyard and look for nests in the lilac bushes, she thought groggily. She remembered digging in the front flower beds and seeing the robins hopping among the overturned sods, searching for earthworms, so close that she might have reached out to touch them. The instinct of birds and animals to care for their young is amazing, she now considered. Then her thoughts shifted and everything rushed back to her—Brendan, the car, the chair rocking in the night, Dolly's stories of Charlotte.

The alarm clock said six thirty a.m. She jumped out of bed, rushed to the window and looked down into the driveway. There, exactly where she had left it when she returned from her counselling session, was her red car. She exhaled in relief, hardly able to believe what she saw, and turned to hurry down the hall to the bathroom. She stopped in front of Brendan's room. His door was shut, but even from the hallway she could hear the steady, raspy rise and fall of a soft snore. It sounded amazingly like a chair rocking.

"He's still not up?" Rupert demanded, rising from the lunch table. Lily couldn't tell if Rupert was exasperated, angry or relieved that the teen had returned safely and that the car was back. Possibly a combination of all these things. It was close to three o'clock when she heard Brendan coming down the stairs. Please God, let me handle this well, she prayed, and when he swung into the kitchen, opened the fridge, unscrewed the lid of the orange juice jug and tipped it back for a long slug, she didn't correct him.

"Brendan," she said, sweeping her hand toward the pine table in the alcove, "sit down, please. We need to talk."

When he had explained what happened, she nodded. Then, hoping that her words were not laced with angry frustration, she said, "I don't understand why you didn't just ask me. I was home. You could have come to the house and asked permission to use the car. I would have agreed."

"Because!" he said, his voice exasperated. "I told you! I was late. My appointment was two o'clock in Kingston and it was already almost one. You know that it takes an hour to get there, and besides, I didn't really know where I was going. I needed all the time."

"Okay. Okay. I get it, but didn't you realize that your Uncle Rupert and I would be worried sick? You might have called to explain or sent us a text. You a new driver, too. We almost called the police, you know."

"You didn't need to do that. Don't you guys trust me at all?"

His voice had risen, and Lily could see that his face was flushed. A mental image of the robins caring for their avaricious, hungry young, their greedy beaks upturned and open in the nest, came into her mind. The young can be so demanding, so self-unaware, she realized. She reached across the table and grasped Brendan's hand. "Well, Brendan," she said gently, "you've got to understand that you've given us a few hard times around the trust issue. I'm hoping—and I'm sure your Uncle Rupert is too—that we can move on from this." To her surprise, he did not pull his hand away, and when she removed hers, she stood up and said, "Now then, you must be starving. Why don't we order in a pizza?"

It was left to her, once again, to explain to Rupert what had gone on. She knew Brendan wouldn't do it. Toward five o'clock, Brendan told her that he was going for a walk on the boardwalk by the lake. Lily nodded, realizing that he was not yet able to face his uncle, expecting a much less sympathetic reception.

She began by telling Rupert about finding the book of tattoo designs under Brendan's pillow. "I give Dolly credit for pushing him to find a job that isn't illegal or dangerous," she said. "Seems he decided to explore something that fascinates him, something he's good at. He decided to become a tattoo artist."

"What?" Rupert exclaimed. "What nonsense. If God had intended us to have designs all over our bodies, he would have made us like that."

"Tell that to all the women who have varicose veins," Lily muttered.

"Pardon? Oh, never mind. Go on, go on."

"He said that some people study art at university as a pathway to becoming a tattoo artist, but he didn't want to do that because it would take too long. Besides, he said, he has been creating designs since he was a little kid and he has a good idea of the kind of designs that work on skin. He took along about one hundred of his drawings, many of them originals. He explained that he could do tattoo designs on a two-dimensional surface but he didn't have the experience of doing them on three-dimensional forms like bodies. He asked around—apparently there are lots of people in New Hopewell with tattoos—and found the name of a reputable tattoo studio in Kingston that has a high standard for its art but also an excellent standard of health and safety. They take apprentices, so Brendan was in touch and he had an interview yesterday at two o'clock to show them his art and to ask to enter their apprenticeship program."

"Does he get paid to do this?"

"No. Seems that the mentor charges a fee, but Brendan didn't mention how much that is. Maybe he doesn't know yet. He finds out next week if he is accepted."

"It still doesn't excuse him for taking your car without asking," Rupert muttered.

"I said that, too, but he told me that he was running late and was in a bit of a panic. He didn't want to miss his interview, so he just jumped in the car and went. Then he was so excited about the possibility of living in Kingston, he went exploring, looking at apartments for rent. That's why he was so late getting home."

"Still…I'll have a firm word with the boy when he comes home," Rupert said gruffly, but Lily knew that wouldn't happen.

CHAPTER 36

Lily boarded the train to Toronto and stowed her overnight bag and her laptop into the overhead bin. She leaned back into the fabric of the seat, impatient for her journey to begin. As the train inched out of the station and began to pick up speed, the rhythmic clacking of the wheels soothed her and the melancholy hoot of the train filled her with excitement. The world of New Hopewell receded. This was her third trip into Toronto, and it amazed her that what had previously been nerve-racking now felt almost comfortable. Anxiety was a familiar and unwanted companion in her life, she had confessed to Ruth, her therapist. Her fear and nervousness had kept her from trying many new things.

"You seem to be making up for that in the last year or so," Ruth commented, smiling. "Perhaps you're ready to branch out, to discover something totally new about yourself. I've always found, though," she mused, "that having a little fear or anxiety at times can be a good thing. It keeps you on your toes. Even though I have been a counsellor for twenty years, I feel a twinge of anxiety when I meet a new client."

"Really?" Lily made a mental note to ask Rupert if he still experienced a little nervousness on Sunday mornings as he prepared for worship. She had no idea how conducting a worship service affected him.

"I had a bit of a new understanding about being fearful," Lily admitted. "When I'm excited, the feeling in my body is so similar to when I'm afraid that I can't tell them apart. I can't tell if I'm excited or frightened. So that got me thinking...what would happen if I took the things that I'm afraid of and thought of them as excitement? I recently learned to drive a car. At first, I said, 'I'm afraid to drive a car,' so what if I had said, instead, 'I'm excited to learn to drive a car.' The feeling would be the same—butterflies in my stomach, sweat in my armpits."

Ruth laughed and clapped her hands softly. "I love it. We therapists like to call that a reframe, in this case taking something that might be considered negative—anxiety—and turning it into something that might seem positive—excitement. Give me another example."

"I'm nervous about enrolling in architectural studies, or am I excited about studying architecture?"

"Any more?"

"I'm nervous about having a relationship with another man, or is this just the most crazy, exciting thing I've ever done in my whole life?"

"Another man?"

Lily closed her eyes, thinking of Philip, trying to remember every detail—how his hair curled at the nape of his neck, the golden hair on his forearms, the lopsided way he grinned, the way he tucked his hand under her arm as they crossed a busy street, his exuberance. She was tired but too excited to sleep. She glanced at her watch. Four hours until she would see him again.

This time, she knew to drop her bag at the hotel, understood which subway stop was closest to the Daniels Building, knew where to find room 204. When she arrived, Suzanne was setting up the PowerPoint projector. "Hey, Lily. Nice to see you again. What have you planned for us this month?"

"I'm a little nervous about this one," she confessed. "I've taken a more philosophical approach."

"About?"

Before Lily had time to answer, Evelyn and Philip walked in together. Evelyn greeted her warmly. Philip smiled and nodded. Lily was flooded with anxiety...or was it excitement?

At the conclusion, Evelyn was the first to speak, declaring that Lily's presentation, *The Problems and Promise of Being a Female Architect Today*, was well-researched, provocative, and raised as many questions as it answered. Had Lily come to any personal conclusions as it related to her desire to possibly study architecture? Suzanne wanted to know what she had concluded about why the province of Quebec had far more female architects than other provinces in Canada. To Lily's relief, this time Philip, too, asked questions. Why did she consider it important to have more women in architecture? Had she a sense of why architecture has historically been so male-dominated? In her opinion, is this male dominance coming to an end?

When the hour was up and when they had asked Lily about the theme of her third and final presentation in July, they stood up, preparing to leave. "You may want to see a couple of notes I made," Philip said, handing her a folded paper. She felt a blush rise in her cheeks and turned quickly to gather up her things, hoping that the women didn't notice.

In the subway on the way back to her hotel, opening the note, she read: *I'm dying to hear how things turned out with your sister escapade. Dinner tonight? 6:00 okay?*

The following day, Philip picked her up at nine in the morning as he had promised. "I remembered that you told us you would like to be more knowledgeable about modern architecture. Today, I'd love to introduce you to some of the exciting newer projects of Toronto. Why don't we start with the Art Gallery of Ontario? The famous Canadian-American architect Frank Gehry added onto the AGO. Completed it in 2008. Took four years and it cost 296 million dollars. Worth every penny, I'd say. His designs are so full of movement. They just curve and bend in such unexpected ways. I've always loved Pablo Picasso, too, and I've read that some of Gehry's asymmetrical designs were inspired by cubism. We'll need to compare the old original gallery and the new elegant glass and wood façade. We have to go inside, too, Lily. It's a must to see that iconic baroque staircase that literally soars upward. When I see that, I just want to run up and fly off the roof."

"Please don't," Lily laughed, charmed by his enthusiasm.

They explored the Art Gallery longer than Philip had expected. "Time for lunch. Two of my favourite pubs are around the corner on McCaul Street. Which one would you like to try? *The Village Idiot Pub and Grill* has a great Brome Lake duck confit and a delicious impossible burger. *The Sin and Redemption Pub* has a sinners club sandwich. You have a preference?"

Lily laughed. "You choose. It's too difficult for me."

"Let's go, then. Get some fresh air and good food."

They lingered over lunch, talking and laughing again over the whirlwind explosion of Lulu's impact on the staid and pastoral community of New Hopewell. "Brendan has never moved with such haste and respect, and I think the whole episode made Rupert more appreciative of me. Those church ladies will never complain about me again. I'm definitely a better option. I would never have had the courage to set it up if it hadn't been for you."

"Hey, I give you all the credit," Philip laughed. "It *was* my crazy idea originally, but it was you who pulled it together. What a coup!" He reached out for the bill, smiling and shaking his head. "I love spending time with you, Lily. You know that, don't you?" He covered her hand with his own and his long, slender fingers caressed hers. "When do you go home?"

"Tomorrow morning."

He nodded. "Sadly, I can't spend the evening with you. My sons are in a drama presentation at school. But I am so looking forward to your next visit and presentation. We have time this afternoon for a quick visit to the Royal Ontario Museum, if you're up for it."

When they arrived, Philip explained that it had originally opened in 1914. He pointed out the arched and bay windows on the building's western façade, a joining of Italianate and Neo-Romanesque styles. They gazed at the decorative eave brackets, quoins and cornices, and both laughed at the controversial and newly added crystal which jutted out on the top. Inside, they stood with a group of school children gazing up at the mosaic ceiling of the rotunda with its gold glass tiles. "It's a great example of Byzantine architecture," Philip told her, "and I suppose it was one way the architect could decorate without creating interference with the exhibits in the centre and around the room."

They walked outside along Bloor Street and stood for a long time gazing at the new addition, the Michael Lee-Chin Crystal. "This addition has been described as one of the ugliest buildings in the world while others say it's a monument. I've never known a structure in Toronto that caused such a controversy. I heard that the architect, Daniel Libeskind, was inspired by the ROM's gem and mineral collection and first sketched his idea for this addition on a paper napkin while attending a family wedding at the ROM. Cost 300 million."

"Amazing. That's more than the art gallery addition."

She noticed Philip glance at his watch. "I wish we had more time. I would have shown you the Aga Khan Museum up in the Don Mills area. The architect, Fumihiko Maki, won the Pritzker Architecture Prize for that project. It's fascinating because he used light as his inspiration to enhance and animate the building in dozens of ways. Maybe next time," he smiled down at her. "Come. I'll get you safely back to your hotel."

Lily nodded but didn't smile back. She knew that if she looked at him, she would cry. Whatever this beautiful thing that had happened between her and Philip might be, she now sensed that it was coming to an end. Lily felt a wash of desolation; next month would be her last presentation and perhaps the last chance to spend time with him. It felt like an ache; she wanted these moments to last forever.

Was this merely an infatuation, or had she fallen in love for the first time in her life? She had never imagined that two people could be so drawn to each other, that the yearning she had for him would be so delicious and overpowering. Her mood shifted as she realized, with a start, that she, a married woman, had no business falling for a married man who claimed to love his wife. Her brain told her that it was madness, but she didn't want to listen to that nagging protest in her mind.

When they had parted on the previous evening—exactly ten o'clock, as it had been on their first night together—he told her that he had to get home to make sure his sons got off to bed. "We're a big basketball household," he told her. "The boys are six foot four," he laughed. "All those boxes of cereal they ate when they were young. Both are being scouted for college basketball in the States, but we're hoping they'll do their university in Canada. We have to be up at 5:30 for practice. Hard on the old dad." He grinned, patting his stomach.

And in that instant, Lily understood, with the bleakness of defeat, that this was the way their future would unfold, if there was to be a future at all.

CHAPTER 37

When she returned to New Hopewell, she felt herself sinking into a dark and terrible place. She knew she should make an appointment with Ruth, but she felt too tired to do it. Negative thoughts lodged in the ruts of her brain. From the living room window, she could see that the flower bed, so tenderly planted two weeks before, now needed weeding, but she couldn't summon the energy to find the hoe in the garden shed. One day she forgot to shower and wash her hair, and she began ordering in food from the Main Street diner, too weary to shop for groceries or prepare a meal.

Rupert, she knew, was worried. Even Brendan, in his self-focused world, seemed to notice that she was depressed. One day, in an act of random kindness, he brought a slice of her favourite pizza—double cheese and black olives.

"You decided yet where you're going on vacation, Lily?"

She jerked her head to look up at him, amazed that he knew that she and Rupert had argued about this. She shook her head.

"Dolly told me about a really cool place in Nova Scotia, close to where she used to live. It's called Five Islands and you can rent a lighthouse and stay in it. Cool, huh? Wanna see the picture and stuff Dolly gave me?" Lily shook her head again. "I'll just leave it here. Maybe later," he said, shrugging before swinging out of the room.

How long had she been slumped in a chair in the snug, not thinking, not caring? She sighed and stirred, but before she rose, she glanced at the material Brendan had left by her chair—two yellowed articles, cut from old travel magazines. As Brendan had said, there was a lighthouse with a compact kitchen and living area on the main floor. The article described the many exciting side trips a visitor could take to explore Nova Scotia. Five Islands, where the lighthouse was located, was a small community of three hundred people, situated in an area called Minas Basin with the highest tides in the world, she read. Lily liked the rugged natural beauty she saw in the photo and the amazing fact that nine rivers flowed into the Basin. One article provided an intriguing history from the 19th century where the area was described as having the largest wooden ship building industry in Canada. What was most attractive, though, was the photo of a couple sipping wine in a hot tub on the deck at the base of the lighthouse.

She picked up her phone. She needed to talk with Ruth and get back on track.

"Since this has never happened to you before," Ruth told her, "I think you don't need to consider medication. There are lots of natural ways in which we can help ourselves when we feel depressed and sad and anxious. I made a brochure for people who were going through similar things. People tell me it is helpful. Consider this your homework. Try to follow these steps and we'll make an appointment to see each other in two weeks. If there is no improvement, we'll figure out some next steps, but I am quite confident that you will feel your spirits lift in the time ahead."

To her surprise, Ruth's brochure listed ordinary things, things that seemed possible to do. Every day, go for a walk outdoors. The movement and outdoor light increase your endorphins, the hormone that improves your mood. Practice positive affirmations. List the things that help you feel good about yourself and repeat them as many times as possible—today, I feel calm; today, I have more energy. Eat healthy foods. Some specific foods increase serotonin levels, the feel-good chemical that carries messages between nerve cells in your brain and throughout your body, helping you to be more focused, emotionally stable, calmer. Eat plenty of salmon, eggs, cheese, turkey, tofu, pineapple, nuts, oats and seeds.

Rupert did not understand what had plunged Lily into a great sadness, but he was relieved that she seemed happier lately.

"There are so many interesting things happening at the church this month, Lily. You must mark June 11 on your calendar. That's the date for the history presentation from the book that you and Margaret prepared. There's to be a short drama, and people can buy copies of the book. We'll set up a table where the authors can sign copies. You'll be famous," he teased.

Their vacation plans, too, had fallen into place. He had called about the lighthouse in Five Rivers and booked it for three weeks in August. "It's perfect!" he declared. "We can take a leisurely road trip there and back. Maybe stop off for a day or two in Quebec City and Montreal. It will be wonderful, Lily. You'll see. Oh, I almost forgot. I found this in my vacation research. We definitely need to make it one of our side trips."

Lily glanced at an article he had printed off about Randall House, a late 18th century wooden Georgian-style farmhouse in Wolfville, Nova Scotia. She was pleased that Rupert had remembered her interest in the Georgian style. From the picture, she could easily pick out the familiar symmetrical five bay façade, steep-pitched gable roof, returning eaves with cornice, pedimented gable porch on Doric columns, and a chimney on each end of the building. The interior, she read, had the original bake oven and floor, a dry wall stone cellar and seven original fireplaces. Something bothered her about the building, though. It seemed eerie. Was it the ugly and barren landscaping around the house? Was it because the name of the town—Wolfville—was frightening? Lily shivered. It was now a museum, the article said, and the woman who works as the curator and manager of Randall House claimed that the building is haunted. Her cell phone, she explained, does weird things when she walks into the house, stops working and starts again when she leaves. Light bulbs throughout the house go off and on, even when the switch is turned off. People report hearing voices, particularly that of a child. There were tales of a child dying tragically in the house. The curator claims that she senses a female presence in the dining room, where the cupboard doors open on their own and the dishes are moved around.

She hears knocking on the mantel in the living room and one room is perpetually and mysteriously cold.

Lily set down the article as if it were something hot. Was this a tourist hoax? Had Rupert read this? Did he really intend to take her to visit a creepy haunted house? Would he laugh at her fears? She tucked the article under a stack of newspapers so Brendan wouldn't find it. He would announce that it was cool. And she definitely didn't want Dolly to spot it if she dropped in on one of her random visits. Dolly, she knew, would believe every word of the article.

The next morning, Lily woke with a start and realized that there were only two weeks left before she had to return to Toronto for her third and final presentation. It was as if she had been stumbling through a fog lately. She felt a wave of panic rise within her. She still intended to do her report on historic buildings of Kingston and needed a few days to explore, but there was no bus or train running between New Hopewell and Kingston. She would have to drive. How could she summon the courage to drive into Kingston by herself? Perhaps she should cancel her final presentation, but this thought filled her with shame. She would have to come up with a plan.

When he came home, Lily was armed with her arguments. "Brendan, I'm wondering if I can talk you into doing a little field trip with me." She explained that she would like him to accompany her on her drive into Kingston. Embarrassed to admit that the presence of someone, even a kid as fractious as Brendan, could give her courage, she hurried on. "Since you are hoping to be accepted as a tattoo apprentice, we could scout out places where you might stay. And find some good places to eat."

"Nah. I don't want to go dragging around looking at dusty old churches."

"Oh, no. You wouldn't have to do that. Take along your sketchbook. Find a nice café and hang out near the university. Who knows? You might make a new friend. We'll find a place to stay overnight, and I'll take a cab to the buildings I want to see."

"No way, José. Zero interest."

Lily stared after him as he turned into the hall, heard him grab a granola bar from the kitchen cupboard and head out the back door.

She waited until the next day, and when he came downstairs in the morning, she was armed with a new approach. “Brendan, I know that you weren’t all that keen to go into Kingston with me, but I’m wondering if you are interested in this. I did a little internet research and made a list of scary haunted spots in Kingston. This article says that Kingston is a ghost’s dream city. There are tons of dark alleys and creepy old houses. While I’m exploring my dusty old buildings, as you call them, you could go visit these.”

She handed him the article and watched as his eyes scanned down the page. Fort Henry is transformed into Fort Fright, and the ghost of Nils von Schoultz, who was imprisoned and hanged for his role in the 1838 rebellion, can be seen roaming the fort in his tattered blue uniform. There is a 90-minute walk with stops at haunted hotels and hidden burial grounds, stories of hangings at the old courthouse and a visit to a dark alley to spot Teresa Beam, murdered in 1868. There are ghosts lurking in the Kingston Penitentiary where murdered inmates vowed to get revenge. A visit to the Agnes Etherington Arts Centre provides an opportunity to spot Agnes herself. She died in 1957 but often comes in to play the piano and remind people to turn out lights. A visit to the grave of Sir John A. Macdonald invites the visitor to wonder why grass won’t grow at the base of the tomb. The famous Grad Club, formerly the beautiful Victorian home of a doctor, has slanted, disorienting hallways. Be careful not to bump into a ghost, the article warned.

Brendan had started to grin. Then he laughed. “This would be totally awesome, totally cool.” He tucked the list into the pocket of his jacket. “When do we go, tomorrow?”

“Sure,” she replied, smiling too.

“One more thing,” Brendan added before swinging out of the room. “I’m going next door to invite Dolly along. She would totally dig this.”

“Dolly Inkpen? I’m going on a little getaway trip with Dolly Inkpen?”

The excursion into Kingston was more expensive than Lily had planned. She hadn’t considered the parking, the meals, the number of taxis needed. Nor had she thought through the sleeping arrangements. Everyone would need his or her own room. There was no way, absolutely no way, she would share a room with Dolly Inkpen.

When they had checked into the hotel, Dolly was girlishly enchanted and thrilled with everything. She had her own private room overlooking the hotel swimming pool and the harbour. There was even a plush chair by the window where she could see the boats on Lake Ontario. She bounced up and down on her king-sized bed, decorated with a towel folded to look like a swan. She turned on and off her huge flat screen television and was thrilled to discover there was a little machine where she could make her morning coffee. She inspected the bathroom with its large, tiled, walk-in shower and enthused about the pile of white, fluffy towels. There was even a bathrobe, she declared, hung behind the door! It made Lily wonder if she had ever stayed in a hotel before, and for a moment, she felt a tiny pleasure, glad that she had been able to gift Dolly with a memorable experience.

After their day of exploring, they agreed to meet at the *Lone Star Texas Grill* at eight o'clock in the evening. It was late enough, Lily figured, that they could have a meal, then return to their hotel for bedtime. As the restaurant maître d' ushered them past the mirrored bar, Lily caught sight of the three of them. Leading the way, she looked prim and tidy in a pink cotton sundress and sandals. Dolly, with her frizzled red and white hair, wore a long flowing flowered skirt, a purple blouse and cowboy boots. Brandon had shed his black hoodie because of the heat of the day, but his wolf tattoo and spiked earrings were profiled above a black T-shirt featuring a skull and crossbones and the inscription *Instant Death*. What a trio we are, Lily thought. A loud and lively band was playing on the patio, making conversation almost impossible. I'm sure they don't want to hear about my historical research any more than I want to hear about things that will scare me in the night, she considered. She could see that both Dolly and Brendan were brimming with excitement and energy. They dug into their southern fried chicken, tacos and fish and chips while she picked at her garlic shrimp on a bed of rice, grilled peppers and onions.

By the end of their second day, Lily had enough material to create several presentations. They were all tired and ready to go home. Against her better judgement, she let Brendan drive and, feigning a headache, lay down in the back seat, praying that they would all arrive home safely.

CHAPTER 38

Something was wrong. Terribly wrong. Rupert's face was ashen and drawn. Lily put her hands on his forearms. "Rupert, I can see that you are upset. What is it?"

At first, he refused to speak, but when she pressed him again, he said, "I just don't get it. I don't get how you are able to buy a car—even though it is a used one—and go off into Kingston for a couple of days. How are you doing this?"

Lily broke into a cold sweat. Oh, I have been so stupid and careless, she thought. She realized that she had been so absorbed in her own life and activities that she had not stopped to consider how things might look to Rupert. She sank down into a chair. She could not bring herself to look at him. "I should have told you this long ago," she began. She explained about the lawyer asking her to set up a personal account, which she had done in Toronto without informing Rupert. "I used my own money for these things."

"But why, Lily? Why didn't you transfer the money to our joint account here in New Hopewell? Don't you trust me?"

She realized, with a start, that she didn't totally trust him, but she couldn't say that. She glanced up from her clasped hands. "You must try to understand things from my point of view, Rupert. I am forty years old and have never had much of my own. I wanted to savour this money, to be the only one to make decisions for its use. I have hopes and dreams for using it."

"Well, those hopes and dreams obviously don't include me. You think you're the only one with hopes and dreams?"

"Please don't shout, Rupert. I know that there are things you want to do. But your plans and desires are different from mine. I had already made up my mind, though, to pay for our three-week stay in the Nova Scotia lighthouse." It had not occurred to her to offer this before, but she saw it now as a conciliatory move. Rupert grunted. Maybe she should offer to make tea. Maybe she should suggest they go out to dinner. How long would it take for this tension to ease? Days? Weeks? Months?

"There's another thing," Rupert declared. "Follow me." He turned toward the snug. "What is the meaning of this?" he asked, pointing to a bundle of clothes sitting on a chair. Lily gasped and found herself unable to speak, even unable to breathe for a moment. "I found them in the bottom drawer of the desk in your office," he said, peering at her. "What is the meaning of this?" he demanded again.

"What gives you the right to go through my personal belongings?" Lily shouted. She felt her knees go weak. She sat down quickly, fearing that she might faint. There in front of her on the chair were the Lulu clothes—the jeans with ripped knees, the crop top shirt, the heavy gold medallion. She looked down at her white, clasped hands. "I had to do something, don't you see? I had to make things change—all the demands from the church people, from Brendan, from you. I was drowning, losing myself." She sat quietly for a minute. Rupert waited, frowning, his arms crossed. "I made a friend in Toronto," she continued. "He suggested the plan to me. At first, I thought it was the most outrageous thing anyone had ever dreamed up. But the more we talked the more I thought that it would be the most exciting, liberating, audacious thing I could ever do for myself. I remembered my high school drama course and how easy it was for me to pretend to be someone else. It was like I was finding something new inside myself for the first time. Maybe it wasn't the real me, I don't know, but it felt as if Lulu just came alive in me."

"Alive in you?" Rupert shouted. "You're not like that at all! You came home pretending to be your contemptible twin sister and tricked all of us."

Brendan, startled by the shouting, had crept to the door of the snug, trying to make sense of the scene before him.

"Where is she, then? This so-called twin sister of yours?" Rupert demanded.

Lily slumped in her chair, staring at the floor. "I've had a report back from the search agency. She died three years ago in California. A boating accident."

Flooded with despair, Lily looked up at both of them before her face crumpled in tears. She had made a complete mess of things. Rupert would ever trust her again.

Lily wanted to die. If she thought she had fallen into a deep, dark hole in the previous month, this time it felt as if there was no way out. Rupert had moved into the guest room and had begun to eat his dinner at the New Hopewell diner. He arrived home late and went straight to his room. How long would he continue to punish her with his distance and silence? Brendan had disappeared again, probably back with Dolly Inkpen. Worst of all, she could find no solace in her architecture presentation on Kingston. There were only six days left until she was to go into Toronto again and she hadn't even started. Could she pretend to be ill? She called *New Beginnings Counselling Centre*, but Ruth was away on vacation. The receptionist asked if Lily would like to see someone else. She said no and punched the end button on her cell phone.

In the late afternoon, as she sat slumped in a chair, the front doorbell rang.

"Lily! What's the matter? What's going on?" Margaret exclaimed. She was alarmed at Lily's appearance—her hair hanging oily and limp, her shirt stained, her face ashen, her shoulders drooped. Margaret was troubled. "Come, come, come," she said briskly, ushering Lily into the snug. She plunked down a pile of the church history books. "I came to get you to sign some more of these, but I can see that we need to talk. Spill the beans, kiddo. What's going on?" She reached for the tissue box and handed it to Lily.

It was like a dam breaking, an enormous catharsis. Lily told Margaret everything, and when she had finished, she was drained, emptied. "You must think badly of me," Lily moaned.

"Oh, on the contrary," Margaret exclaimed. "I love complicated things. That's why I make such a good high school principal." Margaret took her hands, "Lily, my dear friend, you have just done yourself the most amazing favour. It's more than a favour, really. You've miraculously rescued yourself."

"I have?"

"Absolutely. Without a doubt. The first time I met you I gave you some probably unwanted advice: don't let this place gobble you up. I could see the tenderness and fragility in you. But that scheme of being your evil twin sister—bwaa-ha-ha—oh, I *love* that! I wish I had the guts to do something so dodgy and dramatic."

Lily looked up in surprise. Margaret was admiring her nerve?

"Where do you need to go from here, Lily?"

She sat quietly for a long time, lost in thought, considering what might lie ahead. Finally, she raised her head. "I need to make peace with Rupert. I need to go next door and ask Brendan to come back home. I need to take a shower and change my clothes. Then, I need to phone the Daniels Building and postpone or cancel my last presentation. I'm not ready."

CHAPTER 39

Lily had finished typing the material in Elodie's red journals and was relieved that this odious task was done. After she heard Rupert leave for the day, she gathered together the journals and the transcription which she had printed off. She opened the door of the guest room and set them in a tidy pile on Rupert's dresser. It had been several days since their shouting match and neither had taken any steps to make amends. Lily couldn't figure out how to do that. Maybe Rupert can't either, she considered. She stood looking around the guest room. It was tidy, the bed carefully made, almost as if no one had slept there. She wondered if he had moved all of his clothes out of the closet in their room or just some that he needed right away. It might give her some indication if he was thinking this was a permanent or temporary arrangement.

She opened the top drawer. A few pairs of socks, some underwear. The next drawer held a pair of pajamas, some summer T-shirts. She was about to close the drawer when she saw the envelope which had been tucked under the T-shirts. Feeling uneasy but curious, she picked it up and discovered that it contained a letter from the Ontario Provincial Police requesting an interview with Rupert regarding an alleged theft under $5000 while he was living in British Columbia. There was a stern and terrifying warning of the dangers of being charged with petty theft: the conviction will show up on a criminal record check, which can be a problem with future employers or volunteer positions. It would also show on a customs check. Those found guilty could face a maximum of two years in prison, probation, fines, and a permanent criminal conviction. The letter issued a terse suggestion to seek legal counsel.

Lily quickly tucked the envelope back under the T-shirts but not before noting the date at the top of the letter. Rupert had probably received the letter in the morning mail on the day when Lily, Brendan and Dolly were arriving home from Kingston. She felt as if she could hardly breathe. Not only had Rupert been brooding about her money and the curious set of Lulu clothes, he had a much more urgent worry plaguing him. She knew him well enough to know that if this accusation were true, it would be the most shameful thing in the world for Rupert. Even if it were not true, she knew that he would be terrified of this news becoming public. Furthermore, she wondered how his modest income could stretch to include a good lawyer. Suddenly, she saw a way forward.

The next morning, she woke early and prepared something that she knew Rupert loved—a full English breakfast with bacon and eggs, toast, fried tomatoes, baked beans. When she heard him come down, she went into the hall, put her hand on his arm, and looked up into his face. She was shocked by how grey and drawn he appeared, as if he had aged ten years overnight. "Come into the kitchen. I've made your favourite breakfast."

When they had finished eating, she began, "I know that you were upset about the money and about my Lulu escapade, but I think there is something else bothering you. Won't you tell me about it?"

He hesitated for a moment, then told her briefly about receiving a letter—although he didn't mention the police—that accused him of taking money from his last church.

"Rupert, that's a terrible thing. So worrisome." She jumped up and began clearing the table. "We must get a lawyer. And a good one."

"But, the cost…"

"We will use some of my inheritance money. This is important."

"You can't spend your money on a lawyer! I won't allow that."

"Rupert," she said, sitting down at the table and taking his hand, "this money from my mother was an unexpected gift, really a gift from heaven. I did nothing to earn it. It just dropped into my lap. I think you theologians have a word that describes this. Grace. By the grace of God, I was given this money, and it feels right for me to share some of it with you in this way. Now, off you go to work. I am going to my computer to research the best lawyer in Kingston."

Lily had decided to see Ruth, who was now back from her vacation. She needed to make sense of some of the things that had been happening lately. She had to set the appointment for after ten o'clock, though, when she had her car back.

Brendan had, for the past few days, asked her if he might borrow her car daily to drive Dolly to the same town where Lily went to the counselling centre. "Dolly has a part-time job at a grocery store," Brendan explained. "Nine to one o'clock. She has no way to get there unless I drop her off and pick her up."

Lily had hesitated, then reluctantly agreed. After Brendan left on that first day, she walked into the living room and, standing behind the curtain, shook her head in bewilderment. Dolly was climbing into the little red Honda wearing her long, flowered skirt, the purple blouse and a pair of the most beat-up running shoes that Lily had ever seen. Dolly had a small bag and a piece of cardboard tucked under her arm. How and why would a grocery store manager hire someone looking like that? Maybe they need someone to scare the ghosts out of the produce department, Lily considered.

Her counselling session finished at noon. Lily felt drained but at peace. She had offered to wait to pick Dolly up at one o'clock, but Brendan had been adamant. "No. You come straight home. I'll go back to get her at one. She counts on me." Lily had shrugged, but now that her counselling session was over, she decided she would pop into the grocery store. There *were* a few things that she needed, but mainly she had a ghoulish curiosity about Dolly's job. She parked the car, grabbed a shopping bag and headed toward the store. As she rounded the corner, she stopped abruptly, stunned, unable to comprehend the scene before her.

There, outside the entrance to the grocery store, stood someone who she would recognize anywhere. Her red frizzy hair was tangled by the wind. Her legs above the battered shoes were twisted and distorted so that it made her look lame. She was looking down, but one hand held a little bag and the other a cardboard sign with a handwritten message: *Widowed, hungry and lonely. Please help. God bless you.*

When he came before one o'clock to get the car keys, Lily was ready. "Brendan! I saw her! Outside the grocery store. What is going on here?"

Brendan looked sheepish, then peeved. "So? She said she did it in Nova Scotia. It's a good living."

"But panhandling! Why?"

"We gotta eat."

"I suggested to your Uncle Rupert that we should be giving Dolly something for your room and board. I know she doesn't have many resources, but panhandling! Honestly, Brendan, don't you think it's a bit disgraceful?"

"You and your middle-class morality," Brendan stormed. "You just don't get it. I promised her. She said if I gave up smoking and selling weed, she would earn the money for us."

"For us? Brendan, don't you remember that your home is here with me and your Uncle Rupert? We promised your mother we'd look out for you."

"Well, Dolly needs me," Brendan muttered. "You guys don't need me."

"We *want* you." After she said that, Lily felt surprised. She realized that this was now true. Even though he was still a challenge, she had become at ease with him living with them. She felt out of sorts when he stayed away for days. "What did you mean about Dolly needing you?"

"She looks out for me. I look out for her. She told me she needs me in her life. It's a reason to get out of bed in the morning."

"Oh...I see. I think I see. Well, you'd better be off to fetch her then. She'll be tired and hungry after standing in the wind all morning."

She could put it off no longer. Tomorrow was the day she was to give her third and final architectural presentation. She would need to cancel. Digging through her purse, she searched for a contact number. She wanted to call Suzanne. It would be easier to make her excuse to Suzanne than to Evelyn or Philip, but to her dismay, the only phone information she had was Philip's. She felt very reluctant to call him.

In the next instant, a strange thing happened. Her own cell phone rang.

"Lily?" It was a male voice.

"Yes?"

"It's Philip. Philip Karpen."

His voice had a muffled, nasal quality. "Philip? Is something wrong?"

"I hope I'm not disturbing you. I'm terribly sorry to call you at home, but I have some tragic news and I'm afraid we will need to cancel your presentation tomorrow."

"Philip, you're scaring me. What's wrong?"

"It's Evelyn." Lily heard his voice catch and she realized that he was crying. "This morning, she collapsed in her office. Her administrator called 911 immediately, but by the time the ambulance reached the hospital, she was gone."

"Gone?"

"Passed away. Dead, Lily. A heart attack, they said." She heard him blow his nose. "It's been a terrible shock to all of us, but especially to me. She was a valued colleague. I could tell her anything. She was like a mother to me."

Lily could not think of anything to say. She was stunned, shaken by the news. Evelyn had been a warm and nurturing person, kind and motherly to her, too. Finally, she said softly, "Philip, if I were there with you now, I would put my arms around you and hold you tight."

"I know you would, Lily. I know you would."

CHAPTER 40

When Rupert returned for the evening, Lily had prepared one of his favourite dinners—shepherd's pie. It was easy to persuade him to move back into their bedroom. They were both ready for things to return to how they had been. She urged him to move his clothes back into their closet while she was putting the finishing touches on a salad. After dinner, they lapsed into a quiet but comfortable silence and Lily wondered if she might share with him the sad news of Evelyn's death. But before she could do that, he stood up and peered through the kitchen window.

"Lily, there's a storm brewing. Come and sit on the side porch with me to watch it."

She knew that there was nothing more exciting to Rupert than to be in a sheltered place and watch a storm blow in. The wind had been strong all day, but now it was gusty, rough and howling. The trees in the backyard bent and swayed, the rain lashing against them. The lightning snapped, followed by a menacing boom of thunder. "Do you think we should go in? Are we safe?"

"We're safe and we're dry. Isn't this wonderful, Lily?"

Hardly how I would describe it, she thought. It's tumultuous, turbulent, chaotic. She wrapped her arms around her body, remembering a phrase from her high school English class: pathetic fallacy—the attribution of human feelings and responses to inanimate things or animals. The teacher had written on the board: *The sun smiled upon her. The raindrops wept for him.* This evening is raging for me, this is my stormy life, she considered. In the past year, my life has erupted around me, inside me. It has been agitating, changing, confusing, but there were also periods of serenity and tranquility, and there were times of tension when I sensed the lull before the storm. There have also been mountaintop experiences of exhilaration and passion. In that moment, she realized that, as upsetting and muddied as the previous year had been, for the first time in her life she felt really alive, overcome with excitement, awash with the wonder of life. If I didn't worry that Rupert might become alarmed, I'd like to run out on the lawn and dance in the storm, she thought with a smile.

A lightning crack followed by booming thunder was so close and loud that it made them both cry out. They heard a snap like a gunshot, a great rush and a racket of brushing. Jumping to their feet, they watched in horror as a huge broken tree fell into their driveway.

"Oh, my God!" Rupert shouted. Lily backed up against the wall, her hand clasped against her mouth. "It's the Manitoba maple from the backyard," Rupert shouted into the thunder. "Those trees are so unstable, top heavy. What a mess!"

When the wind had eased and the rain slowed into a soft and even patter, they continued sitting on the side porch, wondering how long it would take to clean up the obstruction in the driveway. "At least it didn't damage our cars, so there is really nothing to do but clean up," Rupert said.

"Look, Rupert! Do you see this?" Lily had moved to the edge of the porch and was pointing. From under the broken leafy mass, they could see that the Berlin Wall had snapped under the weight of the tree trunk and now lay flat on the ground in Dolly Inkpen's backyard.

Tragedies and accidents always have a silver lining, Rupert told her. Lily doubted that, until the telephone began to ring. Mrs. Hardy told all the women of the Missionary Society, and the church secretary phoned all the Sunday school teachers. The church treasurer told all the men at the coffee shop, and the Chair of the Board—Margaret's husband—reminded the men to bring their chainsaws. There was to be a work bee in the driveway of the Old Manse. Anyone who wanted firewood for their cottage fireplace could fill their trucks, and women were to bring sandwiches and squares.

When Mrs. Hardy called her, Lily was surprised to hear how solicitous she was. "That must have been quite a terrible shock for you and Reverend Cameron," she said. "I hear you were sitting on the side porch when it happened. Imagine! Land o'mercy. If, but for the grace of God, it had landed right on your side porch, it might have killed you both."

"Oh! I hadn't thought of that." Was that meant to be a comforting thought? Lily wondered.

"Now, don't you worry about a thing, Mrs. Cameron. Me and the ladies of the Missionary Society will bring the refreshments and the tea and milk. We don't like them flimsy cardboard cups, so we'll bring a basket of mugs from the church. We'll be bustling in and out of the kitchen a bit, but we'll try not to make a mess."

Lily thanked her. That would be the drama for tomorrow, but today... today brought worry and stress. In an hour they were off to Kingston to meet a lawyer.

The lawyer ushered them into a small meeting room and urged them to sit down. Lily clasped her shaking hands together and buried them in her lap. She glanced at Rupert, who looked stiff and formal. The lawyer informed them that he would like to ask some questions for clarification. Were they comfortable with that? He explained that in Ontario, theft under $5000 falls under section 334b of the Criminal Code. If charged and found guilty, the penalty depends on factors in the case. Hence, his need to know as much about the circumstances as possible.

"May I begin?"

Rupert nodded and swallowed.

"Have you ever been charged before, even if the charges were withdrawn and fingerprints destroyed?"

"Never!" Rupert replied. Lily glanced at him. She could see that he was dismayed.

"Have you had police warnings from any police force in Canada?"

"No. Once I got a speeding ticket and the officer told me to slow down."

"No warnings about theft?"

"Never."

"Have there ever been prior findings of guilt, discharges, fines, probation, suspended sentences, conditional sentences like house arrest, or prison sentences?"

"Good heavens, no!"

"Have you ever taken something, without his or her knowledge, from a vulnerable person such as a child or someone mentally challenged or an elderly person?"

"Never."

"Have you ever shoplifted from a store or been accused of such?"

"No!"

"Have you ever taken anything from your place of employment, which I believe in your case was a church?"

"That treasurer in my last church had it in for me from the moment I went there," Rupert erupted. "He had this insane idea that someone was taking the loose money from the church offering plates. If he could find a way to frame me and accuse me of doing this, I'm sure he would find it. I never trusted him from the first moment we met. How do we know that it wasn't him or the church secretary who was taking the money?"

"Well, based on the story you told me, it's entirely possible that when we receive the disclosure of evidence from the Crown prosecutor, I will find there is zero evidence to support the accusation that it was you taking money. In that case, with there being simply no proof, I'm quite sure the case will be dropped."

Relieved and exhausted, Rupert and Lily pulled into the driveway of the Old Manse. To their surprise, Mr. Cruikshank and a man in a white hard hat were standing at the corner of the porch, pointing and bending forward to peer at something. Mr. Cruikshank turned toward them and exclaimed, "Oh, there you are. Nothing to worry about, and it's an easy repair. Seems that we were so focused on the mess in the driveway that we missed the fact that the trunk of the tree glanced off the side of the house here by the porch. The damage is around the corner where none of us noticed it." Lily and Rupert could now see that there were, indeed, some crumbled and broken bricks at the corner of the house, exposing the beam and plaster inside.

"We'll cover it with plastic for now," the man in the hard hat told them. "Then, we'll be back to begin the repair in the morning." He laughed suddenly, opening his hand to show them what he had been holding. "This was a real puzzle to us until your neighbour came along—her name's Dolly Inkpen, I believe?"

Lily and Rupert stared down at the small object lying in the palm of the man's hand. It was floppy and yellowed with black scuff marks on the heel but was clearly a small child's leather bootie. "A shoe? You found a child's shoe?" Rupert said.

"It was in the wall. Must be at least a hundred years old," the man mused. "I haven't seen this before when I've done house renovations, but I've heard of it. Apparently, it was an old Scottish tradition or superstition to put a child's shoe in the wall of a house when it was being built. It wards off the devil and evil spirits, your neighbour said." Both men chuckled. "Dolly said to give you a message."

"Yes?"

"She said you'd best get that wall fixed up as soon as possible and make sure this shoe goes back into the wall. Otherwise, she said, it will upset someone called Charlotte. Any idea what that means?"

CHAPTER 41

Lily had no time to consider yet another strange tale from Dolly. With the nerve-racking visit to the lawyer behind them, she now had more pressing things on her mind.

She began to think about Evelyn. Until her mother had died, Lily had never considered how important it is to most grieving people to have some ceremony or ritual, some comfort that comes from gathering with others as you say your goodbyes. She wondered if there would be a public funeral or celebration of life for Evelyn. Searching through past copies of *The Globe and Mail* and the *Star*, she found a glowing obituary of a kind, thoughtful scholar who left behind a bereft husband, daughter and son. The column described Evelyn as a supportive encouraging mentor to many architects, who saw herself, especially, as being a role model for young women in the field. Her meticulous care as a teacher had influenced hundreds of architects. There was to be a private family funeral. Donations could be made in her memory to the Daniels Building Development Fund, University of Toronto.

So, that's that, Lily thought, her spirits sinking. She began thinking about the significant people she had lost through death: her beloved father in a tragic car accident, her stoic mother so shaped by suffering, an identical twin sister who she had never met but still someone with whom she sensed a deep bond, and now Evelyn.

People talk about closure, she mused, but somehow in death there is never any real closure. All you can do is hold close the memories of the person you loved and then soldier on. Some days will be fine, but then, on other days, some small thing will set you off—the feel of someone holding your hand, the sharp yellow of a perfect lemon, a cello solo—and suddenly you are tumbling back down a rabbit hole of grief. What is this closure thing that people are always talking about? Does it mean that the pain becomes less frequent? That the body and soul become stronger, more tempered like a metal, so that a person can not only cope but may even find happiness again? She didn't know.

The next day, she turned on her computer and found an email message from Philip. It was written in a formal tone. Perhaps he was conscious of it being sent from his university account—or perhaps he worried that Lily and Rupert shared an account. He expressed again his grief at the loss of their dear colleague and friend, Evelyn. He then suggested dates when Lily might travel into Toronto and, instead of preparing a presentation, have an informal conversation to wrap up her portion of the pilot project.

When she arrived at the hotel where she always stayed, the clerk at the registration desk said, "Welcome, Ms. Kaltyk. Your room is ready, and we just sent up a delivery."

"A delivery?"

When she opened the door, she caught sight of a dozen red roses in a crystal vase on the bedside table. Her hands trembled as she opened the card. *My darling Lily, I have known you for such a short time but will remember you always. You have no idea what this has meant to me. May I take you to dinner today? 6:00 okay? Philip.*

For a long time, she sat on the bed. She had to think this through. It was as if there was a decision to make, but she couldn't figure out what it was. Finally, after what seemed to be a very long time, she rose, walked to the bathroom, stripped off her clothes and showered. She brushed her teeth and hair and put on a fresh dress. Glancing at her watch, she grabbed her purse and took the elevator down to the lobby.

At six o'clock he came through the revolving door. Her heart beat wildly as she rose, smiled and walked toward him. He wrapped his arms around her and said, "You look delicious."

"I'm impossibly sentimental," he told her as they walked into the same restaurant where they had shared their first meal. Again, he ordered two filet mignon meals, medium-rare, and when he noticed that she had clasped her hands together in her lap, he reached under the table to take her hand. "Perhaps we need a drink," he said, signaling to the waiter.

Their conversation was slow and languorous, full of small pleasures. They talked of Evelyn and he told stories of their work together. He inquired about what Lily had prepared for her final presentation. Though reluctant to admit that her concept had not been fully fleshed out, she explained that after exploring Kingston, she had decided to research one of the top architect firms in the city and describe the six main areas in which they did their work, focusing on the projects that involved historical renovations. This would, she said, not only describe the diversity of projects with which an architectural firm might be involved but would also point to the need for flexibility, openness and resourcefulness. And most of all, if it were a historical renovation, it would display the firm's dedication to maintain the integrity of the original so that it melded smoothly with the new.

"Ah, it's that old palimpsest issue again," Philip laughed.

They spoke about summer plans and Lily told him about renting a lighthouse in Nova Scotia.

"That sounds awesome. I love the part about the hot tub." He caressed her arm. "Everything better at home now, Lily?"

"We're getting there. I think."

"Good. Glad to hear it. Our boys will be off to university in Ottawa, it seems. We're pleased that they agreed to stay in Canada, and Carlton University in Ottawa seems to have command of the Canadian university basketball world."

Their conversation faltered until Philip asked, "Have you made a decision about enrolling in our program yet?" She looked at him, saw the hope and expectation in his face, then reached out and ran her fingers along his cheek. He placed his hand over hers. "What's holding you back, Lily?"

"I can't explain it very well. I've always been a cautious person, so perhaps I'm just the type to take time arriving at a conclusion."

"Well, that hardly seems the case when you have only a month to pull together a brilliant PowerPoint presentation on architecture," he laughed. But then he became instantly sober. "There's something I have to tell you, Lily, and this is very hard for me." She withdrew her hand. "If you do apply to our program—and I fervently hope you will—you will not have to worry about me being your professor." Lily felt as if she could hardly breathe. "It's my wife, you see. She has been offered an amazing opportunity. She's been invited to help design and structure a community health clinic in Nairobi, Kenya. She'll take a two-year leave from her current position, and I have applied for a leave, too, so I can accompany her. Not sure yet what I'll do there, but I'm sure there are opportunities in my area. That's what I'm exploring at the moment."

Finally, Lily exhaled. "Well, perhaps it's time for me to get back to my hotel," she said.

When they pulled up in front of the hotel, Philip turned off the car, grabbed his keys and said, "Wait here. I'll open the door for you."

"No. No thanks. We'll say goodbye here," she said, turning toward him, looking into his face. He looked surprised, his eyes wide. Then she saw that his eyes were beginning to fill with tears.

"I love you, Lily Kaltyk."

"And I love you too, Philip Karpen. You have no idea what you have meant to me." And she, too, began to cry.

He kissed her cheeks, her forehead, her lips, their tears mingling. "I'll never forget you. I promise you that." He kissed her again, and then she twisted around to open the door.

"Please..." he said, but she held up her hand, opened the car door, stepped onto the sidewalk and walked through the revolving door.

CHAPTER 42

At first there was just silence. Silence, despair, pain, darkness. Lily knew she should open her mouth and speak, but she could not find the words. Rupert brought her tea, but it cooled, untouched, on her bedside table. The doctor came, then left. Margaret came and helped her change her nightgown. When she woke, she could not tell if it was night or day. Her pillow was damp with tears, although she couldn't remember crying. The blinds were down, the curtains drawn. Had Brendan come into her bedroom, tentative and awkward? She thought so, but she didn't know for sure. How long had it been? She didn't know.

Then, one day, something changed. She heard a voice from far away. "Mrs. Cameron. Mrs. Ca... Lily. Sit up a bit now, that's a good girl. We're going to have a bite to eat and then I'm going to pour you a lovely warm bubble bath and wash your hair. I've always admired that glossy hair of yours. We'll make it shine again." The woman bustled around the room, plumping pillows, raising the blind, setting a small invalid's tray over Lily's lap. "I thought you might be lonesome for some of your own food," she said, setting out a bowl and spoon. "I've never made this before, so I hope it's almost as good as your mother's." She ladled borscht into Lily's bowl. It was full-bodied and fragrant, emitting the rich aroma of the soil in which the beets had grown. Floating in the soup were light, fluffy dumplings. She suddenly felt very hungry. "Here now, Lily. Let me fix your pillow. Here's the spoon," she said, tucking a tea towel around Lily's neck. "Take a sip. There's nothing like beet soup. It puts the blood back in you."

By mid-July she was strong enough to walk by the lake, content to sit on the bench by the boardwalk, listening to the waves and allowing the sun to warm her cold hands. Rupert had hauled two suitcases from the attic and began to pack for their vacation. He didn't speak of what he came to think of as her "time away." His tenderness and patience brought tears to her eyes, and when she couldn't tolerate any more weeping, she rose and walked and walked.

After they had settled into their cozy lighthouse cottage, they made a list of all the places they wanted to explore in Nova Scotia, and Rupert quipped that three weeks might be entirely too little time. By the end of their stay, they had motored the Cabot Trail on Cape Breton Island, regarded as one of the world's most scenic drives. They spent a day in Halifax, strolling on the waterfront and visiting the Halifax Citadel National Historic Site with its distinctive clock tower. Another day they discovered the Fortress of Louisbourg, the largest reconstruction in North America, which invited visitors to experience what life was like for early European settlers from 1713 to 1758.

They had the luxury of time to talk of many things. They puzzled over why Brendan was so fascinated with the world of spirits, wondering, too, if he would follow through on his desire to become a tattoo artist. "We must go to see Peggy's Cove tomorrow and take some photos," Rupert insisted. "He's sure to ask us."

Lily was enchanted with the incredible number and varieties of lighthouses along the rugged coastline. "This little gal from Emerson would never have dreamed that there would be so many lighthouses in one province," she laughed.

Always, there was good food and drink around each corner—a lobster boil on the beach, wineries, cafés. And when they returned from their exploring, the highlight of their day was relaxing in the hot tub on the deck, watching the sliver of moon float over the treetops as stars began to appear.

It was on their last night that Rupert asked her something about which he had inquired before: "Lily, are you happy?"

"This has been a wonderful vacation. I'm glad we did it."

He noticed that she had not really answered his question, but he let it slide. "You see that? A shooting star off to the east."

"My mother used to tell a little story about me as a child. It was the time of year for meteor showers in southern Manitoba—April, I think—and my parents took me out into the backyard where we cuddled under blankets in lawn chairs and watched for shooting stars. They kept saying, 'There's one, there's one,' but it would be gone before I could spot it. Finally, I said, 'Mama, if you blink really fast, you see a whole lot of shooting stars.'" Rupert and Lily chuckled together.

"You were a smart little thing from away back." Rupert glanced over at her in admiration but was astute enough to realize that there was a depth to Lily that he could never know, a mystery that would always elude him. "I'm reluctant to face the autumn with all the church programs and meetings starting up," he confessed, sighing. "A new cycle begins. Only five more years until I can retire. How are you feeling about things, Lily?"

She didn't answer for such a long time that he began to wonder if she had been listening. She turned to him in the hot tub and said, "There's something I need to tell you." He waited while she seemed to be thinking something through. "You remember on the way when we stopped for gas at the roadside station outside Kingston?" He nodded, and she continued, "I went into the convenience store and picked up a cold drink and a copy of the *Kingston Whig Standard*. After we arrived, on a morning when you had gone for your walk along the shore, I read the paper and saw a job posting that was so exciting to me. The ad said that the Kingston Historical Society, Tourism Kingston and the Greater Kingston Chamber of Commerce had teamed together to create a position called 'Historical Animator.' It's a bit like being a glamorous tour guide," she hurried on. "You give tours on a bus, pointing out the history, purpose and architecture of a site."

"Oh! You intend to apply for this?"

"I already have," she said quietly. "I applied online. It's perfect for me. I have an interview the day after we return home." She didn't tell Rupert that she was confident—more than confident, she had a deep conviction—that she would get this job. Nor did she want to spoil their vacation time by telling him that she had put in an offer on a tiny three-room coach house in Kingston that had been part of a palatial estate in the 18th century. There was time in the future for all these things to unfold. For now, it was enough to think through how the interview might flow, how she would insist, gently but persistently, that these tours would *not* use yellow school buses. They must build into the cost of the tour a luxury coach with plush seats, ample leg room, air conditioning, a good PA system, panoramic windows, and above all, a proper washroom that emitted no odours.

Lily closed her eyes, smiling, enjoying a flute of champagne in the hot tub, a suitable way to toast the end of something and the beginning of something else. Perhaps it was never meant to be that she would become an architect. Maybe her dream had become a tyranny which she could now set aside, but even this reflection did not diminish her yearning to introduce others to handsome buildings and structures that she had grown to understand and love and about which she would become an undisputed expert.

She knew that she was in a hot tub in Nova Scotia, but Lily imagined herself in the front seat of a luxury coach in Kingston, Ontario, smiling and greeting people as they boarded the bus. She could hardly wait for the bus to start rolling. She felt excitement stir in her stomach as she prepared to help people fall in love with beautiful old buildings.

Notes of Thanks and Explanations

The ending of this story

When I sent this manuscript to beta readers (test readers of an unreleased work who give feedback to the author from the point of view of an average reader), I found them rather evenly divided in their opinions about the ending. Some liked that the story is open-ended. They realized that Lily is still on a journey but heading in a new, self-defined direction. Others wanted to know what happened to Dolly, Brendan, Charlotte, Rupert, Philip. Since this is primarily Lily's story, the answer to these questions is, "I'm not sure." If you enjoyed the open-endedness of this story, don't read the next paragraphs.

I liked the comment of one of the beta readers who said that readers don't necessarily want or need everything "tidied up" at the end of a novel, but in the process of reading, they become attached to the characters and want to know what happens to them.

To you, dear readers, who really want to know what happened to the supporting cast, I would say, "I think Dolly probably just goes on being Dolly. Brendan may or may not become a tattoo artist. (I hope so, for his sake.) Charlotte the ghost may settle down now that the tension has decreased in the Old Manse. Rupert will move toward retirement and any relationship he had with Lily will be greatly altered. Will Lily ever reconnect with Philip? I doubt it. He has his own life. Did Lily inherit her twin sister's half of Krystyna's estate? Yes."

Identity formation in women

At many points, Lily's story becomes our story. We may have different traits, strengths and weaknesses, but we share the commonality of developing an individual identity. This, of course, is never done in isolation. Our family, schooling, social networks, life experiences, and the environment in which we live all play a part.

At some point in the 1990s, I became fascinated with the whole issue of identity development in women. I read and reread, highlighted and jotted notes in a book entitled *Finding Herself: Pathways to Identity Development in Women*, written by Ruthellen Josselson, who was a clinical instructor in psychiatry at the Harvard University Medical School, associate research scientist at Johns Hopkins University, and assistant professor of psychology at the University of Toledo. What I most appreciated about Josselson's writing was her pushback on what had come to be thought as normative for personality development, a schema established by Erik Erikson. Erikson, Josselson argues, saw personality development as stages to be moved through, as content, and as such, this description is and was better suited to the male experience. Josselson, on the other hand, saw the personality development of women as a relational process as they moved toward a more solid and reliable sense of self.

Josselson's longitudinal study followed young women, interviewed as they were about to graduate from university and then again twelve years later. She was exploring how "normal" women—that is, women without major mental or health problems—formed their identity and made their choices. What she found was that there were significant and varied ways in which women form relationships, raise children, pursue careers and develop values. She identified and described four divergent pathways that women followed, but one of these pathways was not "better" than the other. Each had its own unique struggles, challenges and rewards, but all women moved toward becoming their unique selves, just as Lily does in our story.

After I had finished writing this novel, that book by Ruthellen Josselson popped into my mind. After locating it on my bookshelf, I reread her description of the four pathways in which she describes how women form identity. I will not burden you with the official names Josselson attached to these identity paths because, quite frankly, I found them distracting. However, I will divulge one which she labelled "The Moratoriums." They were, by and large, young women who were acutely aware of and sensitive to social problems and psychological closeness or distance, and when interviewed twelve years later, had been held back or stalled in some ways. They had declared a "moratorium," a temporary pause, on life. When I reread that chapter, I was struck by how many characteristics Lily shares with the Moratoriums. (But she doesn't fit all of them, of course, nor would any woman.) Here are ways that Josselson describes Moratoriums: frequently experience torrents of intense feelings; this moratorium period is upsetting for some women but not indicative of long-term difficulty; moratoriums often define themselves by how they feel; they may accumulate a good deal of rage because of what they experience to be failures at achieving their dreams; may struggle with independence/dependence but sense that they must "cut loose," "be crazy," in order to be themselves; often need to look outside their homes for models and options on how to conduct the rest of life; have a great capacity to tolerate and integrate guilt.

Perhaps, in your mind as you read this story, you may have considered Lily a slow starter, engaging in this identity exploration when she was already approaching forty. But perhaps, as Josselson describes, she was merely a "Moratorium." And, like many of us, what she *thought* she wanted —to fulfill her dream by becoming an architect—was not what she really *needed* in order to find her strength. She needed to find her courage, her voice. She needed to learn to stand on her own two feet. At least, that's what I figured she needed.

What a reminder to all of us, regardless of our gender, age or circumstances, that we are constantly in the state of becoming.

The world of ghosts and spirits

In the lovely old stone farmhouse where I grew up, there was a small sitting room in which the piano was housed. We spent hours there practicing our piano lessons, playing duets and trios together. It was only when my brother, Stewart, and his partner, Nan, were raising their children in that house, that they had an opportunity to read the will of Robert Robertson, the original Scottish settler who had the stone house built. In his last will and testament, Robert decreed that, upon his death, his daughter, Charlotte, *would permanently assume ownership and control, with unimpeded access, to the south upstairs bedroom and the sitting room on the main floor, a cow, and fodder for said cow, all bestowed in perpetuity.* We know Charlotte Robertson to have been a real person, the fifth child of seven, who emigrated with her parents from Scotland to Canada in the 1850s. Even today on the farm, you can spot a barn board where she inscribed her name. Because of the wording of the will (bestowed in perpetuity), my brother and sister-in-law imagine that the lingering presence of Charlotte came with the house and farm, whether they wanted her or not. From that time on, any mischief or missing items, any occurrences that made the dog howl in the night, any creaks of the floorboards were attributed to Charlotte. Unlike Dolly Inkpen's Charlotte, though, our farm ghost Charlotte is perceived by the family to be friendly and congenial, and she must be musical, too, to say nothing of being patient, having listened to so many Brown children stumble through their études.

Once, earlier in my life, I spent some time in Nova Scotia doing a series of leadership development events. While at the airport giftshop, I picked up a book about the ghosts of Nova Scotia—Nova Scotia has a rich history of these—and after reading these stories at night, I became so frightened that I slept in my hotel room with the lights on. One weekend, I drove in my rental car to an event held at Camp Geddie, near the small community of Merigomish on the Northumberland Strait. The previous night, I had read about the mysterious ghost ship, blazing with fire, which sails up the Strait, so I knew the place would overflow with mysteries. I arrived after dark, and just before I turned off my car, I saw some large white thing dancing and waving in front of the hood of my car. Terrified, I screamed and ran to the shelter of the camp lodge. Only later, when I had located my courage, was I able to creep back to the car to retrieve my overnight bag.

There, in front of my car, was a tangle of sprawling bushes on which a large clear plastic bag was caught, dancing in the wind. I had a good laugh!

So...do I believe in ghosts? I certainly do when I'm in Nova Scotia. Even if they are not real, they make for some terrific stories.

Thanks to my committed, faithful beta readers and editor

When I had finished writing this novel, I passed it along to a faithful core of beta readers and looked forward to their comments, suggestions and responses. I am always profoundly grateful that people take the time to do this. It helps me see changes—both big and small—that strengthen and add depth to the story. Then, I'm able and happy to go back to the drawing board and make revisions. Thank you Ivan Brown, John and Sylvia Congram, Peter Van Katwyk, Mabel Williamson, and Marian Crockford. I am especially grateful to David and Jackie Brisbin, former residents of Emerson, Manitoba, who painted a picture of the town for me. Thanks to Dionne Chambers, who corrected and amended some of the "lawyer talk." And a huge special thanks to Lawrie Carter for his guidance on the world of architecture. I am always grateful for the sound, wise, generous and thoughtful guidance of my editor and designer, Tim Faller, and for the support I enjoy from my spouse, John, who is always my first reader. He wants to make sure that I haven't put him in the story.

Food and recipes

As usual, it is my trademark to add some recipes at the back of my novels. My almost obsessive enjoyment of food and cooking keeps seeping into my storylines, and I think it is fun to include recipes that emerge from the story. It always delights me when people tell me, from previous novels, "Hey, I made your sourdough bread," or "Kep's Lenten Heathen Quiche was delicious." Let me know if you attempt the Kyiv cake or borscht.

Some books that helped shape my thinking as I wrote this novel

305 Lost Buildings of Canada, Raymond Biesinger, Alex Bozikovic
(Goose Lane Editions, 2022)

Folklore of Nova Scotia, Mary L. Fraser, Introduction by Ian Brodie
(Formac Publishing Company Limited, Hallifax, 2009)

A History of Nova Scotia in 50 Objects, Joan Dawson
(Nimbus Publishing, 2015)

The Long Way Home: A Personal History of Nova Scotia, John DeMont
(McClelland & Stewart, 2017)

The Promise of Canada: People and Ideas That Have Shaped Our Country,
Charlotte Gray
(Simon & Shuster, 2016)

A History of Canadian Architecture, Volumes 1 & 2, Harold Kalman
(Oxford University Press, 1994)

A guide to Canadian Architectural Styles, Second Edition,
Shannon Ricketts, Leslie Maitland, Jacqueline Hucker
(Broadview Press, 2004)

Finding Herself: Pathways to Identity Development in Women,
Ruthellen Josselson
(Jossey-Bass, 1987)

More Ghost Stories of Nova Scotia, Vernon Oickle
(MacIntyre Purcell Publishing Inc., 2019)

Where the Ghosts Are: A Guide to Nova Scotia's Spookiest Places,
Steve Vernon
(Nimbus Publishing, 2018)

The Architectural Review,
architectural-review.com

Lily's Borscht

When Lily falls into a deep depression, the dreaded Mrs. Hardy tenderly feeds her borscht (beet soup) and dumplings, promising her that it will restore her to health. The beloved soup from her childhood draws Lily back into her present world.

Prep time: about 30 minutes
Needed: skillet, large soup pot, another large pot in which to cook dumplings, mixing bowl, a food processor (if possible) for shredding the vegetables, otherwise a box grater
Cooking time: about 1 hour
Makes: about 8 servings

4 pork sausages (omit these if you want a vegetarian soup)
8 cups of water or vegetable broth
3 medium beets, peeled and shredded
3 carrots, peeled and shredded
3 medium potatoes, peeled and cubed
½ medium head cabbage, cored and shredded
796 ml (28 oz) can diced tomatoes
1 medium onion, chopped
3 cloves garlic, minced
1 tsp white sugar
Salt and pepper to taste
For garnish: sour cream, fresh dill or parsley

1. If using sausage, cook in skillet in a little oil over medium heat about 10 minutes. Remove from heat and set aside.
2. Fill the soup pot with 8 cups of water or broth and bring to a boil.
3. Slice the sausage into bite-sized chunks and add to the water.

4. Add the shredded beets and cook for 10 minutes.
5. Add carrots, potatoes, cabbage, diced tomatoes, onion, tomato paste. Cook for another 20 minutes.
6. Stir in minced garlic.
7. Stir in sugar, salt and pepper.

Garnish with sour cream, dill or parsley.

Dumplings for Soup

6 cups water or chicken broth
1 bay leaf
2 cups flour
½ tsp salt
¼ tsp sugar
2 eggs, beaten
1 tbsp sour cream
6 tbsp melted butter

1. Bring the 6 cups of water or chicken broth and bay leaf to a boil.
2. Sift the flour, salt and sugar into a mixing bowl.
3. Make a well in the centre of the flour and add the eggs with 1 tbsp sour cream. Fold together with a spatula. Your dough might look like scraps of cloth at this point.
4. Pour in the melted butter and stir/knead until the butter is well mixed in and the dough is uniform in texture.
5. Put the dough on a cutting board. Separate into 2 pieces. Roll and squeeze each piece into a long slim log. Cut into thin slices. (This dough expands in cooking.)
6. Using a slotted spoon, set the dumplings, in 2 or 3 batches, into the boiling water and boil gently for 10 minutes.
7. Remove bay leaf and add cooked dumplings to soup.

Makes about 30 dumplings.

Krystyna's Kyiv Cake

Don't even think about making Kyiv cake if you're in a hurry. Most Ukrainian cooks make it over a day or two, and Lily's mother claimed that it was better assembled the day before eating. This is definitely a special occasion cake. It is, essentially, an 8-layer cake. It consists of three main parts: a sponge cake, a meringue, and butter cream, all held together with jam. You could cheat and buy a sponge cake, but that would be no fun. There are a lot of steps to a Kyiv cake, so read all the instructions carefully before beginning.

Prep time: an hour or two over 2 days
Cook time: 6 hours
Needed: round cake tin, electric stand mixer, roasting pan (for water bath), frosting piping bag or a zip-lock bag with a diagonal slit cut across a bottom corner
Makes: enough cake for 12 people

To make the sponge cake:
1 cup all-purpose flour (gluten-free all-purpose flour with xanthan gum works, too)
½ tsp salt
6 eggs, separated
½ cup milk
⅓ cup vegetable oil
1 tsp vanilla extract
½ tsp cream of tartar
⅔ cup white sugar

1. Adjust oven rack to middle position. Preheat oven to 300°F.
2. Prepare a water bath. Using a roasting pan that is larger than your cake pan, add hot water to a depth of ½ inch.
3. Trace around the round cake pan on a sheet of parchment paper. Cut out so that the paper sits in the bottom of the pan. Grease the bottom and sides of pan.
4. Whisk together the flour and salt in large bowl.
5. Add the egg yolks, milk, oil, and vanilla. Whisk until smooth.
6. Using stand mixer, whip egg whites and cream of tartar on low speedy until foamy, about 1 minute. Increase speed to high and whip whites to soft, billowy mound, about 1 minute.
7. Turn mixer to low and gradually add sugar.
8. With a rubber spatula, gradually fold the egg white mixture into the flour mixture until there are no streaks in the batter. Pour batter into prepared pan.
9. Set cake pan into water bath and bake for 1 hour.
10. Allow cake to cool, then invert it onto a flat plate, remove parchment paper and slice horizontally into two slabs.

To make the meringue:

6 egg whites
1 cup white sugar
1 cup hazelnuts, chopped (chopped walnuts may be used instead)

1. Whip egg whites on high speed in stand mixer until they are doubled in volume.
2. Gradually add sugar until combined.
3. Line a baking sheet with parchment paper. (Hint: if you wet the baking pan, the parchment paper lies flat.)

4. Using a piping bag or the modified zip-lock bag, use about half of this meringue mixture to pipe out 12 small rosettes onto the parchment paper.
5. Add the chopped hazelnuts to the remaining meringue batter.
6. Using the same round pan that you used for the cake, put the egg white with nuts in the pan and smooth.
7. Bake both the cake pan and the tray of meringues in 250°F oven for 4 hours. If the rosettes are getting too brown, remove after 2-3 hours.

To make the butter cream:

3 cups icing sugar, sifted
½ cup cocoa powder (optional)
1 cup butter, at room temperature
2 tsp vanilla extract
1-2 tbsp cream, if needed

1. In the bowl of a stand mixer, add the icing sugar (and cocoa if you want chocolate butter cream) and butter. Mix on low speed until well blended, then increase speed to medium and beat for another 3 minutes.
2. Add the vanilla, beating on medium speed for 1 minute until creamy and spreadable. Add a little cream if necessary to make the butter cream thick but spreadable.

Gather together:

1 cup chopped hazelnuts (or walnuts)
1 cup strawberry, peach or apricot jam
½ cup semi-sweet chocolate.

Putting it all together:

Essentially, the Kyiv cake is an 8-layer delicacy. Starting from the bottom:

- first half of sponge cake
- jam spread on sponge cake
- thin layer of butter cream
- hazelnut meringue
- another thin layer of butter cream
- second layer of sponge cake
- jam spread on sponge cake
- butter cream spread on top and sides of entire cake

When assembled, use your hands to press the chopped hazelnuts into the sides of the cake. Place a ring of the baked meringue rosettes around the outside top of the cake. In microwave, melt ½ cup semi-sweet chocolate (about 1 minute). Allow to cool but not solidify. Carefully pour liquid chocolate onto the top centre of the cake. Allow to set slightly, then score the chocolate into 12 slices (between the rosettes). This makes it easier to cut as the chocolate will solidify. Store in the refrigerator. To serve, cut slices with a very sharp knife with a rosette on the top of each slice. What decadence! Enjoy!

About the author

Dorothy Brown Henderson lives in Waterloo, Ontario, Canada, with her husband, John Henderson. She has enjoyed a variety of careers: music teacher, mental health worker, Christian educator and leadership developer and, before retirement, the minister of Caven Presbyterian Church in Exeter, Ontario.

When she retired, she decided to become a full-time writer. Besides *Becoming Lily Kaltyk*, Henderson is also the author of the cookbook *Loving it Local: Preparing Delicious Fresh Local Food* (2014), and four novels: *The Season for Strawberries* (2018), *Happy Are Those* (2019), *Dr. Bloom's Event* (2020), and *Dreaming in Grey* (2022).

Henderson holds an ARCT in piano (University of Toronto), a BA in Religious Studies (University of Waterloo), an MA in Religion and Culture (Wilfred Laurier University) and an MRE, Master of Religious Education (University of Toronto). She also holds a three-year diploma in Christian Education from Ewart College, Toronto. In 2006, Henderson received the *Educator of the Year* award from the North American Association of Presbyterian Church Educators.

Henderson enjoys spending time with her three grown children and their spouses and her five grandchildren. She also loves time at the family cottage on Lake Huron, writing, reading, cooking, and is an avid gardener, growing plants of all sizes and shapes.

Manufactured by Amazon.ca
Bolton, ON

40754361R00129